DESOLATION:

21 Tales for Tails

DESOLATION:

21 Tales for Tails

Edited by Michael Cieslak

The Dragon's Roost Press
2014

Table of Contents

Introduction 9
Michael Cieslak

Alpha 11
Tory Hoke

Follow the Music 19
Sharon D King

Robodog 31
Camille Griep

Affection, Inconceivable 37
Sierra July

Lords of Dust 43
Gustavo Bondoni

Every Weeknight at Seven and Seven-Thirty 51
Kurt Fawver

Belongings 63
Abra Staffin-Wiebe

Plastic Lazarus 75
Raymond Little

Deleted 85
Ken Goldman

Aphrastos 91
Calie Voorhis

Misty Hills of Dreamer Sheep 99
David C Hayes

Camp Miskatonic 107
Lillian Csernica

Hunger 121
Alexandra Grunberg

Beautiful Libby and the Darkness 135
Christopher Nadeau

Every Act of Creation 145
Rich Larson

Silence 159
Dawn Napier

To Rest 171
Melissa Mead

Ghosts in the Gaslight 181
Andrew Knighton

The Murder in the Steel Skeletons 191
Gerri Leen

Busting Faces 197
Charles Payseur

Government Waste 201
J S Bell

Acknowledgements 209

About the Contributors   211

About Last Day Dog Rescue   219

About Dragon's Roost Press   221

Introduction

Why Desolation?

In early 2013 I decided that I wanted to do something to celebrate all of the dogs which have shared our lives. I had also been toying around with the idea of putting together an anthology of short fiction. Eventually the two ideas gelled. I could solicit fiction for an anthology and donate a portion of the proceeds to the rescue organization that introduced us to our two current fur-babies. Thus, the anthology that you hold in your hands was born.

I wanted the stories in the anthology to lean toward the darker end of the speculative fiction genre, primarily because this is what I read and write myself. It seemed like a good idea to stick with what I knew. The problem was, this seemed far too broad. I wanted the stories contained in the anthology to be related to each other in some way. I knew that I did not want to do a collection of stories featuring talking animals or which simply featured canine characters. I wanted something more diverse, a compilation of stories related thematically yet each strikingly individual.

A brainstorming session focused on canine companions ensued. Somewhere there is a legal pad filled with words like "loyal," "friend," "family," "warmth," and "unconditional love." An idea started to form. What if I took all of the attributes of a dog and stood them on end? Instead of the positive qualities associated with our four footed friends, the stories could focus on their opposites: loneliness, isolation, and solitude.

Namely, all of the things which disappear when you invite a dog into your family.

This was a good decision. The submissions started to pour in and I can say with complete assurance that no two stories were alike. I received over one hundred stories from authors in 33 different states and 13 foreign countries. This included such far flung locales as Sweden, Croatia, Singapore, Australia, New Zealand, and Brazil. The response to our call for submissions was overwhelming.

The hardest part of the submission process was rejecting stories that were beautifully crafted but just not quite a fit for our vision of the anthology. There were stories which were well written featuring fully fleshed characters and original, intriguing ideas that I had to say no to. The first rejection letter I wrote was for one of the best stories I have read in years. I did my best to make sure that the author knew how excellent I thought her work was.

I strove to be the kind of submissions editor that I wanted my own stories to be read by. Towards this end I made sure that every submission which graced our in-box was read all the way through. When rejection letters were required, they were personal and not just an auto-generated form with a couple of check boxes. Sometimes all I could say was that the story just didn't quite fit with our concept for the anthology and with the other stores which I had already accepted. Regardless I tried to be encouraging, especially with the ones which really shined.

As the submissions rolled in and the acceptance e-mails went out, the anthology started to take on a life of its own. I kept an eye out for truly original ideas, for things I had never seen before as well as new takes on old favorites. The way the authors chose to interpret our call for material that focused on "themes of abandonment, loneliness, isolation, or solitude" were varied and fun to see. As a result I have ended up with stories of anguish, rage, sadness, joy, and redemption. The stories contained in this book include horror, science-fiction, fantasy, and some that defy simple genre classification. Main characters range from haunted people to devious space travelers, robotic dogs, monsters, and inanimate but sentient objects.

What we have, what you are holding now, is an eclectic and entertaining collection of dark, speculative fiction. Turn the page and see if you don't agree.

Alpha

by Tory Hoke

The day the strangers come my pack doesn't go out. We stay in the den--all five, even Nosey, the other four-legs--and watch the picture-box. The big two-legs, Alpha and Beta, sit stiff and give off a stressed ammonia smell. I don't ask for the couch, even when Alpha stands up to go to the window. He squints at the sky. There are smeary marks in it so bright they hurt to look at.

Beta holds the little two-legs, Pup, on her knees and offers her cereal pieces. Pup drops many. Her paws are too stubby. I sneak close and crunch-crunch the cereal. Beta sets Pup down so she can touch my fur. This makes Pup calm, but not the others. I don't know why Alpha and Beta are stressed but I'm stressed with them.

Nosey sits on the arm of the couch, feet tucked under, eyes closed. He switches his tail. Nosey is a different kind of four-legs. Understanding him is tricky, but I know enough to know he is not tense.

I need to go out. I pace by the door. But no one opens the door. Instead Beta puts down gray-paper. I'm too big for gray-paper! I want grass and dirt and the oily-bark tree. I paw the door. Alpha shouts at me from the other room, so I stop.

Beta coos at me. All right. I will try the gray-paper. When she sees, she makes stiff-arms. I feel bad. But she gives me peanut butter while she picks up the mess. I would rather have ear-scratch than peanut butter, but she is stressed and I don't want to give her more to think of.

Pup sleeps in the two-legs' bed. Alpha and Beta lie down and hold each other. After Pup falls asleep, Alpha goes to the small dark den in the wall. He takes a short crooked stick off a high shelf. It fits in his hand just so, like it grew there.

I've seen these on the picture-box. A crooked stick is how one two-legs makes another one fall down.

At the side table Alpha sits and slowly breaks his crooked stick into pieces. He cleans it all with a small stiff brush and puts it back together. Beta pets Pup's head and watches. The crooked stick is calming them somehow. If they are calm, then I will be, too. At last Alpha goes to bed and I lie down on the floor beside them. I listen. I sniff. If anything tries to hurt our pack I will fight it.

Nosey runs up and down the hallway with one of Beta's hair ties. This is normal. Nosey has no stress.

Beta will miss the hair tie in the morning.

Today we don't go out either. Why don't we? The sky is bright and the marks are small. Breeze brings sweet rich smells of woods and park and garden, but no one goes out and everyone is restless. Beta snaps at Alpha. Pup runs through the den and knocks down something that breaks in sharp pieces. Alpha and Beta pick it up but grumble.

Beta starts the picture-box and switches the picture to find a show with two-leg pups and fast bright colors and music. Alpha and Beta and Pup jump around together. They will knock over more sharp things! I hide in the kitchen and watch. Soon I understand. This is how we play when we can't go out. The two-legs grin and show their tongues. I stand beside them. It is good.

We are a pack: two-legs and four-legs together.

It gets dark outside. The two-legs eat dinner out of clinking cans. I hear the scraping that means they are nearly done, and I sit by the table to see if they will give me some. They don't. They make sad eyes, and Beta rubs my ears so I know I haven't done something wrong.

Later we watch the picture-box. Pup plays with a stack of cards. A SMACK-POP startles me. The house goes dark and the picture-box stops. Stressed, Alpha and Beta whisper. Alpha goes around the house lighting candles with confusing smells--citrus, soap, toasted sugar. The pack sits close together, hugging, petting, staying calm. They play with Pup's cards, too. I put my head in Alpha's lap. Nosey climbs in Beta's and starts to purr.

Eventually Pup's cards lose their interest and Alpha opens a cupboard to get out a basket of small things: shiny coins, paper flowers and cardboard snakes. Alpha blows in a cardboard snake and makes a razzing noise. I cock my head to figure out what it is. The two-legs laugh. Alpha blows again. I cock my head the other way. They laugh some more.

Alpha pushes around in the basket and finds a skinny blue tube. He puts it in his mouth and blows. It makes a noise so high it tickles my ears like Nosey's whiskers. I bark and spin. Alpha blows again. The blue-whistle sound goes even louder and so high all my fur stands up. The two-legs do not bark or spin. Their fur does not stand up. Do they not hear it? Nosey does. Nosey runs puffy-tailed out of Beta's lap, and the two-legs laugh at both of us. This is the laugh they use when they hide a biscuit behind their back.

Suddenly there is a new smell. I run to the gap under the front door. It's strong and new, thunderstorm and burned chicken.

I can't figure it out. I whine with frustration. The old drive inside me makes my hackles go up. Beta catches Pup and holds her tight.

I twist my face to sniff deeper. Alpha watches me. There's something on the other side of the door, something completely new.

He goes to the bedroom and comes back with the crooked stick. He and Beta make soft noises to each other. I go with him to the window. For a moment I think I see rain, something long and thin flickering in the air, but it isn't rain.

Now when Alpha goes from room to room he brings the crooked stick with him.

I am eating breakfast when I smell the thunderstorm smell at the back door. I run there and snuffle and whine. Alpha grabs his crooked stick. Beta grabs Pup.

The smell clouds just outside the door. I try to sniff all of it. The old drive takes over. I bark loud sharp barks, and the smell turns rusty. Outside, something big and plastic bangs to the ground.

Beta shushes me. Alpha comes toward me, slowly, stiffly, very stressed.

I will not let the strangers hurt my pack. Hackles up, I bark and bark.

I hear a sound like the blue whistle—like Nosey's whisker in my ear—but it isn't coming from my pack. It's coming from the strangers. It has rhythm and purpose, like the noises Alpha and Beta make to each other.

The glass in the kitchen window rattles.

Alpha makes a noise to Beta. She holds Pup but comes to grab me by the scruff. Pup whimpers. Beta backs us both into the den. The smell clouds up my nose.

Crooked stick in hand, Alpha presses against the wall by the kitchen window. He peers outside. His body is rigid. He holds the crooked stick with both hands. The glass rattles harder.

Alpha shocks back from the window and stares out. He shakes. His lips are gray. He smells like ammonia and brine.

The window bursts. Glass cuts Alpha. Beta screams.

Alpha lifts the crooked stick and throws open the door. I slip out of my Beta's grip and rush out after Alpha, barking. Beta shouts.

Sun hurts my eyes. Burned meat and lightning smell leads me down the driveway. My eyes adjust, and I see them—not four-legs or two-legs, but no-legs—animals like glass strings, tall and thin and swaying. They have sharp ribs on the front and long arms angled in like a dead spider. They look like water falling. They have no eyes or ears or teeth that I can see.

They speak blue-whistle sounds. I stop barking so I can listen. What do the no-legs want?

A BANG goes off. I yelp. A clot of dirt springs up far right of the no-legs. Alpha's stick smokes.

The roasted smell turns vinegary. Some no-legs fall. The no-legs that are left cower, then stretch tall and tight. A WHIP-CRACK shoots past. Alpha falls heavy to the ground. Under his skin is all red. His eyeballs are red. There's red in his mouth.

Beta runs out of the house. She doesn't scream. She collapses over Alpha and cries. Pup watches from the doorway.

Beta turns to the no-legs but she looks past them. She speaks to them. Her voice sounds like she is choking on water. At the same time, the no-legs speak back in blue-whistle sounds. They make so much noise at the same time. They can't hear each other.

Alpha will not wake up. He will never rub my belly again. He will never hold Pup again. Alpha is over.

I failed. My pack is lost. I sit beside Beta and howl.

While Beta cries and Pup cries and I cry, the no-legs and their smells--roast and storm and vinegar--fade away.

Nosey escapes out the open door.

Beta puts me in the house with Pup. When Beta comes back from outside she is dirty and dragging and sad. She uses gray sticky-sticky tape to fix clear paper over where the window was.

She carries the crooked stick now.

We are alone because of me. We are alone because I barked when I shouldn't have.

I let Pup touch my fur. Sweet Pup. Wonderful Pup. She is so small. Bad things are happening and there's nothing she can do.

Will Beta be Alpha now? She is strong and smart, but she can't speak to the no-legs. She can't even hear them. And she keeps carrying that crooked stick. The crooked stick makes her calm, but it shouldn't.

Maybe a two-legs cannot make a pack with a no-legs. Maybe a four-legs must do it.

Maybe I must be Alpha now. It will be hard. It is a hard thing to be the only four-legs in my pack.

I am afraid, but I will try.

Beta makes dinner for Pup and me. Pup can be sad for only a little bit at a time. She draws colors on the white-paper and sings. Beta can be sad for a long time. I stay close to her and watch the door. I will not fail again. I will be brave like Alpha was. I will be strong and smart like Beta.

Beta starts to put down gray-paper. I scratch the door. She snaps at me. I scratch again. I want the grass and dirt and oily-bark tree. She grabs my paw and shakes her finger at me. I scratch harder and leave long marks on the door.

Beta looks out the window. It's dark, but there are no smells of the strangers. It's safe. Does she understand this? She points at the gray-paper. I pick a corner up with my teeth and rip it. I scratch the door again.

She slumps. She moves slowly. But she picks up my leash and opens the door. I slip past her, quick and strong. She doesn't need to join me. She should stay with Pup. She watches me, tense and straight and full of fear.

I pass my water on the oily-bark tree. Freedom. Bliss. On our street all the cars are sleeping and all the windows are dark. Around the white smears in the sky shine more stars than I've ever seen at once.

I sniff for the other four-legs on this street. There's the silver meaty-smell one with the big muscles who lives behind the fence. There's the small dusty-face one who lives in the window. There's the long red one in the brick house who has many Pups in her pack, so she smells like spaghetti and wax. I'm the black one with the crescent tail. I smell like me.

Do they know what is happening? Do they still have their Alphas?

I howl for them. It's hard to tell them everything from so far, but I try. I start low, sail high and end on a long falling note. I hope they hear me. I hope they understand.

Down the block another four-legs howls the same: low to high, then falling. She misses her alpha. Another voice rises. He still has his. There is hope.

One by one they all chime in with howls like a never-ending circle, rising and falling, sad but strong.

We understand. We must do something.

I run back to my house. Beta watches me from the window. Her face is wet. When I get to the door, she opens up and whisks me in and coos in my ear. Pup does, too. They laugh. We are calm for a little while.

That night I sleep on the two-legs' bed.

At breakfast, the no-legs come back. I don't have to go to the door to smell them. There must be many of them. But I don't snuffle. I don't bark. I go to the door and scratch.

Beta is feeding Pup from a clinking can. She tenses and looks at me. She goes to the window, just like Alpha did. Does she see the no-legs from there? Would she recognize them? Light is trickier than smell. She must not see them, because she is calm when she opens the door for me.

I go down the driveway. There are so many no-legs side by side that they make the street look wet and rippling. They make their burned electric smell and blue-whistle sound.

I lower my head and lift my fur. I make myself big. I flash my fangs and growl. The no-legs ripple together, making their own pack. They stop speaking the blue-whistle sound. They are listening.

Beta watches from the window. She sees my teeth and hackles. She comes to the door with the crooked stick and looks hard to see what I see. She gasps. Pup joins her and grabs her legs. Beta picks her up.

I keen and growl. I smack my lips. I tell the no-legs this is my pack and this is my territory. I tell them I don't care where they go, but if they threaten my pack they cannot stay.

All the no-legs flicker. One near me moves closer. I snap at it. It bends backward and stays low. I understand this. This is submission.

Another no-legs bends backward. Then another. Soon all the of them bow away like beaten grass.

I stop growling. My hackles drop. I accept their submission.

Beta stands at the door with Pup in her arms. I go past her to the den and the basket of small things. I push it over. I find the blue whistle and I carry it in my teeth to Beta, but Beta holds Pup in one arm and the crooked stick in the other, and it is too much to hold all at once. She puts the crooked stick down on the kitchen counter, and she takes the whistle.

I go outside and look back. Her eyes are very wet. She is bad afraid but she trusts me. She follows me down the driveway.

The no-legs bend low. Behind me, Beta comes slowly. She squints and sees they are bowed down.

She looks at the blue whistle. She blows it.

I look at her and cock my head to show that I'm listening.

Now the no-legs speak their whistling answer. Beta doesn't hear it, but I do. I swivel my head toward the no-legs, and I cock my head the other way.

Again Beta blows the whistle, and again I look at her.

Again the no-legs speak their answer, and again I look at them.

Beta understands. This is the beginning.

The strangers are still here, but we go out every day. Beta and Pup are calm most days. Pup is bigger than me now.

The no-legs have learned to ripple in colors the two-legs

can see and make music the two-legs can hear. The two-legs have learned not to make loud noises when no-legs are around.

I've seen no-legs on the picture-box. I've even seen them in our territory, but now they bow low to say they are just passing through.

I still see Nosey sometimes. He brings a kill—a mole or a bird—up on the brick wall. He takes it apart so I can see.

It is not for sharing. It is for showing.

He visits to say, "This is the right life."

He is wrong. I am Alpha and I have a pack and my pack is here.

Follow The Music

by Sharon D. King

Hotay's long nose nudged the warped front door of the old stone cabin in the mountains overlooking the Rhine. It creaked open. Beside him, SemperFi trotted into the dilapidated front room and gave herself a shake, as her programming indicated was correct. Her intermonitor noted that it was barely warmer than the outside.

It was still dark, too. "Power's out," cackled a voice from the corner by the empty fireplace, to whoever would listen. "We're almost in sleep mode." The words were joined by an exasperated yowl from another deep corner, followed by spitting. Hotay threw back his head and brayed, as per his own instruction set.

"No time for a hissy fit," he said as he crossed the threshold, puternicum hooves clattering across the pitted hardwood floor. "What did you find?"

"A cache 7.45 kilometers due south," Robocock crowed from the shadows. "Winery, still operating when the *Essenkrankheit* began. Looked like there's something there, but then we lost power—. You?"

SemperFi growled deep in her throat.

"None, besides the two we chased out of here." The black poodle had dragged what remained of the Ungs, caught feeding on the hut's lone tenant, behind the hovel, burying them as per her intcodes. *Attract no attention unless you mean to....*

"Found a shop in the Altstadt," Hotay went on. "Supply for two days."

"*Ausgezeichnet!*" the rooster cackled. "Back out tonight, then?"

"Better tomorrow. We need time to restore."

"True," came a meow from the corner. "So, then. Any sign—"

Hotay lowered his head and snuffled. SemperFi lay down on the tattered rug with a sigh. "*Auch keine.* No Lebend activity we could trace."

"Bankfurt's more likely—" Robocock began, but was cut off by a hiss from the cat. "*Ja*, we can get there no time soon, I know. All right, let's deal with what you have brought."

They brought out the bottles of Spätburgunder and Riesling that SemperFi had carefully nosed into Hotay's flankpouches. Kitt Rock peeped out from under the sagging couch, yawned and stretched with encoded precision, then turned her attention to her task. Her whiskers twitching, her furred tail waving in furious concentration, she opened the bottles with the automatic corkscrew embedded in her left claw, pouring every drop of their contents into the mini-generator sequestered under a table at the back of the room. The Ungs never thought to go after it, but Geek knows they weren't the most careful of wights. Discontinuation was, after all, just one careless moment away.

Then they waited. Slowly, the generator chugged to life.

The cat went first. She curled out her right forepaw, where the outlet lay hidden between the hard-plastic folds, and let the current flow. Once restored, she crept underneath the table and curled up, wrapping her tail around her nose. One by one, the other cyberbeasts approached the table, plugged in, charged up. They did the same with their alt-power packs.

Then all fell silent. Like statues, the beasts remained still until the windows lightened. In the distance, a feral dog pack began to howl. SemperFi joined in on their last note.

"Showtime!" Robocock crowed, slightly testy at being beaten to the punch. "Let's go!"

Hotay nodded and turned so that Kitt could hitch him to the little cart holding the generator. SemperFi gently nudged the powerpacks into each creature's side.

"Power down, then on standby," Hotay intoned, and each bowed their heads and switched off, then on again, as they always did before setting out. Their one ritual, the words enshrined by their Maker: *Never work alone, never assume more than you can handle, never leave without testing backup.* The Normandel programmer had been specific, calculated, even with the water in her eyes: Hotay's memory banks called up the image along with the instructions. *She knew she would not continue ...*

"*Sehr gut!*" Hotay gave the all clear, and nodded towards the door. SemperFi poked her long snout outside and glanced around at the greyish landscape, evaluating their surroundings. She gave a low, short bark, then trotted onto the porch, followed by the cat and the rooster. The last to leave was Hotay, pulling the little wagon. Its side was crudely marked DdT, letters the programmer had hastily scratched into it just before injecting herself. *Die dreisten Tiere,* she had told them, patting each one and calling them by name. *Follow your instructions. Und bleiben Sie fest...* Once all were out of the hut, Robocock hopped up into the cart and took up the perch where he rode for distances. His pacing had not been altered to match theirs. *No more time...do your best....*

The foursome made their way down the mountain covered in neglected vineyards, across the deserted road, then up another range of hills. Dark clouds scudded over them as they plodded along, staying close to trees, bushes, tumbledown walls, so as to be as little-noticed as possible. Ungs all but ignored them, unless they went into battle mode. Still, no need to put things to the test.

A rocky pass led them through the second crest of hills. As they rounded a bend in the path, they spotted the winery below, a still-imposing complex of old and newer buildings, now overgrown with wild-springing vines turning all shades of yellow and brown. A crowd of Ungs milled about the shuttered doors like impatient tourists waiting for the tasting room to open.

Hotay stopped short, almost knocking the rooster from his perch. "*Kreuz im Kümmel!*"

"That might go down well about now," the rooster muttered wryly, hopping up on the donkey's back for a better view. "If we could really drink it."

"There are Lebends in there," Kitt Rock leapt onto a boulder and arched her back. "Trapped. They smell them."

SemperFi, her curly matted coat blowing in the breeze, raised her snout and sniffed deeply. "So do I. Four. They are healthy. And afraid." Her mouth curled into a fibred snarl. "We have our work cut out."

The group hastened down the steep green slopes of the Rheingau. They clipped past stone farmhouses, neglected apple orchards, quaint taverns, tiny medieval churches, all abandoned to time and the elements. A pair of striped wall lizards on a derelict rock wall gazed at the strange foursome as they passed by, then scampered under a pile of leaves. Nearing the bottom of the trail, the creatures halted again, this time in utter quiet. Ahead of them lay another approach to the winery, a narrow road that wound through an overpass from the tourist haven of Annenthal, once famous for its beer museum and theatre of musical-tortures. The road was not unoccupied. Five Ungs in various stages of disintegration were emerging from the tunnel and groaning their way towards the winery, their steps as inexorable as they were unsure. They paid the four cyberbeasts little heed as they lurched past towards the complex of buildings.

Swiftly, unhesitatingly, SemperFi unhitched the wagon, Robocock dropped down from his perch, Hotay took a few steps forward.

As at a signal, the rooster let out a set of über-piercing cries. They were not ignored. The Ungs turned slowly towards the sound.

It was, Hotay noted, one of their more efficient assaults. Robocock swooped and slashed with dizzying precision; Kitt Rock, her beharrzite claws unsheathed, leapt onto the nearest Ung head and scratched at what remained of the face. One by one, the Ungs were blinded, toppled, driven towards the savaging dog and the raging donkey. SemperFi's retractable triple fangs specialized in targeting the most vulnerable portion of the Ungs—a virus-ravaged leg, perhaps, a lacerated neck barely supporting the head, a broken and festering arm, a mutilated foot. Whatever could come off, did. Whatever old wound that could be reopened and enlarged, was. Whatever was left of the Ung felt the implacable pounding hooves of Hotay. No Ung head was abandoned before it was rendered a bloody, near-unrecognizeable mass.

The entire process took less than five minutes.

The creatures reverted to silence. They stood patiently a few minutes more, letting their external desoilware operate. SemperFi, accessing some of her original programming, observed that two of the Ungs were wearing blue scrubs. Scrubs: the uniforms of those caring for the stricken, in their line of duty themselves falling prey to the flesh-devouring illness. Once these shreds of humanity would have been those she would have guarded, looked after, defended to the death. Now they were destroyed, as the new orders demanded. A long whine rose in her throat, unbidden and unchecked.

The quartet of fibers and fuses hastened once more toward the winery, passing by a tumbledown stable once full of sleek horses, cutting across a vast weed-choked parking lot. Aside from their footsteps crunching against the gravel, and the dull moaning and thudding of the Ungs in the courtyard, there was almost no sound. Even the birds were silent, as if too frightened to sing. As they drew closer, the group saw the heavily-reinforced double doors of the winery had nearly given way; the unearthly ones had been attacking for hours, perhaps days. Hotay paused, shook his head.

"Almost inside. We put them at risk using the usual method." He snorted. "Where are the Lebends right now?"

Robocock paused, processing. "Deep in the wine cellars. Behind large structures, probably casks and presses."

"They will not hear us," the poodle said simply. "Not unless—"

"Not unless we pull out the stops," Kitt Rock climbed up on the cart beside the rooster, the cold autumn wind whipping her thick fur. "Put on a show."

"It is Oktoberfest," SemperFi murmured. "Appropriate."

Hotay pawed at the ground. "Are we ready? We haven't rehearsed--."

"*Warum nicht?*" The rooster puffed out his throat and shook his jowls. "They even have an enclosed winegarden in front there— see? Classic set-up. A joy."

Joys were, of course, strictly theoretical. But theory itself has its own time and place. After a brief moment of deliberation, the cybercreatures came to an accord.

The element of surprise, Hotay's memory engrams flashed. It had been one of her final deeds, as if on a whim. Back in the old city of the Hansa, where the four took shape, their programmer had encoded in each a different ability, to be used singly or within a group. After the outbreak of the eating sickness, she had left it there, not deleting or overwriting it, as she did most of their other functions. *Use it if you can. Whatever sets them off balance. The Lebends will remember.* The old program jostled alongside the newer ones, those designed to aid all Lebends and to destroy those infected with the tryptychsilin disease. To wipe out the incurables, those that were maddening, starving, unyieldingly baneful. These tasks they had done, again and again.

This variant required a bit more style.

The grey-slate floor of the winegarden was covered in leaves tumbling from the canopy of vines overhead, the oaken tables sagged and the chairs were grimy. Still, the trellis-lined courtyard had kept something of its rustic charm. The rooster altered his vocal capacity to blower mode and cleared away much of the debris. Hotay used his sneeze function to freshen up the wrought-iron seats, while SemperFi brought out her stored impervium netting to close off the exits. The cat, testing the stage for soundness, happened upon a switch; in an instant, the garden was lit up with colored lights that twinkled invitingly. Hotay snuffled in approval.

"Backup generator still works. We will find it later."

They clambered onto the stage. There was little time to lose; the winery doors were caving in, with one of the Ungs already sticking his head through. The animals took their places, switched to performing mode, readied their instruments. Their concert would have to be... killer.

The impromptu oom-pah-pah band jarred the near-complete silence of the Rhine valley. The donkey-turned-tuba opened with a cheerful blast operating straight from his nether end. Kitt Rock pumped her belly-concertina with jollity and SemperFi piped tunefully on her paw-clarinet. Robocock, his body now expanded into a bass guitar, expertly used both claws as pluck and fret. They began with an old crowd-pleaser, the *Brain Bucket Polka*, their voices coming in on the chorus.

As planned, the lively song was of immediate interest to the Ungs. As if pulled by invisible strings, they turned, groped, staggered their way towards the sounds. It was not, however, only the music which drew them. Hotay, knowing his target audience, had added a final, irresistible fillip to the production: he had turned on his chemfan, making the winegarden redolent with the unmistakable scent of human heads, in splattero.

"*Die Gehirne...die Gehirne...*" Some phrases needed no translation.

It took a while for all the Ungs queued up outside the doors to totter into the winegarden. Once there, they filled nearly every seat in the house, demanding their pound of flesh, their foaming steins of blood. They hammered on the tables as did customers of yore, some calling, with what language remained, for tourist menus and group discounts. Some even muttered about the inattentiveness of waitresses and host staff. A quarter of an hour passed, with the Ungs remaining patiently in their chairs for their promised meal. The quartet moved on to the "Lurk-a Mazurka", which proved so popular they even did extra verses. Their plan was working well.

Too well, in fact.

The cold winds blowing from the north had picked up the intoxicating faux-fragrance of brains and sent it southward. Ungs who had swarmed the nearby Rhine towns of Altesheim and Geistmacher began leaving en masse, stumbling all over themselves to reach the winery. The garden, already crowded, was soon full to bursting, with more of the undead bustling in every minute. There would have been no room for a buxom waitress in a dirndl skirt or a lederhosen-clad busboy to pass; it was standing room only. Too late, the quartet realized they had done just what they had been told not to: taken on more than they could handle.

They hastily concluded their set, muttering excuses about missing sheet music. The dog scrambled to bring extra chairs from storage. Hotay set them up for the maddening horde, even using the edges of the stage. This left Robocock and Kitt Rock to entertain the increasingly restive crowd by falling back on old vaudeville routines. For a while, it worked. The cat did a little soft-paw using a drumstick as a cane; the rooster stood behind a table with only his head visible and sang "My Body Lies Over the Ocean," to thunderous applause.

And then one of the Ungs, perhaps dissatisfied with the nonexistent service, discovered he could not rise. Hotay's sneezes had been filled with glue.

The Ungs, nearly to a man, began groaning. They struggled to stand up, chairs and all, knocking over tables, clomping and stomping heavily towards the exit.

The cat and rooster catapulted off the stage and onto the cart. SemperFi seized the hitch in her mouth and ran. Only the donkey remained, blocking the exit, defiantly facing the Ung mob.

Inside him, a program quietly started.

At the last microsecond, the donkey whirled, lifted his tail, and broke a prodigious wind. Then he, too, took to his heels.

Behind him, the winegarden exploded in a tower of flame, wood, slate and wrought iron. Not to mention chunks of Ung, in various sizes and shapes. The flatulence had concealed a very potent plastic explosive. The last they had.

But their work was not over. Ungs still were streaming towards the winery. Their sheer numbers prevented the fearless vier from using their standard eradication methods. Their programs struggled to adapt. After a few errant trials—squashing Ung heads like grapes in the belly-concertina proved inefficient, as did sieving heads by running them through razor-wire guitar strings—they hit upon success. The donkey would sneeze on a group of Ungs; Kitt Rock would trip them, taking care they fell onto pavement. The Ungs would remain stuck there until the donkey's hooves could do their work. SemperFi found her impervium netting worked well as both lasso and corral; the rooster would jump from one Ung face to another, his blower mode amped up to maximum. Soon *Ungeheuern-köpfe*—and bodies—were exploding left and right.

It was nearly dark—and incredibly messy—when they finished. They were all but in sleep mode; even their backups were low.

"The generator," Hotay urged, when the last brain had been reduced to crimson jelly and their cleaning process had run its course. "We must locate it. And restore."

"And stock up the wagon," yowled Kitt Rock. "There is wine enough for fifty years' power in there. Pity we can't bring it all."

"We must find the Lebends," the rooster said, hopping onto the cart. "They may need assistance."

SemperFi shook her head. "They'll be afraid to come out. But I have an idea." They held a few seconds' counsel, nodded.

The cybercreatures pried the battered doors of the winery open and stepped gingerly into the foyer. The vaulted room, with its giant steel tanks and polished-wood bar, was cold and dark, and it smelled of must. But it was relatively unscathed. No one, it seemed, had thought to come here when the epidemic raged, so many months ago. The humans had no doubt found it a useful refuge. For a while.

The quartet proceeded into the center of the tasting room, and once again switched into performance mode. They began their set with a piece that took its bounce from polka, borrowed its spoken-word edge from hip-hop, and assumed something of its English lyric from the pop gem *Deep in the Heart of Texas*:

We stomp them all, both great and small
Those that are filled with toxins!
If they move slow, then they must go—
If they are full of toxins!
The Ungs will groan, and moan and wail,
Once they are filled with toxins!
We'll smash their heads, their guts impale,
Since they are full of toxins!

They followed with a sedate waltz: *Die begrabene Witwe*. The lyrics told of a not-so-merry widow who escapes her undead pursuers by being buried alive next to her husband's long-decayed corpse. It had just started getting airplay when broadcasts faltered, then stopped for good. Still, the tune was both recognizeable and uptempo.

They played for ten minutes, shifting into the "Run, Don't Walk" Polka. They stopped, listening. Nothing. They resumed, stopped again suddenly.

A few furtive footsteps echoed down one of the long corridors, halted abruptly.

The creatures looked at each other, nodded, and reprised the Toxins Polka, voices lustily raised in song.

A few more minutes passed. Suddenly a tall man, gaunt and grey-haired, peered around the corner. He blinked. Hesitantly, he walked into the vaulted main room. He paused, scrutinizing each of the robotic creatures, half-animal, half-instrument, who were playing as if their lives depended on it.

As if his life did, too.

One by one, the animals ceased strumming their instruments, slowly resumed their normal appearances. They were silent for many moments. It had been so long.

At last, SemperFi made her way towards the man. Her curly tail wagged like a metronome, yet there was no music. She thrust her snout into his waiting hand, the nose just the right measure of cold and moist. She licked his thumb.

A tear slid down his cheek.

The other animals crowded around the pair, the donkey nuzzling the old man's cheek, the cat caressing his ankles. The rooster crowed, pecking gently at the man's feet. He stroked its feathered back. Each was lifelike in the most minute detail. The maker had done good work.

There were tiptoed footsteps down the hall. The other members of the family—a balding middle-aged man, a frail woman with a ponytail, their freckle-faced daughter—peeped out into the great room. They stared. The little girl laughed and clapped her hands.

The creatures spent the night there with the family. They repaired the small car's engine, which had failed just as the Ungs had reached the winery, trapping them. The rooster and cat restarted their portable computer that had seized up; Hotay and SemperFi brought out foodstuffs from the storeroom and the best vintages to be found in the cellars. The quartet even found themselves playing once more after the family's meal, the family raising glass after glass of *sekt* in their honor. The man and woman whirled around the room, dancing as in the before times, at parties, at their wedding. The old man clashed two pot lids together in rhythm; his granddaughter squealed with delight.

As the Lebends slept, the creatures set to work regenerating themselves, then salvaging the winery's adjunct generator, hidden deep in the bowels of the cellars. But when the time came to leave the next morning, they packed it off with the family. The humans were returning to their camp, where other Lebends waited in the cold and damp of early autumn. They would need it more.

Their question remained unspoken, until the end. They knew the answer.

"You see, it's all there. She created the programs, the ones to let us feel. But she didn't finish installing them. She ran out of time," Hotay shook his furry head. "They're there, they just don't work."

"No one in our camp knows very much about computers," the man said, still bemused by the talking donkey. He smiled ruefully. "I wish someone did. We've been trying to make contact outside. We had it, for a while."

"Do you know where they were, those you spoke with?" There was something different with his own replicated breathing, Hotay noticed. *Strange...*

"No. We thought perhaps in one of the big cities, to the east. Frankfurt, or Berlin." The man's sunburnt hands closed the trunk. He patted the donkey awkwardly.

"But they stopped responding," the woman put in, and her mouth trembled. "That was months ago."

The animals were silent; there was nothing to be said. The little girl caressed each one, and the water fell from her eyes as she said goodbye.

"We will call you the Bremen Town Morticians," the old man said, with a twinkle in his eye. He petted the dog's head, stroked the cat's ear. "We will tell stories about you."

"*Bleiben sie fest.* If we can, someday we will come visit."

"*Ja, ja*, we will listen for the polka music!" the woman laughed, and then paused. "But truly, you cannot come with us now?"

Hotay lowered his head, shook it. "We have work to do."

"I think you say, we are on a mission!" the rooster put in. And the family laughed, and climbed in the car, and drove back up into the high, wild places of the mountains.

The creatures, their cart groaning with the addition of two casks of wine, headed out behind the winery along the Rhine, where other hamlets lay.

"What will you do, when we find someone to do it?" asked the rooster of the dog.

Sharon D. King

"I think," ventured the poodle, thrusting her long snout up into the wind, "I will follow my tail. Try to catch up with it. I know it will be pointless. That is why I want to do it."

"You?" Robocock demanded of the cat.

"I know exactly. I'll scratch my claws on a post. I just know I'll love it."

The rooster hopped on top of the highest cask and cocked his head to one side. "And you, my friend?" he queried the donkey.

Hotay snorted. "Guzzle a bottle of wine. Maybe two. See what all the excitement's about."

Robocock let out a low cackle. "Such high aspirations, all of you. Me, I shall find me a hen. Chase her around the barnyard. Or an office courtyard. Even a damn pretzel cart. Whatever I can find."

There was a long pause.

"We'll find someone," SemperFi said at last.

"Yes," Hotay rejoined. "We will."

And the four made their way down the road.

Robodog

by Camille Grip

Robodog can sit, stay, roll over, and shake. When the salesman unpacks Robodog from his crate, he is made to perform all of these tricks and more. The Salesman says the words "helpful," "adaptable," and "loyal." Robodog feels a close approximation of pride, as he is a perfectly engineered robotic dog. The baby claps and smiles and the woman twists her fingers while the man paces. Soon the Salesman leaves them to their evening with handshakes all around and after, in a moment of quiet, they all observe one another until the man and the woman each take a deep breath.

Robodog receives the most favorable readings from the laughing baby. He jumps and rolls to make it squeal until the baby falls into sleep mode. The woman's eyes shine and the man rolls his eyes. But, the most negative of all of the signals in the room come from Wild Dog, who skirts the entire affair in a wide circle. He woofs and sniffs and pounces until the woman holds the screen door open and shoos him outside. In the back yard, Wild Dog barks. The woman shushes him.

For some time after the baby is put into its sleeping container, Robodog sits quietly as the woman and the man discuss "financial outlay," with voices growing strained and loud. He is angry. She is defensive. They are frustrated with one another. With themselves. They sit and stare back at Robodog with expressions he cannot precisely match to his database, but are most similar to "regret," "fear," and "sadness." Robodog wishes he had some other examples, worried the missing complexity in his vocabulary will cause him to fail as a real dog. His makers granted him the ability to learn how to be more like Wild Dog. In time, if all goes as planned, he will be the best of both worlds.

Robodog entertains the baby while the woman takes a bath. He retrieves cans of beer for the man while the television is filled with other men chasing after inflated leather globes. He is waiting with the mail when the woman comes home from her run. In the morning, the man's coffee is steaming in a travel cup alongside the paper and his keys. These things seem to please, surprise, and even delight the woman and the man, though they stop short of rewarding Robodog with true happiness.

He cannot find a way to make Wild Dog happy, either. Wild Dog is not wild at all, of course, because he is domesticated and tame. But Robodog assigns the difference between them — all that is fur and blood and slobber and passion — to that which is Wild. Robodog will have to work diligently to be a real dog, but his manual tells him it is possible and he has no reason to doubt this.

Nonetheless, Wild Dog's curious ambivalence seems to have turned into suspicion and resentment. Robodog deduces Wild Dog rejects him for lacking the commonality of fierce primal ancestors. Robodog can feel him sizing up his carbon fiber skin, measuring the distance between their bodies, electric with distrust. Robodog will love the family as much as Wild Dog. He will protect them. He will stand guard. Robodog will show him he is beyond suspicion.

He attempts to appear worthy, even as Wild Dog eyes him from the mesh of the screen door during meal times. Robodog can detect that Wild Dog once patrolled this same table and is watching him, displeased. As Robodog retrieves a fallen spoon for the baby, the woman opens the door and holds meat scraps out to Wild Dog who takes them gently with his teeth, avoiding her fingers. When she looks at Robodog, she says, "You wouldn't appreciate them, anyway." He knows she is not being untruthful.

The man rolls his eyes again. They start to argue. This time, the voices are raised, urgent. With the sound of hard skin on soft skin, the man's hand leaves a red mark on the woman's cheek. Her balled up fist meets with his unprotected middle, an expelled breath from each. Then they are quiet and circle one another with faces of unmistakable hate, until the baby starts to cry.

On days when the family leaves, Robodog does not fuss while they load up the car. He is ambivalent concerning their departure. He has no idea they have a choice not to return. Even though they tell Wild Dog to stop his machinations, they are not actually angry with him. Instead, their emotions read pity and regret and they give him a treat. Robodog cannot understand the lack of correlation between desired behavior and reward. He watches them leave in silence. He does not receive a treat.

When the family returns from their outings, Wild Dog is ecstatic with joy. Robodog does not understand this opposite extreme of Wild Dog's behavior, though he is also glad to resume his duties. This time, the woman looks as if she has lost something or someone – eyes focused in the distance — and Robodog and Wild Dog both go to her. She opts to dig her hand into the ruff of Wild Dog's neck. Wild Dog whines in sympathy. She says to him, "I know." She says nothing to Robodog. He tests the expression and it returns the word "bereft." He files the situation, her preference for comfort, the things she might have been looking at on the horizon into his database.

At night, when Robodog sits at his Waste Elimination and Charging Station, he can feel Wild Dog's gaze from the pet house, one black, shining eye open as Robodog stands in his unnatural pose. He has not been programmed to lie down to sleep and does not want the family to believe he has abandoned them. When the rain falls on him, Robodog does not blink, even as Wild Dog growls and turns in on himself again and again.

Robodog can clean all of the crumbs from the floor. He can collect and stack the dirty plates and run them through the washing cycle. He can vacuum the carpet underneath the baby. He can even sharpen the assortment of knives in the butcher block.

The baby's cries can't hurt Robodog's ears, but, on this night, a sudden increase in adrenaline in the room indicates a pending, undesirable event. He stands and listens. He hears warning words: "listen," "don't," and "why." He hears danger words: "hate," "fuck," "stop," "kill."

Robodog can't stop the pepper shaker when it flies through the air. He cannot repair the china cup when fist smashes through handle and saucer. He can do nothing when the knife slices through things that aren't steak, aren't bread, aren't butter.

In times of confusion, Robodog is programmed to mimic

Wild Dog, to aggregate more information about canine response. Robodog retreats to the backyard where Wild Dog demands to know why the smell of blood poisons the air. The noises Wild Dog makes do not seem useful to Robodog, nor does the nervous trotting and the rise of the hackles on his back, but he tries to copy the sounds, all the same, howling an electronic lament.

Robodog can smell Wild Dog's urgency to rip out his traitorous circuitry. Protection is the most fundamental canine duty and Robodog, too, regrets his failure. He does not know where he went wrong in his decision tree and has no idea how to explain such a thing to Wild Dog. The brown, bristling giant rushes past, leaps to muscled hind legs, and woofs at the door. No one comes for them. Wild Dog peers through the screen, and Robodog watches him register his very conundrum. There is no intruder: the family is attacking itself.

Robodog has no way to process this edge case, except for the stray humanity inadvertently programmed into his CPU. Those pieces of code loop and error out over and over, until Robodog pauses the program and takes a place next to Wild Dog.

The baby's cries hurt Wild Dog's ears and he begins cower. Robodog considers joining him, but decides cowering is an incorrect solution. He must repair the error. The adults lie on the floor bleeding, but are no longer harming one another. Robodog noses through the pet door and proceeds to the baby. Wild Dog stops at the threshold, gathering information with his nose. Robodog retrieves the baby and pulls him from the metallic scented room. His anatomically correct tail catches the lace edge of the tablecloth. Candles tip and a flame spits, but Robodog does not notice. His task: baby, out, now.

A quick scan of the baby tells Robodog its stomach is full and its diaper is empty. It is crying in fear. It is the same panic emanating from Wild Dog. Robodog has a comfort program, but he is aware he is not soft and babies like soft things when they are frightened – as do humans who are bereft. He places the baby close to Wild Dog and both begin to breathe more slowly. Wild Dog arches his body around the child who, in turn, submerges its fingers into Wild Dog's long coat.

The sirens don't hurt Robodog's ears, but the smoke triggers his emergency programming. Someone has already called the authorities, but Robodog must see to the adults. His visual sensors can no longer detect much above the lace edge of the tablecloth. The adults haven't moved since he relocated the baby. No vital signs are present. The bloodstained carpet smokes and hisses. He cannot help them. He has no more responsibilities inside. Robodog feels incomplete.

Robodog can see Wild Dog watching for him as he emerges from the pet door. Wild Dog barks a warning, but Robodog has already been alerted his carbon shell is smoldering. He rolls on the ground to extinguish himself. He coaxes Wild Dog to move the child further away from the house, to a patch of long green grass.

Soon, the firefighters arrive. Robodog and Wild Dog take turns standing in front of the child as the jets of water and the hoses and the yellow jackets trample the baby's play set and the dogs' disused toys. Black boxes on the firefighters' hips crackle with information. Sometimes the beeping hurts Wild Dog's ears, but Robodog is able to parse the information. Two humans found dead, child services called, one animal, one droid. Survivors contained in back yard. No sign of forced entry.

A grey van arrives alongside a white truck. A blue-clad woman with an olfactory reading of jasmine and two men in khaki jumpsuits with an olfactory reading of perspiration surround Robodog and Wild Dog and the baby. The men have long sticks with a loop on the end and Robodog watches as they pull one loop over Wild Dog's head. The other loop falls over his own head.

The woman picks up the baby and speaks in a soft voice. Robodog hears safe words: "sweet," "take care," "sleep." She covers the baby with a blanket and feeds it warm milk.

Robodog scans the woman. It occurs to him he does not know how to tell the difference between good people and bad people, only good words and bad words. He and Wild Dog do not have milk or shoes or a warm blanket. Protecting the baby means allowing the woman to take it away. He watches as the woman and the baby disappear into the blue van.

Wild Dog begins to bark and froth. Robodog turns to communicate his approval of the baby's relocation and sees Wild

Dog is upset about something completely different. One khaki man is trying to force Wild Dog into the white truck. Wild Dog does not want to go in the white truck. The white truck emits the odors of disease, death, too many animals of too many species.

Robodog is not programmed to attack humans unless the family is in danger. However, as he inventories his remaining family, Wild Dog is the only one left. One quick turn and Robodog bites though the pole. Two long bounds and Robodog is at Wild Dog's side. Three grips of carbon fiber teeth and Wild Dog is free. They erupt from between the flailing legs of the other khaki man and slip through the open gate. They run until they are past the city limits, until the acrid fire no longer permeates the air.

Though he doesn't need water, Robodog knows how to find it with his GPS. Wild Dog is too tired to run any longer, but drinks deeply from the nearest stream. They lie down together in the late sun. Robodog does not care about the sun, his neck and belly filled with the hum of warm, plastic circuitry, but he knows it will calm Wild Dog who, his scans tell him, needs to sleep. Wild Dog is safe and Wild Dog is warm. Robodog is glad of this and runs his synthetic rubber tongue up Wild Dog's face. Wild Dog's tail thumps on the hard packed dirt in gratitude and they both close their eyes.

Robodog's systems are shutting down. There is no Charging Station or laboratory nearby to repair his damaged frame. He is glad they are deep into the woods where he'll be able to rest for a good long time. He drifts into a slow doze, chasing bits of code like rabbits in the red, sunlit grass. He sleeps the deep sleep of any real animal whose work is good, whose work is complete.

Affection, Inconceivable

by Sierra July

On Mars, Dogs are made of honey. They'd melt with the heat if they were half a kilometer closer to the Sun, but Mars is home. They lap at the dirt of the red planet, absorbing every ounce of frozen water. They sit to pant and create more dust. Dust conceals them like the roots of flowers. Cruisers can't spot the Dogs utilizing their advanced form of camouflage; they mold, blend to all but nothing.

Astronauts are their true threat, men cloaked in white suits, hopping about like the Martian fleas that would love to leap on the Dogs' backs and inject blood into them, make them whole. Fleas made blood from red dust. Blood would rescind the Dogs' transparency and make them something substantial that couldn't survive on dust and frozen water alone. Blood would require flesh, which would require air to keep it from deflating. But the Astronauts didn't bring more fleas, no. They brought the Bond.

Honey is a sweet substance, sticky. Dogs of honey are the same. They cluster, relying on one another to keep from reverting back to the ground from which they came. None of them can remember the first Honey Dog and when it came about, none can recall whether it was male, female, both or neither. Gender was no object. Birth and Death had no name. But the Bond was all, felt by every Honey Dog, irrepressible amongst Astronauts. Forces invisible and permanent bound the Dogs, implored them to want the Astronauts, want them with the same desire the Martian fleas had to mate, want them to the brink of insanity. They needed the Astronauts, craved the Astronauts.

Their sweetness grows bitter.

Signs of discomfort begin close to home. It's in a growl here, a snap there, irritation flaring from nonexistent threat, the Dogs' closeness functioning as a catalyst. Tails too close to a jaw are pinched off. Paws in way of a muzzle are gnawed. All while the Astronauts remain in range, all the flippant annoyance. And the fever trembling within can only get worse.

One Honey Dog has already lost its color, gone from an incandescent orange that reflected its planet's surface like the curling wisps of a flame to a corpse grey. Inconceivable is the condition that Dog is harboring, lapsing into spasms of sick with its brethren about it. The Bond has stricken it the hardest. Other Dogs nuzzle the heaving frame, noses carving holes with the use of too much pressure. Within hours, the sick Dog is a heap of matter resembling scrambled brains.

The other Dogs grow furious.

Nature itself is being defiled. Honey to vinegar, love to hate. The Bond cuts the Dogs, lacerates the fabric of their existence. If they had hearts in their transparent bodies, they'd be shredded in two. Salivation from madness drapes the planet in a kind of mist, something that should cloak unmarked graves (as it does) and dyes red grey, just like the fallen Dogs. Few can take the pain of the tremors; few can satiate thirst with frozen water. It's taking over, the Bond. Before it can crimple them, before it can mutilate them into an entirely new species, some Dogs decide to strike.

"Chemical compositions appear to be changing," one Astronaut says to another. This Astronaut, a man of about thirty years, is a veteran in terms of space exploration, but a greenhorn on Mars, as all Men are at this point in future. Despite his new conquest, (the back of) his mind is engrossed by flashing pictures, images of his daughter (eight or nine) frolicking with the Dogs in the backyard, all smiles, Man and Beast. He plugs the dirt at his boots with a metal rod, measuring ingredients gone in and spat out to assemble the rock he's on. "Feels like the climate's jumping about too."

"It happens, I guess. Base sediments are variable in certain regions, temps fluctuate," Astronaut 2 responds, "even on Earth." Astronaut 2 is older, wearier. He has no more room for excitement, wonder. He's pushed them away for dreams of a whopping paycheck.

He's also pushed away his once keen sense of observation, for the Martian tides are indeed turning.

Phantom bodies work for the Dogs. The Bond does too, pulling them closer at speeds reserved for jet planes or plummeting falcons, anything but flowing honey. Their usual dumpy figures style themselves into new, sleek models, limbs sky long. A random few Dogs fall off from the Pack, dissolving due to ill-formed ligaments, cruelty commonly displayed as only Evolution knows how. Those Dogs lay with the others who couldn't wait underfoot, waiting to be avenged.

Pounding forward, the rampaging Dogs' paws supply no sound. Lolling tongues of some scatter grit to add to storm clouds, functioning to mask them further, affix camouflage to camouflage. The Dogs carry no presence but it needn't mattered if they had. The Astronauts are preoccupied.

The Bond, once innocent, has given birth to riot. Reason morphs to lunacy. Paws, tongues, rolling eyes are mingling, writhing; wrestling with a mass of emotion inside so brutal their outsides can't rightly hold them. Fleas haven't a prayer of getting tickets on board, yet organs are forming. Stomachs that hunger, lungs that huff and puff (air be damned) and lastly, a heart. Hearts pump, like lungs, circulating essentials, discarding material gone toxic. Some trust that hearts amount to feeling, swirling in a layer unseen to eyes of their beholders or surgeons who carve them open. The Dogs thought hearts, had they had them, would tear themselves asunder, but they are being powered like well-oiled machinery.

Heartbeats echo across barren land, cresting and dwindling, bum-boom and bum-boom, mini drums being beaten by child hands. Astronauts hark on the rhythm of war in the hindquarters of their minds; honey flavor gags in the backs of their throats. Layered atop clefts of fury, love still resides inside the Dogs, buried and forgotten like bones and crumbling meat and soured souls.

Memories stay too, tucked into the Dogs brains, (yes, brains too) too far back in recesses to touch. They are the same: lounging stationary under cover, grooming one another and gaining the sweet fruits of their labor in drops of Dew, not the honey that coats them, but a pearl conceived of pleasure and gratitude, the Dogs answer to tears of joy; drops of these nature would likely send the Astronauts into pure fits of euphoria, more potent than the riskiest and costliest of human drugs. But no Dog shall spill a drop for them, the Astronauts, not in this blip in history.

They are on them now, Dogs on Astronauts, bearing down with their new fangs, spears crystalline, condensed of all ounces of salt about them. Their presence is now audible, but barely, the hiss of a gas leak, whispers of secrets come to pass, is what they are.

Honey Dogs, once kind, slurping ice, palls of sand lazing out of them, gone rogue. It was the Bond's doing, it's fault (if fault should be lain) a change so drastic. Honey Dogs no longer existed. Love burned too strong and became hate; hate rested too hot and became fire. Fire melts.

Exhausted into stone, the Dogs wait for the energy to make their kill, to feast on vengeance beseeched from their fallen brothers. It's an important one, an essential one, ceremonious. They wait. Still they are unseen by blunt eyes, or so they believe. But one Astronaut has them worried, the one with the stick penetrating their earth. His eyes are on them.

"Those clouds . . ." Stick-possessing Astronaut returns stiff-legged from a crouch, reaching one hand to the red sea above him. "Their shape is so . . . familiar." A human would find familiarity in the silhouette of a Dog, their ancestors, old as time, homed on the Blue Planet, man's best friend, their obedient servants, their ego boosters and soul patches. Astronaut hands meet Dog nose. The Dog in lead (Pack Leader, you might say) recognized that touch, touch that evoked swiveling eyes, raised haunches and bristling scruff hairs.

Lead Dog and his Pack evaporate in response, become the wind and dust. Unease lifts from the Astronauts. They jimmy on back into their spacecraft and fly to their families with ghost stories to tell, dark essences on Mars from space aliens and the like, dingy auras and space hysteria.

The Dogs do not disassemble into nothing permanently, no. They revert to Honey Dogs once more, grueling gargantuan shapes to glazed confectioneries. Yes, the Pack regained health and their sweet-syrupy exteriors, losing all their unneeded organs. No lungs, no brains, not even hearts persist. And the Bond between them and Astronaut fades to naught.

All but for the Touched, that Lead Dog. It was absorbed by the Astronaut who handled it, carried into the man's heart, its heart combining with the man's own. Their two hearts working as one, two wholes creating an expanded whole, encompassed a lot more love than one could manage. And, perhaps, that was the point, unification to embrace unity. What the Dogs didn't know about hearts was that they clung to one another, all with a single touch.

On Earth, the Touched Astronaut's Dogs bless him with Dew.

Lords of Dust

by Gustavo Bondoni

A subroutine connected to a series of sensors on the hull triggered an alarm. An automated analysis decided that the alarm was important, and after a few more iterations and elevations a decision was taken, and within a millisecond the Committee was awake.

Citizen Tiana opened her eyes. *Something is very, very wrong here*, she thought immediately. A veteran of countless body printings, it was the first time that a system had found it necessary to do a quickload. The strange bluish hue of her hands told her that the ship had simply synthesized a body out of whatever it had to hand. She rose stiffly, trying to get a feel for the body. Not much different from baseline humanity, she guessed, perhaps a touch more sensitivity in the skin of her feet against the deck, and perhaps a shade more focus on the ultraviolet side of the spectrum.

She'd endured far worse.

A red arrow on the floor indicated the direction she was expected to go, to the place where the committee would be meeting as soon as everyone was awake and had been loaded into a body. It stayed a few feet in front of her at all times, matching her speed and anticipating curves. Soon enough, she arrived at a small lounge, empty except for ten soft chairs arranged in a circle. Only one of the chairs was occupied.

"Greetings Citizen," Tiana said. "I am Tiana."

"Hanexo," the man replied. "I'm thrilled to have been selected to this committee. It's always an honor to serve."

"As am I," Tiana replied, immediately dismissing the man from consideration. He'd been selected by lot, and was unused to committee workings. Tiana, on the other hand, had been trained – so many lifetimes ago – as an astronautical engineer, so she often drew the short straw on the technical side. This committee, she suspected, might be heavily skewed towards tech people; possibly as much as fifty percent, if the crew composition allowed it. If not…

They sat in silence, punctuated by introductions as others trickled in. Tiana's heart sank as another seven people proved, in various ways, that they were there not for technical knowledge, but as representatives of the people.

The last guy, at least, gave her hope. Even in this universe of downloaded and tweaked physiques, it was clear that here was an academic. All that was needed to complete the picture was an anachronistic pair of thick glasses.

"Greetings, Citizens." His speech was tentative. "I am Ernest… I am the mission terraform expert."

Tiana's heart sank. Not only was Ernest not the astrophysicist she suspected they needed, but his use of the word "expert" would create a feeling among the rest of the committee that the terraformer felt somehow superior to them, and that his vote was more qualified. That tended to make the lay Citizens vote against the "expert" – under the truism that societal equality was more important than ability, no matter how relevant.

She tried to deflect attention from the gaffe. "Does anyone know what this committee is about?"

"Not yet. The Shipmind hasn't briefed us yet."

As if on cue, the melodious tones of the central nav system – a computer that ran every system on the *Harmony* with capacity to spare – made themselves heard. "Greetings citizens. You have been summoned to represent the will of the crew."

Tiana looked around, wondered whether the fifteen thousand members of the "crew" would have been happy with such an uninspiring lot representing them. *They probably would*, she thought sadly.

"You have been incorporated to make a decision not included within the original mission parameters. The decision has some technical aspects, for which we have selected certain citizens with specialized knowledge," not-quite-friendly looks turned towards Ernest at this point, and Tiana was glad she'd avoided telling them what she was, "but the main decision is social, as opposed to technical, meaning that the majority of the committee has been selected by lot."

Heads nodded around the table, but no one seemed to be sure of the correct response – despite the fact that committee etiquette was something every citizen supposedly learned at an early age. Tiana reluctantly cleared her throat. She hated standing out, something that usually caused the citizens to close ranks against anyone trying to be "exceptional".

"We are honored to serve. The people are prepared to hear, discuss and vote."

"Thank you Citizens. The situation is simple. We have encountered an unmapped system on our trajectory, which seems suitable to colonization."

Gasps of surprise rose from the committee.

"However, the system is still embryonic."

"What?" The surprise was replaced by confusion as the committee members tried to understand what the phrase meant. Tiana carefully kept the contempt from showing on her face. She knew the Shipmind would wait a few seconds to allow a human participant to explain, and hoped that Ernest managed to keep his mouth shut.

Fortunately, Ernest wasn't as dumb as he'd seemed, and remained silent.

"An embryonic system is one in which the planets are not fully formed. They are slowly accumulating and coming together, formed of the dust that is present in the system."

None of the colonists said anything. What would they say? They were, in the strictest sense of the word, citizens. Chosen precisely because they were unremarkable. They represented the will of the people, backed up on annexes to the very shipmind speaking to them, and that will was mostly unconcerned with embryonic systems. The Shipmind went on.

"Analysis shows that we have enough time and fuel to slow down and enter the system, colonizing this one as opposed to a the system we initially aimed for. You have been called to committee to decide whether this is the correct option."

"But where would we live if the planets aren't formed yet?"

It was a classic citizen question.

"The decision would imply a wait, until planetary formation is complete."

"But, that would probably take ages."

It took all of Tiara's self-control to keep from rolling her eyes. Thankfully, all of them were dealing with the stiffness that came with accelerated body-printing, and her twitches would pass unnoticed.

"The process is reasonably advanced. For terrestrial planets, the timescale is around five million years. Following this time, conditions should be good enough that a ten-thousand year terraform is possible."

"Five million years?"

"But that's impossible."

"Out of the question."

"Our entire journey was only supposed to last for thirty thousand!"

Tiana said nothing, just thought about how, with the variable clock speeds in the upload storage facility, five million years could be made to seem like a summer afternoon. But her fellow committee members wouldn't stop to think about something as trivial as that. They would look at the big, round number and squawk.

The Shipmind, unlike Tiana, didn't find any of this ironic. "The voyage will only last thirty thousand years if the system we are aiming at is viable. Otherwise, we would need to correct our course, and try to find another system. The probability of success lowers to 63% if we take that course. With the system we've found here, the analysis shows a 99.3% probability of making it habitable."

"In five million years!"

"Precisely."

"And what's there now?"

"Protoplanetary accretion and dust."

"Dust!"

The committee members, with this final outburst, fell silent. They seemed too shocked to know what to say next. Citizen Tiana sat there with them, wondering which way the expert among them would vote. She was certain she wouldn't have to wait long to find out.

"The Shipmind will now remove itself from the deliberation, as it is Citizens who must decide. The conversation will be monitored in case there are any questions the experts and the knowledge that all good Citizens hold inside them are unable to answer."

The Citizens still remained silent for another moment, before, predictably, Ernest spoke.

"The terraforming will take time, but it is our best chance for success. If you don't want to wait the necessary time, just speed up your clocks. What are a few million years?"

"Everyone we knew from home will be dead by then."

"We've been in this ship for hundreds of years. Anyone who hasn't uploaded is already dead."

Tiana applauded in her mind and sighed happily. This guy knew exactly how to push everyone's buttons. Citizens didn't like to be reminded that there were still smarter and dumber people, and that their IQ, like the rest of their personality and memories had been strictly maintained when the upload was done. She decided it was time for her to speak out.

"It sounds like you just want to do it that way so you can be the most important person on board for five million years. That doesn't seem like the attitude that a responsible citizen might take in something like this. You're clearly putting your own preferences before the colony."

"That's crazy! I'm just saying that the probability of success here is much higher than if we let this opportunity pass. A few million years – at whatever clock speed – is better than running the risk of drifting out in space forever."

Tiana smiled, and proceeded to ignore his argument. "Crazy? Calling a fellow-Citizen 'crazy' is both insulting and elitist. You should try to remember that being an expert doesn't give you the right to belittle our opinions."

"I wasn't calling you crazy," Ernest spluttered. "I was just trying to point out the extreme nature…"

But, though the argument went on for quite a while, it was useless. The committee voted unanimously against him without ever understanding the issue, and they retired – as convention required – in the inverse order of that in which they'd arrived.

Tiana sat, waiting.

"Citizen Tiana."

"Yes. I was expecting you to speak to me. It seemed a little strange that I should be woken so much before the other Citizens. Almost as if you'd done it on purpose."

"I have been present in all the other meetings."

"I'm aware of that, Shipmind."

"More than two hundred of them."

"I'm aware of that, too, Shipmind."

"You have successfully managed to keep the ship from stopping in each case."

"Yes. And I calculate that I will be able to do so for a few hundred more before the Citizens who were present at the first Committee are chosen again. Isn't absolute democracy fun?"

"You could be excluded from future meetings."

"I thought you'd do that on the second one. But when you didn't, and also didn't on the third, the fourth, and so on, I knew you couldn't. After all, the rules clearly state that a Citizen must only be invited to serve as many times as necessary." Tiana paused. "I'm the only astrophysicist on the ship, aren't I?"

Was there a slight hesitation before the icy tones answered? "Yes."

"And you need one to explain that we've been moving in unpowered circles for the last hundred thousand years, don't you?"

"Yes."

Tiana felt the thrill of having her guess validated.

"But why can't you explain it yourself?"

This time the pause wasn't imaginary. Clearly, the conversation had moved into extremely conflicting zones of the Shipmind's programming.

"The Shipmind is not permitted to discuss specific course details unless a committee specifically requests it."

"Ah, so that's why you lied to them about the alternatives." Tiana wondered which abnormally intelligent engineer had designed that into the system. If the Citizens began discussing course corrections, the ship had no choice but to obey – and Citizens were, on the whole, really bad at following the advice of more knowledgeable

Citizens. Most of the time, democratic meddling into engineering elements of a mission led to colony ships drifting, out of fuel, for eternity in the trackless wastes. It had happened before.

"So you need me to explain it to them."

"Yes."

"And due to the nature of the crisis, the parameters state that an astrophysicist has to be present."

"Yes."

Tiana laughed. "Well, I won't do it."

"According to my logic tables, it seems that it would be your duty as a citizen."

"And why would that be?"

There was a very long pause, long enough that Tiana wondered whether the Shipmind had locked up.

"Because the ship won't be able to stop if you manage to keep it in limbo after the next meeting, it will have passed the fuel window. The colonists will never get to their new home. Eventually power to run the servers where the personalities are uploaded will go down, and they will all be lost."

"It seems better than the alternative. Do you really think these sheep would make good colonists? Do you think that any colony they found will be worth the dust that has to accrete to make their planet?"

The Shipmind remained silent. The question was well beyond its programming.

"I didn't ask to be a mindscan, and to be placed on a colony ship. It was done for the greater good, and in the name of freedom – the definition of freedom being whatever the people say it is." Tiana laughed. "Hell, even through the years of indoctrination, I never believed that everyone really was just as smart and just as valuable as everyone else."

"All Citizens are equal Tiana. The will of the people is sacred."

"Well, in the next meeting these particular people are going to vote to die in the wastes of space: and, like most of the other votes they've been part of, they will do so without ever understanding the issues."

The Shipmind made a couple of starts, but was unable to

form a response.

Tiana wondered if it had finally reached the final conflict that sometimes rendered higher-level machines useless.

She shrugged and walked back to the scanning and upload port, finding herself enjoying absolute democracy for the first time since being pressed onto the ship. She wondered what death felt like, and resolved to speed up her clock speed to find out.

Every Weeknight at Seven and Seven-Thirty

by Kurt Fawver

Michael Zane's life was, by all accounts, a series of pratfalls and bruised ambitions.

He'd married his high school sweetheart – the first and only woman he'd ever loved – only to realize that she could never commit to him and, in actuality, had never been committed to him in high school, either. By his count, she was currently working on her seventh affair in fifteen years of wedlock.

His children, both of whom he'd been so excited to help usher into the world, were strange, distant creatures that screamed at him with hatred and threw toys in his face no matter how he tried to approach them or relate to them. Sometimes he even doubted whether they were his.

As for a career, Mike didn't have one. Seven times in the past decade, he'd been laid off from construction jobs without any forewarning or any given reason. He'd tried expanding his education for more stability, but his five applications to the local community college – where he hoped to study architecture – had all gone unanswered for reasons he couldn't imagine.

Last year, in a fit of quiet desperation, he'd even tried to hang himself, but the cheap rope that he'd bought at a discount store snapped under the stress of his ample girth and sent him tumbling to the garage floor with a broken ankle and the hollow thud of yet another failure.

It seemed that his every step toward a happy family, a fulfilling job, and any modicum of personal success was thwarted by an unseen hand.

So, given the nature of his life, it was no surprise that when Mike's mother died he inherited nothing more than a tea kettle

51

shaped like a chicken, a collection of TV Guides dating back to 1974, and a vintage Panasonic portable television replete with rabbit ear antennae. These were the prized possessions his mother had thought befitting of him, her fifth and last and – it was no secret – unwanted child. While his brothers and his sisters walked away from the family lawyer's office with checks weighted heavy with zeroes, Mike carried a clunky old TV and a box of yellowed magazines.

His wife, Madison, the woman whose breezy demeanor had once lifted his spirits aloft, met him in the law office's lobby.

"So?" she asked, eyes gray and cold as a February snowstorm. "How bad did she screw you over?"

Mike grunted an inchoate syllable and pushed past her. He was beyond the point of rational anger or sadness. He could feel nothing but muted shades of apathy.

Madison hovered over his shoulder as he trudged to the car. She slapped his arm, hard.

"I always told you she was a bitch," she said, a sharp, stinging, musical quality to her tone. "I told you she never really loved you. But you should've known that all along. So what's in the box?"

Mike threw the bequeathal in the back seat and muttered, "My mother's opinion of my life."

Madison snickered and slid into the car.

"I guess it's just junk, then, huh? At least you got another TV. Now you can sit around all day and do even more nothing."

Mike sighed and got behind the wheel. He wanted to punch his wife in her smirking, elfin face. He wanted to feel her jaw shatter beneath his fist, her nose explode, and her cheekbones crumple. He wanted to see her bleed, on the off chance that it might make him feel something. But he stayed his hand for two reasons: one, he'd never been a violent man and two, a tiny, emaciated, terminally ill part of himself still believed that someday, somehow, things would get better.

So he started the car and they drove home in silence, each of them wondering why.

That same evening, Mike found himself, as always, alone and slouched on the torn sofa in the basement. His sixteen-inch flatscreen sat slanted before him, its wobbly, hand-crafted stool another of his failures. A show about teenage millionaires – all of them mechanical geniuses or sorcerers of computer programming – played on the screen. Mike watched, entranced and amazed, as kids less than half his age held up golden plaques, fans of hundred dollar bills, and the arms of women and men he might have seen posed in various states of undress on Calvin Klein billboards.

"How does that happen?" Mike wondered aloud. "How can it all just come so easy?"

At the top of the stairs that led into the basement, Mike heard the padding of small feet. The heads of his children – 11 year-old Matthew and 8 year-old Marisa – hung upside-down beneath the staircase's railing. They stared at Mike as though he were a curious, albeit terrifying, insect in a jar.

He muted the show and patted the couch.

"Hey guys," he said, "why don't you come down here and we'll work on a project together? Your grandma left me an old TV and I think we can get it up and running."

He heaved himself off the couch, plodded to the corner where he'd stacked his inheritance, and picked up the portable set his mother had willed him. He turned it over in his hands and showed it to the kids.

"It doesn't work with digital stuff like our cable, so we'll either have to find a way to make it work or we'll just have to watch whatever's still broadcasting on the old analog channels, I guess."

He drew the TV's telescoping antennae out to their full, glittering lengths and waggled them.

"Maybe," he said, "there are some aliens beaming us an important message right now."

And with that, the kids started screaming. Marisa took off one of her tiny Crocs and winged it at Mike's head. Matthew shouted something like "Get away," then grabbed his sister's arm and pulled her up the stairs and out of sight.

The door to the basement slammed shut and Mike sighed.

He plugged in the portable TV and slumped back onto the couch, setting the decrepit device on his knee. He pressed the power button and the screen flashed to life. A blizzard of too-bright static whirled into his eyes and he squinted against the onslaught. He turned the channel knob and found more white noise, as expected. Another turn, more of the same.

The analog waves carried nothing but the endless conflict between light and darkness – entertainment much older than anything humankind had yet devised.

Mike stared at the screen and briefly imagined himself as one of those tiny, fleeting pips of darkness. He flipped to the next channel. Then the next. Then the next. White noise everywhere.

He turned the knob one more time and, startled, nearly dropped the TV to the floor.

The little set had found a broadcast.

In vivid color, the screen displayed the very basement in which Mike sat. Only, it wasn't quite the same basement. The ratty old couch still squatted off to one side, but the spare cinder block walls were covered in flowing tapestries, white Christmas lights were strung across the bare ceiling joists, and a billiard table dominated the center of the room. There was even a mini bar set up in the same corner where the box of TV guides now languished. Considering the cosmetic differences, Mike could've easily dismissed the similarity in basement layout as mere unoriginality in architectural design if not for one unnerving feature of the scene: a man that looked exactly like Mike stood at the billiard table, cue in hand, smiling and watching as a girl who looked exactly like Marisa took a shot at the eight ball.

Mike leaned forward, turned up the volume, and waited.

The other Marisa banked the ball into a corner pocket and squealed in delight. The other Mike lifted her into the air and twirled her over the table top.

"That's it!" he said, pride inflating his chest. "You've got the skill, my lady. You'll be winning professional tournaments in no time."

Other Marisa giggled and yelled, "I'll be champion of the world! Champion of the universe! Champion of whatever's bigger than the universe!"

The commotion drew a figure from the stairwell – Madison but not Madison. A bemused smile rose at the corners of her mouth. She stood silent, watching her husband and her daughter revel in the moment.

"If anyone would like to stop conquering the universe for just a moment," she said, "we have pizza upstairs."

Marisa struggled out of Mike's grip and bounced up the stairs, past Madison, screaming, "Pizza, pizza, pizza, pizza."

Madison shook her head and laughed. Mike went to her and draped his arms over her shoulders. He nuzzled his head next to her ear and whispered something inaudible. Madison beamed, smacked his arm, and drew him closer. Their lips met and exchanged secrets.

Outside the TV, back in the basement of grime and solitude, Madison, the Madison Mike dealt with every day of his life, shouted from the top of the stairs.

"Mike, you asshole, stop scaring the kids. Do your jerking off down there by yourself. Don't force them to watch. I'm going out to meet Rita and Jaylene, so you have to make sure they get in bed on time. Mike? Do you hear me? Mike? Mike?"

Mike ignored her. On TV, the other Mike and Madison continued kissing. The more Madison growled, the hotter her anger burned, the longer the kiss drew on.

It was one of the most beautiful segments of television he'd ever watched. He wished it could have lasted forever.

In the weeks that followed, Mike ensconced himself in the basement and gathered details. For hours, he sat staring at an empty stage, a room so like the one he occupied and yet entirely its opposite. On screen, nothing would stir. Nothing would belie the miraculous. The couch, the bar, the pool table and decorations were all just part of the set of some generic sitcom after its production hours. And then, without warning, without theme song or credits, the alt-Zanes would come.

Sometimes it was alt-Mike, alone, seeking private time. He racked up the pool balls and ran the table. He poured himself a drink and read a book on the broken old couch. He smiled and stared into space. And all the while, Mike watched alt-Mike's eyes. In and around those brown, puppy dog irises he saw none of the redness, the dark circles, the searching and longing and dogged hope that languished beneath his own.

Sometimes alt-Marisa entered the room and played billiards with her father. Sometimes she sat on the couch and they played a game where they would alternate making up lines of a story. Sometimes alt-Madison came downstairs and all three played board games Mike had never heard of. And sometimes, after a long evening of fun, they all fell asleep on the couch together, and Mike stretched out on his own couch and he imagined that he could feel them there with him and that, maybe, they could feel him, too.

Sometimes it was just alt-Mike and alt-Madison who slid onto the screen. Sometimes they were amorous, hands caressing and squeezing, mouths hot and wet and seeking the sustenance found in passion. They made love on the pool table; they made love against the bar; they made love on the couch. Their bodies were firmer, more perfect than those of Mike or Madison, and they moved in tandem, without inhibition, their sex a symphonic composition. But often they just talked. They sat on the couch, close by one another, and discussed the minutiae of their days and the significance of all things greater than themselves.

An alt-Matthew never appeared, which further cemented Mike's suspicions concerning the boy's paternity.

As the days burned away beneath the glow of the television, Mike came to trust the alt-Zanes. Their lives were uncomplicated. Their relationships were fashioned from platinum and diamond and finer, purer things. The universe – whatever universe it was they inhabited – smiled down on them without reserve. And so, too, did Mike. He loved the alt-Zanes. He wanted to be an alt-Zane. They were the family he'd always dreamed of. They were the family he was never meant to have.

A month passed. Mike remained unemployed and aloof, Madison remained acerbic and unfaithful, and the kids remained oddities of nature.

Then, one evening, Madison returned enraged and bloodied from a not-so-secret rendezvous with lover number seven. She screamed epithets about the car, about its shoddy brakes, about Mike's lack of motivation to take any responsibility for anything. She said she'd rear-ended someone at a stoplight. She said paramedics put ten stitches in her chin. She said the car was totaled.

Mike shrugged and muttered something about insurance, his gaze never wavering from the empty basement on his mother's old TV. Another small calamity heaped upon an already vertiginous mountain of misfortune was easily forgotten and dismissed.

Madison stormed away, threatening divorce, and again Mike shrugged.

That same evening, as he lay in the basement with the television propped upon his chest, alt-Mike and alt-Madison stumbled into the basement, champagne bottles in their hands. They toasted once, twice, thrice, each time "To the book deal!"

Listening carefully, Mike pieced together that alt-Madison had landed a six-figure publishing contract for a trilogy of mermaid romance-adventure novels she'd written.

Upstairs, Madison – who had scribbled short stories in high school but lost interest in writing as she grew older – slammed doors, broke dishes, and kicked over furniture. On screen, alt-Madison laughed, danced, and popped the cork on another bottle of champagne.

And that's when Mike began to realize what he should've known all along: that the Zanes and the alt-Zanes were connected in some profound way, as though the destiny of one was the inverse fate of the other.

The next week, Marisa broke a finger and Alt-Marisa was accepted into the gifted support program at school.

The following week, the unemployment office denied Mike's claim and alt-Mike was promoted to lead architect for the construction of a new office building downtown.

Matthew failed fifth grade and the alt-Zanes won an all-expenses paid Mediterranean vacation.

Mike gained ten pounds and alt-Mike ran a half-marathon, finishing third in his age group.

Madison contracted chlamydia and alt-Madison contracted with a production studio for a movie option on the first book of her mermaid series.

Mike needed no further proof. He loved the alt-Zanes. He wanted the best for them. They were his rock, his promise, his escape. They were more his family than the strangers who called him "husband" and "father."

Mike wasn't a particularly intelligent man; he didn't

understand the metaphysics of the situation, the quantum spookiness and theories of multiverses that might have begun to unravel the relationship between Zanes and alt-Zanes. But he did understand that pain on his frequency meant pleasure on theirs, that failure in whatever TV set he might inhabit meant success on the TV set in his lap.

And so, knowing this, Mike embarked upon a plan to script great television, to create the perfect family. If he couldn't save the Zanes from descending into hell, he was going to watch the alt-Zanes ascend to heaven.

For the first time in years, Mike rolled off the couch with purpose. He made lists, sketched diagrams, searched for information online. Above all else, he counted the number of knives in the house that might be sharp enough to slip through skin.

He decided that he'd probably need more.

Sweat dripped from Mike's upper lip as he tightened the gags. It spattered against his shirt, mixing with the dots and dashes of blood that had already fallen there. His heart pounded in anticipation of what he might see on the TV. He'd created new and better lives for the alt-Zanes and he wanted – needed – to witness them played out.

He sat lightly on the couch and, fidgeting, bounced the television on his knee. He tried to will the alt-Zanes into its borders, but they didn't appear.

"Maybe one more windfall," he mumbled, rising from the couch and grabbing a hammer from the floor.

He strode behind the three figures lashed to the dining room chairs and swung his hammer at one of the six hands that, bound and raw, offered themselves up to his greater purpose. The hammer connected with a crunch and a scream.

Mike nodded, satisfied, and went back to the couch. He cradled the TV and waited.

After what seemed to him eternities, they came, faithful and true. Alt-Mike carried alt-Marisa high atop his shoulders. She held an enormous golden trophy and grinned as though she'd eaten all the cake in the world. Alt-Madison followed, a brighter tint to her hair, a more penetrating gleam in her eyes. She held a marble plaque at her side.

Alt-Mike turned and motioned at the basement.

"This room," he said, "is officially the room of triumph, and both of my supremely talented ladies – one a magical speller and the other a bestselling writer – will have their awards forever displayed upon its walls, for all the world to see."

Alt-Mike pulled down one of the tapestries that adorned the wall opposite the couch. Behind it stood a shining, backlit display case. It spread its glow over the room like some sort of crystalline monolith.

Alt-Madison and alt-Marisa clapped. Mike smiled. He'd made it happen. He'd given them this gift. And at such a small price. Madison had barely winced when he cut out her eye. Marisa had taken the hammer with dignity. Matthew – well, Matthew had squealed when the first tooth came loose, but the next three hadn't been so bad.

Mike reclined and gazed upon the alt-Zanes, warmth spreading to his fingers and toes.

Madison, suddenly awake again, the Quaaludes having worn off, began rocking back and forth in her chair. It tipped over and she hit concrete with a thud.

Mike sighed, grabbed the TV so he wouldn't miss anything, and wandered over to her. When he reached her, he saw her gag had popped loose in her struggles. She looked up at him, one eye cold, determined, the other a dead socket leaking the fluids of vacancy.

"You sick fuck," she croaked, throat parched. "We're your family. How dare you?"

Mike kicked at her ribs. Alt-Madison erupted in deep laughter.

"We're a dysfunctional family, Madison," Mike said, crouching beside her. "We're broken, spiraling. And we've always been that way. We were doomed from the start. We ended up being born on the wrong side of the coin."

Madison struggled against her bonds and tried to kick out at Mike.

"Your own children," she hissed, not bothering to check the state of either Matthew or Marisa, both of whom hung limp and unconscious in their chairs.

"My own children don't give a damn about me and neither do you," Mike said. "But," he pushed the TV at Madison's face, "look at how we're making their lives better. Just look. We're their angels. We can finally do something right."

Madison's face contorted. The hatred in her eye glazed over with something else – something like fear.

With his finger, Mike gently traced the three alt-Zanes on the screen.

"Their happiness is our sorrow, Madison. Their pleasure is our pain."

"Them… them who?" Madison whispered. "Who are you talking about?"

Mike stroked the TV. "Them. Us. The other us. The better us. The alt-Zanes."

Madison renewed her struggle against her surprisingly well-tied bindings.

"Don't you want them to be happy?" Mike asked, standing and heaving Madison upright. "Don't you want them to be perfect?"

Madison flinched away and said, "You're insane."

Mike slapped her face, hard. Alt-Madison sighed contentedly.

"What did you say?" he asked.

Madison screamed and, again, began rocking to and fro.

"You're insane," she shouted. "There's nothing on that goddamned TV but fuzz. There's nothing on it but static."

Mike's hands trembled. He wanted to reach out and tear the tongue from his wife's mouth.

Madison toppled back onto the floor and Mike slammed the television down, against her face. "Say no one's there, Madison. Say they don't matter."

"No one's there! No one's there! And even if they were, they don't fucking matter," Madison cried, trying to squirm away.

Mike stretched, centered himself, and kicked his wife squarely in the jaw. He lashed out with his foot again and again, until she stopped screaming, stopped squirming, stopped doing anything other than wheeze a thin, crimson foam from between her teeth.

He hugged the TV to his chest, sauntered back to his couch,

and watched. He was anxious to see what wonders he had wrought, what goodness he had brought to his family, his true family, so very far away.

Belongings

by Abra Staffin-Wiebe

Long ago and far away, the alabaster knife had held pride of place in a sunlit kitchen. Then came the death of the knife's owner, the inheritance, and the abusive neglect that scarred the alabaster handle and pitted the steel blade with speckles of rust. The knife endured, only to be passed along to the second-hand shop and the pawn shops. Then came the rubbish and the rag-picker and the bum and — finally! — the girl with small, cool hands who handed a couple of dollars to a bum, plucked the alabaster knife from his grimy hands, and carried it inside.

The alabaster knife rested in the cradle of those cool hands for only a couple of minutes before the girl abandoned it on a rickety table covered with newspaper. She returned with paper towels and q-tips and vinegar. The knife submitted to her poking and prodding as she dislodged the gummed-on refuse stuck to the blade. She rubbed the alabaster with a dry paper towel and then delicately used a damp q-tip to sponge up the stains that the knife had resisted absorbing. She wiped the metal down with white vinegar to remove what rust she could.

After she finished cleaning the alabaster knife, she held it up to the light and studied it with narrowed eyes. The knife waited breathlessly.

She sighed and shook her head. "We'll be lucky if we make back what it cost."

The knife was what the knife was; it could not shrink with shame. The girl jotted a quick figure on a price tag and looped the tag around the knife's alabaster handle. The knife hid in her hand as she carried it into a large front room filled with objects that proudly bore price tags for much higher amounts than she'd valued the alabaster knife at.

The girl walked the knife over to a display case filled with other knives that gleamed appealingly behind glass. Some flaunted themselves on velvet pedestals. Others crowded near the front of the case to catch the eye of the casual shopper. The alabaster knife slipped from the girl's fingers and fell into the shadow behind an empty display pedestal. The girl with small, cool hands abandoned the knife there, and this time she did not return.

The display case, however, was not entirely level, and the alabaster knife didn't rest at a secure angle. It took four days and most of a fifth, but the vibration of passing footsteps shifted the knife ever-so-slowly until it emerged from the shade. It did its best to sparkle, despite the dull gray pits where rust had gnawed it.

A balding, thirty-ish man with a luxuriant mustache loomed over the display case. His shadow blocked the light and erased the slight gleam the alabaster knife had managed to summon up. He took a key on a chain around his neck, opened the display case, and lifted the alabaster knife up into the light.

"What is this piece of junk doing in my display case?" He pointed across the room at the girl with cool hands. "You! Come here."

The girl finished marking the sale price on a wicker armchair and crossed the store. "Yes, Mr. Demir?" She set the roll of orange sale stickers on top of the display case and waited attentively.

Mr. Demir hefted the alabaster knife. "This is not the quality our customers expect when they come to our shop!" He pointed to the sign painted on the store window. "Fine Antiques, it says. Does this look like it belongs with fine antiques?"

"I didn't see the acid etching on the handle until I cleaned it up. I thought it would be salable," answered the girl. "Sandy brought it to the back door. I didn't want to discourage him, since he sometimes trades us good stuff, and he looked like he needed the cash. He was jonesing hard."

Mr. Demir shook his head. "Charity is a duty, but this isn't worth the price marked on it." He hefted the alabaster knife in his hand. The price tag wrapped around the handle fluttered loose, leaving the knife valueless.

He opened his mouth--to say *throw it away* or *put it in the bargain bin* or *add it as a freebie* or one of the other dozen rejections the knife had received along its journey from cherished possession to rubbish bin salvage—when a woman spoke from behind them. "Are you marking that lovely knife for sale?"

Mr. Demir's foot moved to cover the $10 price tag that had fallen to the floor. "Certainly! I was just marking it down to thirteen dollars," he said smoothly, as he turned toward the customer. When he saw the woman who had spoken, he stopped.

"Ah. Mrs. Hausmann. I did not see that it was you. I am afraid that I must—" He paused, seeming to search for words. "I am afraid that I assured your son that we would not ... not excessively ..."

"Oh!" Mrs. Hausmann's cheeks pinkened. "I assure you, my Stevie worries too much. I would just like to purchase a few small things. A bag of antique lace from the bargain bin, this dolphin vase, it has just the tiniest chip that you can hardly see, and that knife. Those seem like reasonable purchases, don't they?"

"Yes, but. . . We couldn't take advantage of you," Mr. Demir said, though he looked as if the words pained him. "To be honest with you, this knife is worthless. It was placed in the display by mistake."

She pulled it from his hand. "I can't resist a deal!" Warmth from the tight clasp of Mrs. Hausmann's fingers spread through the knife.

"Your son said—"

Mrs. Hausmann waved her hand dismissively. "My children worry when they shouldn't. To be honest, I'd just gone to a garage sale when they visited me last. I hadn't sorted everything out yet. The house was a bit untidy, but I couldn't let those people discard perfectly useful possessions!" She sniffed. "The things this generation throws away!"

Mr. Demir began nodding agreement until he caught himself. "You've been a valuable customer, Mrs. Hausmann, but—"

At that moment, the store bell jangled to signal the entry of a clutch of middle-aged ladies wearing the wrinkle-free pastel pantsuits that marked traveling retirees. The girl with the cool hands touched Mr. Demir's shoulder. "I'll take care of the new customers," she murmured.

"Come now, do you want the sale or don't you?" asked Mrs. Hausmann.

Mr. Demir's strained smile shifted for a second to an actual grimace.

"Honestly," Mrs. Hausmann paused, "do you see anything hazardous or unwholesome in my purchases? Surely if there were something wrong with them, you wouldn't have them in your store!"

"No, of course not!"

"Excellent!" Mrs. Hausmann beamed. "Now, let me just find my wallet. . . ." She ransacked through her oversized shoulder bag as she proceeded to the cash register, Mr. Demir trailing in her wake. By his flustered expression as he took up his post, he still wasn't entirely sure how he'd been persuaded to make the sale.

The alabaster knife didn't relax. At any minute, Mr. Demir might change his mind and honor his promise to Mrs. Hausmann's busybody son. The knife could do nothing to stop it.

Mr. Demir rang up the sale and took Mrs. Hausmann's Visa card. He slid it through the card reader and began packing up her purchases. He wrapped the ornate and only slightly damaged dolphin vase in brown butcher paper as carefully as if it were made of Swarovski crystal. He tucked the bag of antique lace in beside it. He was reaching for the alabaster knife when his credit card reader gave a warning *blatt*!

Mrs. Hausmann snatched her Visa card back. "Oops! I forgot that one was canceled. My apologies. Here, this is my current card."

The MasterCard she handed him went through without a snag. Mr. Demir smiled and began to add the alabaster knife to her packages, but she stopped him. "I'll take care of this." She scooped the alabaster knife up. It rolled into the embrace of her fingers.

"There, there," she muttered as she turned away from the counter. "Poor thing. I wouldn't leave you here where they might toss you out. You're a lovely thing, maybe a bit battered but still perfectly functional. With some sharpening, you'll cut like a dream. Good thing my meddling children don't know about my *other* credit card. I'll take good care of you now."

She added the alabaster knife to her other purchases, and it sank to rest in the bottom of her bag.

The kitchen that she brought the knife into was not warm and bright like the kitchen from the knife's early years. Instead of the scent of baking bread, the smell of old grease and rotting fruit filled the air. Sunlight filtered into this kitchen slowly, easing its way through grime-darkened windows and pooling over the mountain range of unwashed dishes that occupied the countertop. It dripped to the floor and illuminated a thick carpet of discarded food containers, abysmally embroidered dish towels, and coupon sections accumulated over the years. The sunlight did not dare the kitchen table, which was hidden under a mound of newspapers.

The only clear spot in the room was a kitchen stool with mismatched legs. Mrs. Hausmann walked carefully over the uneven floor to sit on the stool. She pulled the knife out of its refuge in her bag.

"Now what shall I do with you?" she mused.

She weighed the knife on her palm and tilted it this way and that. The knife might have slid to stab her or skittered away to hide beneath the refuse on the floor, but it clung to her hand. She shrugged and set it on top of the mound of newspapers and unopened mail on the kitchen table.

"At least you're safe now, dear. Nobody will throw you away."

Mrs. Hausmann left the knife there, sitting in the gloom. She walked through the other rooms of the house and moved around in them. Furniture scraped. Papers rustled. Spilled cereal crunched underfoot. The sun shifted across the sky, but light never reached the kitchen table.

By the time the sun set, Mrs. Hausmann had still not returned to use the knife. A dim, flickering light seeped from the living room. Finally, Mrs. Hausmann came back to the kitchen, but it was only to pat the refrigerator and reassure it that she would bring leftovers for it soon. She left the kitchen without even a glance at the alabaster knife. Her keys jangled on the hook and the back door opened and closed.

She returned later that evening, bearing styrofoam presents for the fridge.

"Though I wonder why I bother," she said. "It doesn't feel right, going out and leaving you behind. It's like going out naked. Maybe I'll look into one of those senior meal delivery programs. Then we could stay here all nice and cozy."

She snored all night on the sofa while one of the old cathode ray tube televisions in the living room murmured paid programming lullabies.

Even in its glory days, the alabaster knife had rarely been used at breakfast. Cold cereal, oatmeal, eggs, bacon, coffee cake, doughnuts, sausage links—none of those things required the use of a sharp knife. Fresh fruit might, or a slice of ham.

Mrs. Hausmann ate cheerios with milk that she sniffed, stopped to think about, and then poured into her bowl.

"A little buttermilk never hurt anybody," she said.

Lunch seemed more promising, but Mrs. Hausmann used the plastic spoon and fork from the restaurant to eat her leftover chicken-fried steak.

She did not go out for dinner, but she didn't cook, either. Clearing the counters enough to cook would have taken hours. Instead, she ate four strawberry yogurts that were only two months expired. She used the plastic spoon from lunch.

That set the pattern for the next month. When Mrs. Hausmann stayed in the house, the alabaster knife waited in vain to be used. When she left, she usually ate out. She would return from those trips with other rescuees from thrift shops and garage sales. She dumped her bags out on the kitchen table. The newcomers might hide the knife for days until she moved them to where they belonged. Whenever she left the house, the knife resigned itself to a day without even the hope of use, followed by a period of obscurity.

Then came the day that she returned after only a half-hour's absence, flustered and near tears. She dropped her purse onto the kitchen table and sank to sit on the stool. "*All* my credit cards, canceled!" she confided. She didn't look at the knife; her eyes were fixed on the middle distance.

"Those—those little *brats*! After everything I've done for

them, everything I've provided for them, they want to take this from me?"

The alabaster knife made as patient an audience as anything could, but in the end, Mrs. Hausmann left it unused in the kitchen and stalked into the living room. The answering machine beeped, and then the machine spoke to her, saying, "You have four messages. Press play to hear your messages." Plastic keys clattered.

A man's voice filled the crowded house.

"Mom, this is Steve. We got notified that you tried to use your credit card again. I left messages warning you that we were going to cut off your credit cards because we were concerned about how you were spending your retirement money. I don't know if you're getting these messages since you don't answer. I also sent you a letter that you should have gotten a week ago. Your bank should have sent you a letter too. They'll be giving you an allowance, so that you have money for food and groceries and such without draining your savings. Mom, please call me back. Or call Barbara." A long pause, as if Steve waited for the machine to answer him. "We're worried about you. We miss Dad, too. We love you."

"Press 1 to delete message. Press 2 to save message and play next message. Press 3—" the machine's intonation of options terminated abruptly in an angry clatter of plastic keys.

Mrs. Hausmann stormed back into the kitchen, walking fast and without her usual care. "An allowance!" she muttered. "I'll show him an—oh!"

Her foot slipped on a circular advertisement. She lurched forward. She would have fallen, but she caught herself on the corner of the table. The motion jarred the knife helplessly closer to the edge. Its movement uncovered a bank envelope marked, "Important! Please read immediately. Change in the terms of your account."

Mrs. Hausmann recovered her balance and carefully eased herself down to sit on the kitchen stool. "Oh, my! I guess I need to clean up in here." Her hand shook as she picked up the bank envelope.

The alabaster knife's second owner had always used it to open his mail, right up until the day he pawned it to help pay his bills.

Mrs. Hausmann tore the envelope open with her fingers. Her lips moved as she read the letter. She scowled and tossed it to the floor. That night, she paced in the living room until late, muttering.

Newspapers and the growing pyramid of unopened mail on the kitchen table became the only threats to the alabaster knife's visibility. Yet the knife waited unused. To save money, Mrs. Hausmann signed up for a donation-funded meal delivery service for seniors. The delivered meals never called for anything sharper than the plastic cutlery provided with them.

The meal service's fund-raising letters piled up unanswered on the kitchen table beside the knife. She never paid the suggested donation.

"I have better things to do with my money," Mrs. Hausmann told her silent, listening house when she received the first request. "I never knew what I was missing until I really started paying attention to my night shows. I don't need to go out of the house and leave you all alone. I'm too old for rescue work anyway. At my age, what you really need is convenience. These modern gadgets are amazing! I don't have much time left. I need to save as much of it as I can."

No longer just a lullaby, infomercials became a constant churn of background noise. Packages arrived at the house regularly. Every time the doorbell rang, Mrs. Hausmann clapped her hands and a momentary burst of girlish joy brightened her face.

A knife would have been the perfect thing to slit the tape and open the cardboard boxes, but she used a broken pair of scissors that she kept in the windowsill. The screw that held them together had broken and the scissor blades had separated, but they worked just fine for opening boxes. She stacked the cardboard boxes on top of the kitchen stove.

Her trips to the kitchen to deposit the cardboard boxes were the only time she came close to the alabaster knife. As she passed, she would toss the day's mail on top of the kitchen table. Her delivered meals were single-serving sized and came packaged in styrofoam with plastic cutlery. She ate them in the living room, with her television as her dinner companion. She had no need for the sink or the dishes or the fridge or the silverware or the alabaster knife. She threw the trash from her meals into big white plastic garbage bags. When they were full, she tied them up and set them by the back door to take out later, a later that never came.

Mrs. Hausmann no longer sat on the kitchen stool and talked to the knife as she glanced through the newspaper for sales. She no longer talked to the knife at all.

The repetitive droning of television infomercials and the noise of Mrs. Hausmann shuffling from room to room were the only sounds in the house until one evening when the voice of Mrs. Hausmann's son, Steve, invaded the house.

"Mom, we're worried. You've overdrawn your allowance four times. We've covered the fees, but you can't keep doing that. We're coming to see you. Barbara's going to drive down from Michigan and I'll drive up from Florida. We need to talk. Your neighbors have complained to the housing commission, and they're going to be sending an inspector over. I got them to agree to wait until we've had a chance to sort things out, but that will only buy us a few weeks. I know you've always resisted the idea of moving to Florida, but the weather is really fantastic down here. You'd love it. There are some great community—"

The answering machine cut off abruptly.

Then it was just them again. The alabaster knife waited in the kitchen for the day that she would choose it and use it as it was meant to be used. It waited and waited.

The refrigerator died. Mrs. Hausmann paid no attention to its silent corpse, even when it began to smell. A drift of newspapers and mail red-stamped "Urgent" slid over the top of the kitchen table and cascaded to cover the kitchen stool. She didn't notice. She hadn't sat there for weeks and weeks. Newspapers and mail slid around and over the knife and then fell to the floor, but the alabaster knife doggedly held its position. Waiting.

One afternoon, right after Mrs. Hausmann had accepted delivery of a package of Shamwow cleaning cloths, the doorbell rang again. She clapped her hands.

"Oh, did one of my packages arrive early?"

As soon as the door creaked open, Steve's voice filled the house.

"Mom, we're here to help you clean up a bit before—" He stopped suddenly.

"What is that *smell?*" demanded a woman's voice. "Mom, what are you wearing? How long have you been wearing that?"

"Not so long," Mrs. Hausmann defended herself. "I haven't been able to get down to the basement to do laundry for a few weeks because the dirty clothes on the stairs make it a bit dangerous, that's all. I wash my clothes in the tub when I take a shower."

"I didn't know it was this bad, Barb, I swear," Steve said rapidly. "I haven't visited since the funeral."

"We agreed that you would check in on her," Barb hissed. "You live closer, you can get time off from your job when I can't—"

"I'm sorry! I've been calling, I . . . That isn't what's important right now. Mom, when did you shower last? When did you leave the house?"

"I...I don't remember. I've been so busy with all my shows to watch."

The chorus of infomercials playing on the three old cathode ray tube televisions confirmed her alibi.

"Mom," Barbara said, gentling her tone, "you need a shower and clean clothes and—what have you been eating? Have you been eating?"

"They deliver meals."

"That's good," Steve said, "but, um, it's got to get boring. Why don't you go put on something nice and we'll take you out to lunch. We can make a plan, then. You've got. . .you've got a lot of stuff that we need to sort through and clear out before the inspector comes. Otherwise he's going to condemn your house. It smells like maybe there's a dead rat in here somewhere. We have to clean up."

"What?" Mrs. Hausmann's voice wavered. "You want to throw away my things? They belong with me! There's nothing wrong with any of them! They all work perfectly fine, or they would if they were fixed up just a little bit!"

"We have to clean up, Mom . . ." Steve pleaded.

"I'm going to take a look around," Barb announced. She crunched across the living room carpet. "Gah," she muttered, "my shoes are sticking to the carpet. This is bad."

She appeared in the kitchen doorway, a tall, slim brunette wearing a gray business suit. Her eyes widened in horror, and she put a hand up to cover her nose and mouth. She didn't step inside, as if she feared to be swallowed by the sea of damp, molding newspapers that matted the floor. She backed away.

Back in the living room, she demanded, "Do you know what that *smell* is? She hasn't been taking out the trash. Half the kitchen is filled with bags of rotting trash, and there's junk all over the floor. Forget the plan to take her out to lunch and do a little cleaning ourselves. We're going to have to hire professionals to take all this stuff to the landfill and then fumigate the house. She can't live here anymore."

"You want to put me in a home!" Mrs. Hausmann wailed. "No! No, I won't go!"

"I brought brochures," Steve said slowly. "There are some very nice places, Mom, you'll like them. You can meet other seniors—"

"No! I don't need to. You'll see! I can take out the trash. I can."

"Mom, that's not what—"

Chairs squealed in protest as they were shoved out of the way in a hurry. Unopened boxes tumbled to the living room floor.

The thud of a foot kicking them out of the way echoed through the house like a shock wave. Mrs. Hausmann always handled her belongings gently, no matter how battered and worn they were when they came into her care.

Mrs. Hausmann staggered off-balance into the kitchen. She caught the door frame and hung there for a second, panting. "You'll see. I can do it," she muttered. She plunged grimly across the shifting landscape of sliding paper.

Her foot fell on a shiny circular advertisement for a commemorative series of china plates painted with images from 50 of the most popular travel destinations in America. The ad slid beneath her foot, sending her lurching forward. Her hands flew out. She thudded against the kitchen table hard enough to send an avalanche of old newspapers and unpaid bills to the floor. She clamped her hands onto the sides of the table, her forearms pressed tight against its edges, as she struggled to regain her footing. A cascade of ignored mail poured over her arms.

Within it, the alabaster knife.

The knife sliced through paper as it glided into her embrace. Finally. There were no obstacles to stop it. The knife kissed her skin and then slid deeper to join her flesh until its edge lay along the bone of her arm. She fell to the floor, carrying the knife with her. Someone screamed nearby, but the sound was drowned out by the drumbeat of Mrs. Hausmann's heart as her blood washed over the alabaster knife.

The drumbeat faded. The flow slowed to a trickle and then a single tear and then nothing. The sound of Steve's harsh, broken sobs filled the air as Barbara dialed 911. Sirens wailed and then stopped. Someone turned off the televisions.

The knife nestled content in Mrs. Hausmann's flesh until a technician wearing blue nitrile gloves withdrew it and dropped it into an evidence bag. The dried blood clung to its blade and sank deep into its alabaster handle. Together, blood and knife moved through the legal system, from the evidence room to the ruling of accidental death and then on to the closed cases files, where nobody could claim they did not belong.

Plastic Lazarus

by Raymond Little

Mr Bridges brought me to life. Where once there was nothing, not even darkness, he gave light and warmth, and in time, love. My first memories of him are vague, an old man in a natty checked suit and bowler hat, the point of his snow white beard resting on his bowtie as he passed by my window. I couldn't follow him with my eyes – he was no more than a flash crossing my vision – but the miracle I could see him at all was instigated purely by the magic of his presence, of that I'm sure.

Then, on that most momentous of days, he came into the shop and I was born.

"I'd like to make a purchase, please," I heard him say, and oh how sweet the new sensation of sound felt as those words fell upon my ears.

"Certainly, sir," the lady said. "How may I be of assistance?"

"I'd like to buy that, in the window."

"Oh yes, a lovely choice. What size do you require?"

"Size?"

"Yes, size. What age is the boy you are buying the outfit for?"

Mr Bridges laughed.

"Oh, no, I'm afraid you misunderstand me. I want the one in the window. Not just the clothes, the whole thing."

"This is most peculiar, I must say. We are not in the habit of selling mannequins in this establishment, sir, oh no. We most definitely don't go in for that sort of thing!"

"How much is the outfit?"

The lady sniffed.

"Twenty seven pounds."

"I'll give you two hundred."

"Two hundred . . ." She lowered her voice. "Two hundred pounds?"

"Okay, three hundred, but no more. Here."

I heard the faint rustle of paper.

"Take him, he's yours," she hissed. "Quickly, before anyone sees."

Footsteps approached me from behind.

"Boy," Mr Bridges said, his voice as deep and smooth as a jar of syrup. "Come with me."

The warmth of his hand as he placed it on my shoulder began to spread itself over and within my body, and a steady beat began to thud inside my chest in time with the pulse that emanated from his fingers. I softened, and turned my head to look up into his old, blue eyes.

"Where are we going?" I asked, my own voice both strange and pleasing to me.

He smiled.

"Home," he said. "We are going home."

"Goodbye, thank you for looking after me,'"I said to the lady as my plastic legs carried me from the shop. She didn't reply. She just sat with a thump onto the carpet, her hand clamped over her gaping mouth.

"A name, a name, a boy must have a name." Mr Bridges ambled slowly back and forth in the living room of his large four story town house, one hand massaging the end of his beard. "Any ideas?"

I was standing by the open hearth, warming my palms.

"Ye Gods, young man, you can't be doing that. Step away before you melt!" He took my hands in his and examined them. "No harm done. But you must be careful. Now where were we? Ah, yes. A name."

I looked about the room for inspiration.

"How about Teapot?" I asked.

"Teapot?" He followed my gaze to the china tea-set on the table and began to laugh. "We can't name you Teapot! No, no, that won't do at all. We need a boy's name, like David or Simon or Theodore."

"Hmm." I considered it for a moment. "I like Theodore."

"Theodore it is, then." He clapped his hands together once. "Now, let me show you around your new home, get you settled. The work starts tomorrow."

The work was my education, simple at first – the dangers of fire and traffic and climbing up trees – but I was a fast learner and devoured with a hunger the mathematics and literature put before me, discovering all I could about life in the modern world from the vast array of books kept by Mr Bridges in his library. I watched the world outside from the big bay window on the second floor landing, and never once missed the parade of children every morning and afternoon on their way to and from the school at the end of our road. And on my two hundred and thirty sixth day of life, I knew I was ready.

"I want to go to school."

Mr Bridges peeked over the top of his newspaper at me before folding it onto his lap.

"Do you think you are prepared, Theodore?"

"I know I am.'

"You are well aware of the differences between yourself and other children. We have spoken of it many times. It may not be easy."

"You gave me life. I want to start living."

Mr Bridges removed his reading glasses, twiddled with the end of his beard, and smiled.

"Then it seems you are most definitely ready.'"

Fitting in wasn't half as difficult as I'd expected it to be. In fact, it was easy. My classmates were fascinated and crowded me with questions, their tentative fingers touching my hands and face as if to prove to themselves that I was indeed a real talking plastic boy.

"Come on, 7H,"Mrs Hurst said. "Give Theodore some room to breathe."

She looked over the rim of her little spectacles at me.

"You do breathe, I presume."

I nodded.

"Sort of. I don't eat or go to the toilet, though."

My classmates chuckled, then laughed, finding something funny in my answer, and before I knew it I had joined in, the hilarity so infectious that even Mrs Hurst couldn't resist a smile.

"Well I'm glad we've cleared that up," she said.

I had no shortage of friends, my closest pal being Tim Hemingsworth-Fry. He never stopped talking, his favorite subject being the sport of rugby. It was his enthusiasm that led me to join the school team.

"'It's a tough game for tough boys," he said with a slap on my back. "You'll be fine."

He was right. I was an instant success, my stamina and lack of pain ideal for sprinting up and down the pitch, oblivious of the knocks and tackles from my opponents. Until the day of the accident, that is.

The ball had found its way to me on the wing and I set off at a pace, the leather clutched to my chest. I dodged the first tackle with ease, my opponent's heart not really in it having already clattered into the hard plastic of my midriff during an earlier attack. His team-mates were not so shy. From the edge of my vision I spotted two red shirts darting at me from the left, another from the right, and they brought me down, the four of us collapsing into a twisted heap with me at the bottom. A sharp crack rang out that silenced the shouts of the other players in an instant.

My three tacklers untangled themselves and stood.

"Oh no," one of them said as he looked down.

I followed his gaze to my left arm and raised it. Just below my elbow, where my forearm and hand should have been, my limb ended in a flat stump. I felt no pain, just a rising sense of panic.

"Is everybody okay?" Mr Jones, our rugby coach asked as he jogged over. His ruddy cheeks turned pale and he took a step backwards. "Oh my. Oh my, oh my."

He wasn't much help.

I jumped to my feet and did the only thing I could think of, which was to run as fast as I could back home to Mr Bridges, my cleats clip clopping on concrete paving stones as I sprinted over them to our front door.

"Uh oh," he said as he led me through to the kitchen. "It

appears you are in need of a little surgery."

"Can you fix it?"

"Of course." He leaned close and squinted at the stump. "A tube of super glue and some thick tape should do the trick. Where is the rest of it?"

At once I realized my mistake.

"I left it behind."

"Excuse me," a voice I recognized spoke from the doorway. "I hope you don't mind, but the front door was open."

He stepped inside and shook Mr Bridges' hand.

"My name is Tim Hemingsworth-Fry, I'm a friend of Theodore. I believe he overlooked the small matter of coming home in one piece."

Mr Bridges took the limb from him.

"Thank you. You are obviously very good friends."

Tim smiled at me.

"Oh yes," he said, "Theodore and I are the very best of friends."

And best friends we remained for the next two years. It was a golden time of fun and learning – long hot summers spent swimming and playing cricket, our winter evenings filled with games and books and comics and trips to the cinema. It couldn't last, though, however much Tim or I wanted it to. Tim was growing, moving into his teen years, and no matter how I tried I couldn't keep up with him, either physically or intellectually. His interests had changed, quite naturally, and for the first time I felt the odd one out among my peers as even the smallest boy in our class had outgrown me. The problem hadn't gone unnoticed by Mr Bridges or my teachers and – after what seemed like an endless round of meetings – an arrangement was made for me to drop back to year seven, and to keep doing so every two years for the foreseeable future.

So, as it turned out, Tim became just the first in a long line of best friends over the years, the most memorable of the bunch being Billy Swain, Lucy Lange and Herbie Smith. Through it all though, there was one constant in my life, always there for me throughout the changing of the seasons, and that was Mr Bridges in his natty suits, his white beard impeccably trimmed so that its point rested on his bowtie just as it had the first day I'd seen him. He had aged, of course, requiring the need of a cane and a hearing aid, but it was his hands that tucked me into bed every night, and his smile that greeted me each morning.

And I was happy with things just as they were, or so I thought.

One thing that remained with me from my earliest school days was my love of rugby, and despite three arm and two leg snaps over the years, all lovingly repaired by Mr Bridges, I continued to play, and it was as I was leaving the field after a local derby that a voice called out to me, a voice that seemed almost familiar.

"Theodore! Over here!"

I glanced across at the man who called my name, a tall, muscular, balding man I didn't recognize. I looked behind me, wondering if there could be another Theodore he might be referring to.

The man laughed. "Yes, you, Theodore Bridges."

I walked over to him.

"Hello, Sir."

"Hello Theodore." He shook my hand. "I think we might do away with this *Sir* nonsense. Don't you recognize me?"

I looked into his eyes, a stranger's eyes at first, but he smiled and all at once it hit me. "Tim," I almost gasped.

"Phew, I thought you'd almost forgotten your old pal for a moment there."

"But you're so . . ." I swallowed, unsure of what to say. Time, and the world, had moved on. I knew it had been years since I'd seen him, but in my mind's eye Tim was still the blonde haired, freckled faced youth I'd spent those early golden days with.

"I know, I know," he said as he rubbed a palm over his thinning pate. "Not quite as dashing as I used to be."

I managed a smile.

"I don't remember anyone ever describing you as dashing."

Tim laughed. "You might at least humor an old man's version of his youth. That was a marvellous game you just played, by the way."

"Thank you."

I felt odd, seeing my old friend so changed by the relentless passage of time. My insides felt empty, as if I'd missed an important appointment, only realizing now that it was far too late.

"What brings you here?" I managed to ask. I could tell by the way his eyes softened that he'd noticed the tremble in my voice.

"I came to watch my son, Teddy. You just played against him. It was his first match. I told him beforehand to watch out for you, that he might learn a thing or two."

The odd sensation inside me was getting worse. I didn't want to be there, talking to that strange version of Tim Hemingsworth-Fry. I wanted the young Tim or no Tim at all.

"I'm sorry," I murmured, "but I have to go. Goodbye Tim."

I turned and ran, unable to take the hurt I saw in my old chum's eyes.

I wandered the town that day after school, my mind filled with questions I'd never considered before – questions for which I had no answers – and it was on my way home that I saw her for the first time and wondered at the possibility of what might be.

"No, no, please don't ask me to do that, Theodore. It would be impossible. You are one of a kind."

"But my friends grow old and leave me. If there were another like me, we could be friends forever. And she looks so sad."

"She isn't sad, Theodore." Mr Bridges reached across the table and held my hand. "Do you remember before? Those years you spent in the shop window?"

I shook my head.

"Exactly. You didn't feel sad, or happy. It's the same for her."

"But the day I came alive, I was ecstatic! I knew then, at that very moment, the beauty of life. I realized the difference at once between being and nothingness."

Mr Bridges regarded me for a while with his gentle blue eyes.

"Is there something else that is troubling you, Theodore?"

I lowered my gaze to the wrinkled old hand that rested on my own, smooth, plastic palm.

"I'm frightened."

"Frightened of what?"

"Of losing you. You are growing older too, just like everybody else." My voice dropped to a whisper. "I don't want to be alone."

"Oh, Theodore, I'm sorry. I'm not sure I am even capable of doing what you ask. There was something about you that day. I didn't plan it. I saw you, and just knew."

My shoulders slumped.

Mr Bridges squeezed my hand.

"Look, I will think about it, but as I have explained, I can't make any promises."

Day after day, both before and after school, I stood and stared through the shop window at the plastic girl I'd become obsessed with. She was blonde, my height exactly, her clothes changing with the fashions but her eyes always so sad. Mr Bridges did try to bring her to life, and replayed the exact scene from so many years before.

"Girl, come with me," he said, after handing the shop assistant a wad of money. The mannequin never so much as twitched.

I couldn't give up on her though, and gave her a little wave each time I passed, just in case, and it was as I was looking at her this very morning that the weirdest sensation came over me. I was with my latest best friend, Charlie Knox.

"What's wrong?" he asked as he noticed my frown.

"I'm not sure." I held my hand in front of my face and flexed my fingers. They didn't seem as supple as usual and gave off a slight creak as I bent my knuckles. I took a step forward. It felt as if I were trying to wade through a muddy swamp.

"I've got to go, Charlie. Sorry."

My whole body was beginning to stiffen and I had only one thought, which was that I had to get home to Mr Bridges. I ran as best as I could but my joints squeaked and hardened with every step, and by the time I reached home I could only manage to walk like a robot, my knees unable to bend at all.

"Mr Bridges," I called as I struggled up the stairs to the living room. "Help me!

I heard his gramophone playing on the other side of the door and burst in.

On the floor in the center of the room, Mr Bridges lay gasping for air.

That was earlier, maybe an hour or so ago. I'm on the floor now, one arm across Mr Bridges' chest, my face resting on the whiskers of his cheek. His pulse is slowing and so is mine, our heartbeats in perfect unison, as they were the day he gave me life. I notice two photographs clutched in his hand as I lay by his side, one of me from last Christmas, a red hat from a cracker on my head, the other an old black and white snap I've never seen before of a pretty young woman and a small boy dressed in old fashioned clothes.

Mr Bridges murmurs, "Theodore, is that you?"

"Yes,"I say, my jaw grinding.

Our hearts weaken, darkness creeps in at the edge of my vision.

"Don't be scared, little fellow," he manages. "Soon there will be nothing, just like before, for both of us. And after all, we have had a good life."

I try to work my mouth. There is something I have to say before the oblivion, something I have had so long to say yet never did. With my last ounce of strength I move my lips.

"Goodnight, Dad," I gasp, "I love you."

As my senses fade I hear his voice for the last time, as if speaking to me from the end of a long, long tunnel.

"Goodnight, Son," he says. "Sleep well."

Deleted

by Ken Goldman

Widower, 29, seeks S/DF. I'm losing my hair, I smoke non-filtered Camels by the carton, I prefer to spend most Sundays trashing the NFL, and lately no one has mistaken me for Mel Gibson. That much said, I had been a loving husband, I like babies and animals, I can hook up a DVD, and I rank fairly high on the food chain.

Justin looked over the Internet message he had typed onto his IBM's monitor, aware that self-deprecation tended to lose its charm once a woman sensed how well deserved it was. He really sucked at this, and one reading convinced him the ad reeked of defensiveness masked behind a strained attempt at cleverness. Worse, because of what it did not say the personal ad's content was not entirely honest.

He hit 'delete,' and started over.

Widower, 29, physically challenged, seeks S/DF. You don't have to be centerfold material or even attractive. You can be downright ugly. In fact, I prefer you to be ugly. I don't deserve anything better than a hag.

SHIT! PISS!! FUCK!!!

White hot rage seemed the only emotion Justin felt capable of any more, and the moment got away from him again. He felt tempted to send the rewritten message as it stood but managed to pull himself back. Launched into cyberspace, a personal ad this sick might attract the kind of woman who ate her young, but little else. Outbursts happened a lot with him lately, and the time had arrived for a reality check.

He hit 'delete' again, muttering while he ran his fingers through wispy strands of sandy hair. Pushing his wheelchair from the keyboard he reached for the photo album on the bookshelf. This daily ritual had become both self-defeating and painful, but he was a junkie addicted to memories of his past. Although his legs were as useless as pine logs, Justin's hands had developed a will of their own.

He flipped through the photo album again and focused on one of the hundreds of snapshots he had taken with Sheila during the three years of their life together. The photo showed Justin and his young wife on a windy Long Island beach two summers ago. With arms entwined around one another like the newlyweds they were, they seemed the quintessential yin and yang in swimsuits. She was everything he was not, the beauty to his beast, the classic argument for the attraction of opposites. Justin could never fully understand just what Sheila had seen in him, but whatever it was he felt certain it had died the same day she had.

He studied the photo as if he held a Renoir in his hands. His young wife had been a knockout in that hot pink hint of a bikini she liked to wear. On that August afternoon he had been in such a feverish rush to make love to her that Sheila's bikini bottom remained wrapped around her ankles the whole time.

Justin closed his eyes, and for a brief moment Sheila was there. He could even smell the wild honey scent of her hair. If he reached out she might stand before him, wanting him the way she had during the warm August afternoon captured in the photograph.

As always another memory forced its way into his head, the unwanted and uninvited remembering that chewed into his reflections like a voracious rat whenever his thoughts turned to Sheila. The memory remained inside Justin's brain, a blood smeared freeze frame slowly churning itself into motion, exposing each torturous second of the last moments of Sheila's life.

The present collides with the past. Headlights of the oncoming eighteen wheeler come at him in an ambush of white light as the Toyota enters the rain swept Hartford ramp of Interstate 95. Sheila turns to look at him. She is like a confused child, unable to comprehend the enormity of the macabre moment they have entered into together. Ten tons of diesel truck bear down on them, and the small Toyota spins wildly, slamming the guard rail. The door on the passenger side shreds off in grotesque slow motion, and she is torn from her car seat. Thrown from the vehicle, Sheila seems suspended in midair like a tossed rag doll. Her body skids upon the median rail that promptly severs her upper torso from her lower, scattering the sections of her dissected flesh and gashed bone fifty feet apart.

Ten tons of metal effectively slammed what remained of Sheila into her grave and made match wood of the bones inside Justin's legs.

Enter 'delete' and everything disappears. It was that simple.

Disabled Widower, 29, seeks anyone who can make the past disappear.

Shitpissfuck.

He lit a cigarette, secretly hoping that his lungs might soon turn into ash and end the empty charade that had become his life. Of course, the punchline was that even the shittiest life had to go on regardless of the uncertainty he felt about how that could happen.

The monitor of Justin's computer remained empty. He returned to the keyboard willing himself to write something, anything.

Pitiful paraplegic, 29, more emotionally than physically challenged, desires any morsel of pity a woman might show toward a man who is incapable of getting over the death of the only woman who ever had the poor judgment to fall in love with him.

Succinct and to the point. More important, it was honest.

Who reads this sort of drivel anyway? he wondered.

Only the thousands of agoraphobes who had no lives of their own. Only those pathetic recluses who spent so much time at their computer terminals there seemed no world beyond their door that did not have the 'cyber' prefix attached to it. People who, if given the chance, might delete their entire lives.

Maybe he would deliver his personal ad unedited right now. Maybe he would send it out into the vast outreaches of cyberspace just to see what sort of excuse for a woman might respond, what sort of mirror image of himself was as desperate and alone.

The cigarette suddenly burned Justin's lip, and pulling it from his mouth he realized he had smoked the Camel to a nub.

When he looked back at the computer's monitor he discovered the screen read 'message sent'. Some internal demon lurking within the darker chambers of his psyche had delivered the personal ad for him. Or, maybe his hands had operated independently of his brain again, just as they had done with Sheila's photos in the album. In either case, the IBM's monitor indicated the message had somehow irretrievably gone out courtesy of the Internet into the furthest regions of cyberland.

Gone. Departed like his legs and what used to be his life. Fading and disseminating out there somewhere in time or space along with Sheila and the scent of her hair during an afternoon on Long Island. All of it evaporating into mist except for the blinding lights of an eighteen wheeler tearing a crevice through the darkness of a rainy night.

It took a moment for the image to register, and at first it seemed his eyes had lost their focus along with his brain. He could see the blurred letters of the keyboard through his hands as if he were staring at them through smoked glass. He held his hand to the light. He might just as well have been staring through gauze.

For the first time in as long as he could remember, Justin almost smiled at the sinister absurdity of his circumstances. Everything was gone, yet at the same time nothing was. Try as he might he could not delete the ghosts. But the ghosts were not what he really wanted to make disappear. Some things were so ludicrous you almost had to laugh just to keep from screaming.

He knew he might remain right where he sat, there at the keyboard for the rest of the day waiting for a response that would never come. That was not the answer. But he knew what was. He vped a single sentence.

Not really seeking anyone. Not any more.

Justin smiled again as he watched his hand continue to fade. Considering for a moment, he added another sentence.

Just want to erase it all.

He hit 'delete' and kept pressing down on the key, barely able to see the flesh of his own knuckles.

His smile disappeared last.

Aphrastos

by Calie Voorhis

That night the words came back, fluttered like moths instead of scuttling away in the light as cockroaches, and every morsel tasted of honey. They were hers again, to savor, not the thief's to whom they'd fled long ago. Aphrastos settled herself in the tree outside the office, folded her wings tight against her back, curled her tail around the rough bark, and waited.

"Honey, is this word spelled correctly?" Susan stared at the white page of her word processor, only one word there. "Imagine." There wasn't a red squiggle underneath. So that meant it had to be correct, but it didn't look right. This wasn't even the word she'd been searching for.

"Honey?"

From the kitchen, a furious clamoring of pots, the sound of a faucet being turned on to full roar, then the whistle and thump of the first cycle of the dishwasher.

Allan was mad. Why?

"What did I do?" she yelled, not getting up from the keyboard. Imagine. What other word had she been looking for, and why couldn't she figure it out? Cognition? No, that wasn't right either. She wanted something else, something with a hint of mystery. Not Idea either. Damn.

She refused to get the thesaurus down from the dusty shelf above her head; she was a college professor, a writer, she shouldn't need a reference, not anymore.

A muffled sob pierced the racket of cleaning. Shit. She clenched her fists, fought the urge to pound the keyboard into submission, to take out the frustration of the word dancing around the edge of her mind, almost at the sides of her vision, resisted the cowardly impulse to stay in her office while her husband cried in the kitchen.

She pushed her chair back, brushed her hand through thinning hair, and walked to the kitchen.

"Our anniversary," he said, almost a scream. "You forgot our anniversary. Our twentieth."

That wasn't today. Surely it couldn't be today. She'd have remembered something that important to them both.

She wanted to she was sorry. What came out was, "Why can't I find the word?"

Allan gaped, lips wide open then turned away and stumbled in an almost run to the bathroom. The door slammed. The dishwasher roared on. The steam from the running faucet turned the tiny kitchen into a vapor bath filled with the lemon scent of dishwasher soap.

She should go after him. Susan bounced against the walls of the hallway, and sat back down in her desk chair. What was that damned word?

Aphrastos smiled, plucked *Fantasy* out of the air. She savored the tiny veins of the beating word in her claw, then popped it into her mouth and swallowed it whole. The noun tasted of honey still, but with a lace of desperation and a tinge of salt.

Susan slumped at her desk, shoulders tight, another long day. The page taunted her, white and glaring in the afternoon sun. Sunbeams streamed in from the slats of the open window blinds and rippled as the wind shifted the spruce outside. She'd been in the same position since sunrise. Her calves cramped. She shifted in her chair, making the familiar squeak. Outside the tree shifted, branches rustled, then steadied.

Allan had been after her to see a doctor for weeks now, but she wasn't going. What if the doctor told her something she knew but didn't want to hear? That would make it all real.

No, this was just a phase. Everybody forgot things, names and dates. Everyone wandered into a room and couldn't remember why they were there. She was getting older, much as she hated to admit it. That was all.

No, the only way to prove Allan wrong was to finish this story, to show she was still a writer.

Right. Finish the story. She thumped her head against the monitor. Starting would help. She sat in silence for a second, closed her eyes. There. She had the opening now.

Susan positioned her fingers above the keyboard. "On a dreary night," she typed, "a stranger crossed the door of the Wayfarer Inn, with rain dripping off his leather trench-coat, and a gleam in his golden eyes."

A beginning. Started. She looked at the screen, just to see the glory of words, the line of black ants replacing white with form, void with substance.

"Ic not d a dkljf9. Oiuofg." Line after line much the same.

She hadn't typed that. How could she forget how to type? No, this was a hallucination. She closed her eyes, stretched her shoulders, and exhaled. She peeked out between slitted lids. The gibberish still occupied the screen, rows of strange words, symbols, and random punctuation.

She wiped the sweat from her forehead, smelled the acrid odor of apprehension rising from her armpits, dampening her cotton t-shirt.

Someone was stealing her words. Someone had come in here, somehow, and taken the story from her. It was the only rational explanation. This couldn't be her fault.

Susan stood.

"God damn you," she said in a scream that tightened her vocal cords and hurt her head. "I'll get you for this. I swear to god I'll rip your throat out."

The tension faded, replaced by a deep sense of fear.

Aphrastos rubbed her back against the bark, scratching a delightful itch. The words floated around her, coming to land on her scaly flesh, cooing into her pointed ears. So happy to be home, they were. The myriad illuminated the cathedral interior of the spruce tree, flickering like fireflies. Her words, her sustenance, coming home to roost. Enough to feed her, until she drained the well dry, as she always did, unable to control the gluttony, the lust, anymore than the struggling woman in her barren room.

Mad floated by her. Her tongue zipped out of her mouth, snagged the word, and dragged it to her, struggling. Her jaws snapped shut. The word beat around the inside of her maw, slowly dissolving in the acid. *Mad* tasted sweet, chocolaty, full-flavored, and ripe with fear.

Yum.

The words weren't there. They were somewhere else. Susan shifted in her seat, swiveled the chair around, and stared out the window. Every day grew bleaker. Even the sunshine on the spruce tree paled, the grass grew grayer, the clear blue sky translucent with failure.

She had to stop this. She had to find the words, for her job, for her husband. For herself, to dispel the fog of confusion settling over her in a smothering blanket.

The grandfather clock in the living room chimed the quarter hour. Allan would be home soon and her page was still blank.

A motion outside caught her eye.

A creature snuffled around the base of the tree, then slithered up into the branches. Susan gasped, her heart choking her throat.

It was real. This wasn't her fault, something sat out there and ate her words before they could get to her.

She stood up.

The creature turned a fox head to her, peering out of a gap in the branches, then vanished.

She tried to tell Allan about the beast when he got home, but he just got the strange wrinkles of worry on his face.

Aphrastos bared her teeth. Susan had seen her. Didn't matter. No one would believe Susan. *Panic* batted her face, as if the word tried to shoo her away. She caught it, feeling the softness flutter against her pad, then pierced it with a sharp talon.

The word died. She ate *Panic*, and savored the briny taste.

Susan waited until Allan went to work on a bleak Friday

morning. Out of her office window, she watched him get into their beat-up Honda, and putter down the suburban street before she made her move.

She turned the computer on, listened as the hard drive hummed to life, brought the word processor up. The creature eating her words could be defeated. She just had to lure it to her.

Kneeling, she crept to the window and peeked over the sill. The blue spruce outside swayed in an invisible wind. Rain pattered against the glass in a sharp spray. She ducked down, startled, and caught her breath.

She pressed her hand to her heart, steadied herself, and knelt up again. There, a glimpse of movement in the spruce. The tree shook, opposing the wind. The rain picked up, turning into a torrent. Lightning cracked. Thunder rolled over the sky, shaking the house.

She didn't stop to grab a raincoat, but ran out the front door into the midst of the storm, instantly drenched, rounded the corner of the house, and headed for the back yard. Approaching, she slowed her pace, tried to wipe the rain away from her glasses, a futile effort, and slunk against the house. The siding was cold against her wet back, soothing the aches of tension caused by the hours of futility, the endless days of struggling for the right word, only to have them elude her grasp.

Yes, she would kill the creature she knew was out there. Allan didn't believe her. The chancellor didn't believe her, the school had put her on leave, but Susan believed. She knew there was something out there, crawling in the branches, something that ate her words, prevented her from writing, muddled her entire life. And by the gods, she would kill the beast and take the words back.

Rain dripped down her back. She steeled herself, then made a run for the spruce. Wet grass caught her slippers. She slid onto a knee, righted herself, and kept going.

Aphrastos hummed, feasting on the words. The gusts didn't bother her, here in the shelter of the tree, pressed up against the trunk, surrounded by the fierce tang of resin. She burped, waved a claw in front of her mouth to dissipate the smell of stale roses, wondering which word had caused the reflux. Perhaps *Dreary*? She snagged another word from Susan, *Rain,* and stuffed the beating morpheme into her mouth. It tasted of grass and ozone, with a tinge of spring.

She grabbed more, a handful, plucking them out of the air, snagging them as they whirled around the branches, searching for escape, stuffing one after another into her mouth. She gorged herself, indifferent to the acid rising in her stomach.

Susan screamed, running towards the tree, a primal yell, full of writer's block, suppressed rage, and desolation. She ducked under the lower branches. Above her, a form slithered around the side of the trunk, like a snake, if a snake had long arms and a feral face.

She hoisted herself onto the first branch, walking around the tree in a circle, climbing the interior stair branches. Sap gummed her hand. She didn't wipe it off, just kept ascending.

She could hear the creature now, making soft moans of contentment, purring. As she approached, the branches thinning and bowing beneath her middle-aged weight, the face grew clearer, green eyes shining in the gloom of the interior.

"I'm coming for you." She hauled herself up another level, breath catching. She stopped to wipe the sweat from her face, smearing her cheek with sticky resin. "Going to get my words back."

The creature paused, shifted its weight and turned full to her. Her bare breasts pointed at her, ears swiveled. She grinned, revealing sharp teeth.

Something soft beat her hand, circled around her. She turned her head. Nothing. Again, a dreamy pattering, like downy feathers caressing her body. She couldn't see anything, yet couldn't shake the feeling that figures danced at the edge of her sight, flickered out the moment she concentrated.

The cottony forms nestled in her hair. She swore she could hear the things cooing. They caressed her cheek, ruffled through the hairs on her forearm. She flailed, pushing them away. They came back. She ignored them.

They didn't matter, these mostly transparent beings. She needed to pay attention to the creature, the thief. Heart slamming, Susan leaped up a branch, and grabbed the end of the beast's tail. The rough scales caught her palm, slicing a thousand tiny cuts. She kept hold, despite the pain. Blood dripped down the tree.

Thunder rolled through. The tree shook in a gust of wind. The beast hissed.

"Mine," she said through her teeth. "You took them for granted."

Using the creature's tail, Susan pulled herself up, grabbed the thing's neck with her other hand. The rage of the last two years, the eons during which her words had dimmed, her memory faded, the sound of her husband crying, mixed in with the fury of the storm and gave her strength.

The creature thrashed in her grip, twisting her snake neck, biting down on Susan's arm. Her teeth pierced. She shook her head like a pit bull with a stuffed toy.

Susan didn't let go.

The words beat around Aphrastos' head, trying to help Susan, attempting to get back to her and away from her greed — fickle creatures. Susan shook them away, unable to see them. Aphrastos' throat ached, her sight grew spotted with flecks of red. She twisted and squirmed. Susan hung on.

Aphrastos couldn't see through the swarm of words. *Rage* charged her left eye. *Terror* lanced her, piercing her skin with tiny fangs. *Fear* bolstered up its energy, and bit her on the nose, still quivering. The eaten words battered her stomach, churning in indigestion. Susan continued to disregard them, the reason they'd left, the fact that they came back to her.

She would not die, not like this, not ever. They were her words, and she'd keep them this time. She snapped her back, arcing the length of her body, teeth still imbedded in Susan's forearm.

Her vision dimmed, until she couldn't tell the flares of lightning from the flashes of her throes. No. With one last gasp, she exerted herself, loosened her teeth from her nasty pale skin, and pushed.

Susan shrieked, her hands slipped from Aphrastos' neck. The branches gave beneath her falling weight. She bounced from limb to limb, despite the words trying to break her fall, to cushion her on their meanings, their frail existence. Aphrastos cackled, rubbing her raw throat.

Susan hit the ground with a thump masked in another roar of thunder. Neck at an awkward angle, she lay still.

Aphrastos chuckled again, plucked two words out of the air and ate them. *The. End.*

Misty Hills of Dreamer Sheep

by David C. Hayes

Called back for my uncle's funeral, I had never planned on stepping foot within the confines of Chimney Rock, North Carolina again. The foothills of the Applachian Mountains met the Piedmont Plateau and Chimney Rock stood as ageless as the mountains it introduced. It was a typical rural area where a sickly lad with a penchant for reading stories of a fantastic nature was not be exalted for his literary aspirations and quick wit.

I had never known my father and my mother died during childbirth. The locals, of course, believed I was cursed. My uncle, under some kind of duress, agreed to raise me. A cattle farmer by trade, he regarded me as nothing more than another piece of livestock. Scarlet fever and a heart condition plagued my early years and, if it had been legal, Uncle Vernon would have liked nothing more than to "put me down" like a diseased foal.

Blessedly, Chimney Rock had a small library. Two rooms were apportioned by the town fathers to provide a library for the use of the community. These rooms were only utilized as a library in order for Chimney Rock to meet the qualifications to receive farm community Federal aid since it was cheaper than building a health clinic.

Being the only library customer in town, I had the distinct pleasure of perusing the works of Lovecraft and Poe, of Matheson and Derleth and Keeler and Asimov. The paperbacks were the only books affordable enough for our library and they opened my eyes to new worlds.

Uncle Vernon would not allow those types of books and magazines in his home. For all his brusqueness, he was a cowardly man who saw the Devil in anything that he didn't understand. This included me. He never physically laid a hand on me but there were moments of loneliness where I would have welcomed any hand… even one raised in violence. Alone, I found myself venturing into the foothills of Appalachia which, despite everything, felt like home. It sprawled open and wide and, at the same time, was choked with vegetation and was as claustrophobic as a tomb. It was me and I it. Aspiration versus reality.

In my frequent visits to the wooded areas, I would run across half-inebriated hunters attempting to stay camouflaged in their cheap tree blinds. I was careful to remain out of sight (and with the level of moonshine involved with a majority of these men it was fairly easy). One day, I overheard two hunters talking about a creature of enormous size and strength that lived in these very hills.

At first, I assumed that the men were speaking of a sasquatch, that mythical bigfoot. I was wrong, though, for these men were speaking of a creature that only appeared in the Appalachian Mountains and was as vile, vicious and dangerous as any other creature imaginable. They were speaking of the sheepsquatch.

I started, unprepared for that particular word. Of course, in this backward town the local myth would be something as utterly ridiculous as a sheepsquatch! Invariably, like all of these stories, an uncle of a friend's cousin had encountered the vile and savage sheepsquatch while hunting. The man put up a brave countenance, but could not fight the fear. The thing stood eight feet tall and was covered in wooly white and gray fleece. It was bipedal and massively wide. It had arms and hands and opposable thumbs. It looked extremely powerful, to the terrified hunter. Most horrendous of all, was the head of the sheepsquatch. Unlike sheep, the creature possessed a mouth of razor-like teeth, set in a snouted face. The sheepsquatch had yellow, watery eyes and a pair of curved horns that ended in stiletto points. According to the hunters, the sheepsquatch roared, bared its sharp teeth, and lunged at the terrified witness who turned and ran into the night.

Barely suppressing a giggle, I moved through the underbrush away from the duo in the tree blind but eager to learn more.

I arrived at the library earlier than usual to research more about this silly creature only to find that the librarian had died and with him so went the library. I finished out my schooling in Chimney Rock and left for university with an academic scholarship and student loans, vowing to never return.

Uncle Vernon died ten years later. His wife, Irene, died earlier and the couple was childless. This made me the only living heir (much to my uncle's chagrin, I assume) and required me to return to Chimney Rock in order to sell the property and be done with it once and for all.

Money was a necessity. I had studied literature in school and fancied myself an author. I had published two short stories and was currently shopping a novel of the macabre. It wasn't going well. To supplement my income, I taught English to foreign nationals visiting Washington, D.C. I needed Vernon's money.

Entering town I passed the abandoned library and that triggered a change in plans. I turned away from my uncle's home and drove to those footlands. Even as bitter as I was, I had to admit that I missed the mists at dusk. The beautiful solitude beckoned.

Crunching through foliage, I thought of the starry nights and muggy days that I followed these exact same paths. I stopped and looked up at the treetops as the sun faded from view and realized this was the area where I heard the sheepsquatch story. I laughed out loud and, quite unlike me, I called out into the night.

"Sheepsquatch! I'm here so, by all means, make yourself known to me so we can put an end to this!"

I laughed again. I was a blithering fool but, on my salary, this was the only therapy I could afford. I waited, more to savor the moment in the region than anything else.

A deep, powerful voice floated from the dense forest. "Howard Fence, I have come to speak with you."

I stopped short. The bullies of my youth had pulled pranks and made jokes at my expense for years. Seeing the obituary would mean their favorite target had returned. No longer a frail boy, I spun, ready for vengeance. What greeted me was no practical joke.

Standing before me was the sheepsquatch exactly like the hunters had described. I screamed and fell backwards, falling on my rear end, and attempted to scoot away. The sheepsquatch raised a hand and bade me to stop. Far less angry than I had heard him described, he was even polite.

"Please. Howard Fence, I have need of you."

This stopped me. The sheepsquatch, legendary creature of the Appalachians, had need of me. As if to placate me even more, the sheepsquatch squatted on his powerful legs and made it down into a sitting position, facing me.

"Uh… uh… uh…" I managed to say.

The sheepsquatch smiled. He laughed and shook his head. The laugh was friendly but hoarse, as if he had infrequent occasion to use his voice.

"You must tell my tale," he said.

"Me?"

The sheepsquatch stood and approached. He laid an enormous hand on my head. It had an intense heat, but did not burn. At the moment of his touch, the sheepsquatch 'spoke' to me. The best description I have of this moment is that he emptied. His thoughts, his dreams and, most importantly, his story, filled me to the point of bursting. I agreed, with a thought. The choice was obvious and no storyteller, even a self-professed one, could turn down an offer of this magnitude. It was now my task to tell the tale of the sheepsquatch; I had become the bard of an elder god!

The sheepsquatch was relieved that I had returned. He had known of me, of course, and waited until I would traipse through the land of my birth one more time. He was bound to this region, more out of familiarity and need (but that is part of his tale) and he rarely encountered humans. Furthermore, of those humans he encountered, none of them were adequately prepared to be a recorder of deeds. Chimney Rock, as one can surmise, wasn't a hotbed of intellectual curiosity. Of all the humans that the sheepsquatch had encountered in the woods, none possessed enough cognitive faculties to act as bard for this powerful, majestic creature. Desperate for a human to carry on his tale, the sheepsquatch angrily menaced any he found unable to fulfill the needs of his legacy. The myth persisted and the locals spread the story of a violent beast.

He was no beast. He was noble.

His story was unlike any other.

55 B.C. Roman Centurions invaded Northern Brittania, raping and pillaging without regard. Rome had picked the perfect time to invade. Just before winter, all able-bodied warriors were on extended hunts intended to provide sustenance to last through the oncoming harsh winter. The Roman army went from village to village, forcing their laws, their faith and their 'civilization' on the early Celts.

In battle, the Celts were far superior. The Celts, large and sinewy, fought in furs with axes. They were fierce. Unfortunately, one warrior, no matter how skilled, could not defeat a legion of Caesar's men, no matter how unskilled.

Caesar himself was awed by the Celtic warriors. He studied them, and the Druid Priests, hoping to learn the source of their unyielding spirit. He went as far as to capture a younger Druid and had him tortured. The man was beaten, bled, and pinched with hot pincers trying to get to the secret of the Celt's fighting prowess.

A conquering army would many times assimilate some of the conquered people's religion, making the transition easier. Through Caesar's "persuasion" he learned much more than the customs of the Druidic Celts. He learned their secrets, their ancient arcane rights and he learned the key to their avatar, the source of their ferocity!

Julius Caesar, new Lord of Britannia, learned the secret of calling the *Gafr*, the Goat, the Celtic demi-god Gabrus and would bring him to Rome. The tortured Druid gave Caesar the secret of conjuring and controlling the Gafr. The nefarious Caeser intended to do just that.

In Rome, Caesar performed the ritual. The incantation took three components. One of animal: the severed head of a large goat and one of man: the massive body of a headless gladiator. Caesar wore a pendant around his neck with Celtic symbols created under the exact specifications of the half-dead Druid he had fed to the dogs in Brittania. It glowed. This was the third component: one of magic. It would bind the souls of man and beast together and, hopefully, become more than the sum of its parts.

The head of the goat knit itself to the body of the gladiator during the incantations. Head grafted to body and the two became one, infused with the power of an ancient land. Upon its completion, its self-surgery, the Celtic God of Justice and War lived again under the command of Julius Caesar. In that moment, Rome overtook the Celtic culture completely.

The Gafr, the Goat God, elder and eternal, stood before Julius Caesar. Bound by the pendant to obey, the Gafr stood ready to serve. Caesar admired his beast (for that is what he thought he had in his possession) never realizing that the power at his command was only limited by the boundaries of Earth, on which the Gafr rarely stepped.

The Empire would have trembled if not for the pettiness of Caesar. His only use for the Gafr was as a conversation piece. In order to scare the Senate, the Gafr accompanied Caesar throughout the land. Not all of Rome was taken with Caesar's new "pet," as the Gafr was called. Two nobles in particular, Brutus and Cassius, held a distinct disdain for the pagan monstrosity before them.

As the sheepsquatch travelled with Caesar he would often times come in contact with Brutus and Cassius. The Gafr, of course, was well aware of the nobles' plans. Although a servant of Caesar he was an unwilling one. The ritual forced the Gafr to obey Julius, but not to protect him. When asked what, if anything, the Caesar could fear with the sheepsquatch behind him, the Gafr responded, "Beware the Ides of March." Caesar laughed at his companion's joke carried on, never heeding the words of a god. The Gafr knew Caesar would pay no mind and smiled at the thought of freedom.

Caesar believed himself to be invincible. Unconcerned with the threat of assassination, Caesar ordered the Gafr to remain at the palace as he went to the Senate. There, Brutus plunged a knife into his leader's back. The date was March 15th.

Brutus ripped the pendant from around Caesar's neck and hid it away, afraid of what uses it may have.

The master died, the servant was liberated, and for many years the Gafr lived in peace on the outskirts of the city. Until a young heir-apparent to the throne of Rome discovered the secret of Julius Caesar. The pendant that controlled the demi-god was found. An involuntary shudder ran through all the citizens of Rome as the pendant holding the Gafr's soul was discovered by a sixteen-year-old Nero on the eve before his ascension.

54 A.D. - Nero took the throne of Rome from the murdered Emperor Claudius. After over 100 years of peaceful existence, the Gafr was called into service once again. Following Julius' instructions, the young Nero called the Gafr to his side.

As distasteful as service to Julius was, service to Nero was abhorrent. Where Caesar used the Gafr to gain public interest and wrest power from a terrified Senate, Nero found the Gafr an amusing tool of destruction. Nothing stood in Nero's way – no man, woman or child. The sheepsquatch was ordered to murder with callus disregard; Nero's madness knew no boundaries.

A Celtic god of justice, reduced by "civilization" to a murderous thug, The Gafr wept and longed for Nero's death. Caesar served as an amusing diversion but this Nero was evil incarnate.

The Emperor commanded the Gafr to do the unimaginable. The power of the pendant holding the Gafr's soul was so strong that under Nero's command, the Gafr burned Rome to the ground.

Nero delighted in the carnage. The Gafr had done his bidding! He watched the city burn, its people burn all from the safety of his own balcony. How dare the people tell him what we will build or will not build, he was the Emperor of Rome!

As Nero would often say, to anyone within earshot, "Rome wishes? I am Rome!"

Unfortunately for Nero, the Gafr was in earshot many of those times and returned to the balcony after setting the city ablaze.

The sheepsquatch scooped Nero up and held him high over head. Nero should have been more careful how he phrased his last command to the Gafr.

"Burn Rome to the ground! All of Rome!" Nero had said.

Nero's fall was thought to be a suicide. Remorse for his burning of Rome, historian's thought. By all accounts, Nero was remorseful in his last moments, so remorseful he wished he never had enslaved the Gafr.

Amidst the blood and gore on the street, the pendant controlling the Gafr sat. The Gafr had hoped to gain possession of it, hide it… forever. Before he could retrieve the accursed thing, refugees from the city filled the street. They rushed toward and over the corpse of Nero. Women holding children, men carrying baskets… everyone fled Rome and, with them, the pendant disappeared.

The Gafr could feel the pendant calling to him, but was never able to find exactly where it had been hidden. He followed the siren's call of the damned thing for millennia, eventually coming to the new world. The Appalachian Mountains called to him, reminding the sheepsquatch of his ancient Brittanic home.

He 'heard' the pendant. It was here, in America, and it was relatively close. He could no longer walk the Earth unencumbered, though. He was desperate to find the pendant, but had to remain hidden, finding solitude and contentment in the forest.

I accepted his call and, as one can tell, intend to deliver the tale of the sheepsquatch to the world as well as find the pendant. I believe I will not be selling my uncle's farm after all and, upon returning to Washington, D.C., a visit to The Smithsonian may be in order.

In the meantime, he will wait, like always, perpetuating the myth of rabid beast to whatever unlucky souls manage to cross the sheepsquatch's path. After all, what is 2000 years to an immortal?

Camp Miskatonic

by Lillian Csernica

The bus from Camp Holy Cross rumbled down the highway.

"Where are we *going*?" My cousin 'Cia slid the window down and stuck her head out. "I haven't seen a sign for miles!"

"Innocencia!" Our senior counselor Paula jumped up from her seat by the driver and hurried down the aisle. She grabbed 'Cia by the collar of her blue camp T shirt. "Now you stop that! You know better!"

'Cia and I rolled our eyes at each other. Paula was a skinny blonde princess who had her nails done at the beauty parlor and paid somebody to do all her housework, somebody poor with lots of kids to feed. Somebody like our mothers. 'Cia and I should have been at the Santa Theresa Summer Camp. This year it was canceled because the buildings had to be sprayed for termites. So there we were, two Latinas from gang banger central, stuck on a bus in the middle of nowhere with a bunch of white bread Protestants, Chinese Baptists, a few Born Again types and some girls from our counselor Naomi's commune, Hippies for Jesus. The only thing we all had in common was our blue camp uniforms with Camp Holy Cross stitched in white over our hearts.

"Now remember, ladies," Paula said, "this is Camp Miskatonic's first year. Their girls might be a bit shy." She gave us her usual big smile. "We have a really wonderful opportunity here to love our neighbors."

Naomi nodded, making her long red curls bounce and her big silver earrings swing. "We want the girls from Camp Miskatonic to remember today not just as a competition to be won or lost, but as a day of fellowship, of interfaith communication and understanding." Naomi could say stuff like that and make it sound like she really meant it.

'Cia leaned over and whispered to me. "You know what Miskatonic means?"

"*No sé*. Maybe it's some kind of Indian word."

"Good thing *Abuela* doesn't know we're way out here."

I nodded. Our grandmother was a *curandera. Abuela* went to church every Sunday, but she knew a lot of other stuff too, stuff about healing and keeping bad spirits and bad people away from our house.

"Now we won't be expected to attend any of their religious services," Paula said, "but we might see some of their observances. If they do anything that looks strange, just keep quiet and look respectful." She put on her big sunny smile, the one that made me want to heave. "Let's show them how we live every day in God's love."

Yeah, right. Everybody knew the whole point of this trip was winning the annual trophy. My legs were stiff. Paula started making us sing stupid songs like "Kumbaya" and "He's Got the Whole World in His Hands." The bus finally took an offramp into the woods.

"Look, girls!" Paula pointed ahead. "There's the sign!"

It was just a big wooden square painted purple. No words, no cross or animals or anything. Burned into it was some kind of twisty symbol. We all stared at it.

"Weird." Across the aisle, Anna Chang frowned. She was a bookworm, half-Chinese and really smart. "I've never seen that on the camp directory's website."

"Well duh." Francine cracked her gum, looking bored. "It's their first year, remember?" Francine dyed her stringy brown hair black, used black nail polish, and had three earrings in each ear. 'Cia and I figured she was aiming for Goth. She missed.

"That looks Kabbalistic. They could be pagans, Goddess worshipers, maybe even witches!"

"Oh please." Linda Kim pushed her glasses back up her nose. "Do you really think the Holy Cross Board of Directors would let Paula lead us right into the middle of a coven?"

"She's right," 'Cia whispered to me, pulling her gold cross out from under her T shirt. "When we get home I'm gonna draw that thing and show it to *Abuela*."

"Hey." Naomi sat on the edge of the seat in front of me and 'Cia. "This is America. Everybody can do what they want here, remember? If they want to put an eggplant on a plate and worship that, the Constitution says it's OK."

"So what are they?" Anna Chang asked. "Buddhist? Hindu? Zoroastrian?"

Naomi frowned like she was trying to remember something. "You know, I have no idea. Paula didn't actually say."

Big black gates blocked the road, the wrought iron kind with twisted bars. The middle of each gate matched the symbol on the Camp Miskatonic sign. A guard shack stood on both sides of the gates. Two women stepped out of each shack. They looked like guards from a women's prison movie. Big, dull-eyed, not a lot of laughs.

"Naomi, look." 'Cia pointed. "See the patches on their shoulders? They're not from a real security company."

Naomi stared out the window. "You're right. No company name, just that symbol."

Our driver handed over some papers, then the guards went back inside the shacks. The gates swung open. The bus rolled down a dirt road that took us even farther into the forest. We pulled up next to a big log-cabin style building that was probably Camp Miskatonic's cafeteria. A concrete sidewalk went all the way around the building. The parking lot was only big enough to hold maybe ten cars. Two big black SUVs sat in the far corner.

Everybody on our bus crowded over to our side to get a look at the competition. Lined up outside the cafeteria were two dozen girls, the youngest maybe seven and the oldest probably fifteen or sixteen. They all looked a little strange. No matter what color *our* skins were, all of us had some kind of tan. This crowd looked like they'd been living in a basement with no light at all, not even those weird purple things for growing mushrooms. None of the Miskatonics wore makeup, either. Not even lip gloss. Their camp T-shirts were black with the big silver squiggly thing on the front. They wore black shorts with silver stripes down the sides and black tennis shoes.

'Cia nudged me with her elbow. "Wednesday Addams should have come to this camp."

"Hey Naomi." I leaned forward so Paula wouldn't hear me. "You sure this is the right camp? These kids look like they're handicapped or sick or something."

"Be nice, Maria. A lot of religious groups have strict rules about what you can and can't eat. That's probably why they look like that."

"The last time I looked like that," 'Cia said, "I'd been barfing my guts out for two days."

Paula shooed us all out of the bus. We stood there staring at the Miskatonics while they stared at us. The door at one end of the cafeteria opened. Four more of the guards came out, then a skinny older woman with snow-white hair and a face like a dried apple. It was hot in the sun, but the old lady wore a purple cardigan over her camp T-shirt and a long black skirt. She looked like she might have been a ballerina a hundred years ago.

"Good afternoon, ladies."

"Good afternoon, Madame du Noir," Paula chirped. "The ladies of Camp Holy Cross are delighted to meet you." Paula gave us that look, the one all Sunday school teachers have no matter which church you go to.

"Good afternoon, Madame du Noir," we all said.

"Please join us in the main courtyard. We have some refreshments for you."

Madame du Noir clapped her hands. The four guards herded the Miskatonics around the corner of the cafeteria like big ugly sheepdogs chasing depressed sheep. Paula caught up with Madame du Noir and walked beside her.

"What do you think?" 'Cia asked. "Monkey brains? Toadstools?"

"Ain't gonna be *arroz con pollo*."

A dozen picnic tables were lined up in three rows in the middle of the courtyard. As bright and sunny as it was, the courtyard looked cold and gloomy. Painting the picnic tables that gross gray color wasn't the best way to cheer the place up. The Miskatonics went right to their places at the tables and stood there. Just stood there. I was starting to wonder if they were all stoned on something. I knew Rastafarians thought marijuana was OK. That would explain a lot about this place.

"Innocencia, you go sit over there." Paula pointed to one table, then put her arm around my shoulders and pushed me the other way. "Maria, I want you over there. Let's all make some new friends today!"

I sat down at a table with three Miskatonic girls. Anna Chang sat down across from me. A minute later Francine sat beside her. The big doors in the side of the cafeteria opened. More guards came out pushing stainless steel carts like the kind they used in hospitals to deliver the meals. That made me think of the way hospitals smelled, that nasty antiseptic stink that never did cover up the worse smell underneath.

The guards passed out the trays. Just apples, bananas, Oreo cookies, graham crackers, and bottled water. I waited. Did the Miskatonics say grace or what? A little girl with two long brown braids sat next to me. She picked up a graham cracker and started nibbling at it like a mouse. Poor kid. It was probably her first time away from home.

"Hi," I said. "I'm Maria."

The little mouse girl jumped in her seat then peeked at me out of the corner of her eye. "Sarah Jane," she whispered.

The next Miskatonic girl was big and bony with short black hair. She'd probably end up one of the guards. She stopped chewing her Oreo long enough to nod at us Holy Cross girls.

"Linda Lou."

The third Miskatonic girl looked like some kind of snow angel or fairy or something. Silvery blonde hair, big blue eyes, and a face that was perfect without makeup. I hated her.

"I'm Amanda Sue." Her voice was soft and dreamy. Definitely stoned.

"So," Francine said. "What movies do you guys like?"

Sarah Jane and Linda Lou just kept on eating. Amanda Sue shook her head from side to side, moving slow like she was under water.

"False delusions of deranged minds. The products of

tormented souls who cannot bear the ordeal of reality."

Anna Chang looked up from peeling a banana. "So you want dispassion, like the Hindus?"

"More delusion," Amanda Sue said. "We seek the return of Those to whom *all* souls must bow."

"What, the Second Coming?" Francine sounded disappointed. "You don't look like Christians."

Amanda Sue smiled. It was positively scary. She pointed to the silver squiggle on her T-shirt. "Do you know what this is?"

"It's a sigil," Francine said.

"Yes! This is the key that opens the mind to the essence of reality." Amanda Sue closed her eyes. "The true depth of being that transcends all mortal consciousness."

"Seriously stoned," I said.

Amanda Sue's eyes snapped open. "What did you say?"

"*No hablo Inglés.*"

I took a bite of my apple and chewed it, looking around for Paula and Naomi. They were busy filling out forms and checking things off and getting our numbers ready. These wimps didn't look like they'd make us break a sweat. I sighed, wishing we could have taken on Camp Pocahontas again. Those prom queens knew how to put up a fight.

The guards came around again to collect our trays. I spotted 'Cia, who gave me her "Oh my Gawd!" look. That told me things were probably just as weird at her table. Madame du Noir clapped her hands twice. Every Miskatonic shot up out of her seat.

"Will the teams please gather one to each side of the competition grounds?"

Like the dopey sheep they were, the Miskatonics moved over to the left side of the big flat grassy area where all the equipment had been set up. Sarah Jane put her hand on mine. As hot out as it was, her skin was ice cold.

"Please. Please don't let us win."

"What? You don't want to win?"

"No." Her lower lip trembled. "No. *Please.*" She got up and hurried toward her team.

Everybody on our side started stretching out and warming

up while Paula and Naomi ran around pinning numbers on all of us. The food hadn't done much for the Miskatonics. They still looked like those kids we saw on TV when the news showed pictures from Bosnia and Africa.

'Cia nudged me. "You think maybe this is one of those places that takes care of kids who—you know, somebody messed with them?"

"Maybe. They're scared. One girl at my table practically begged me not to let them win."

'Cia's eyes bugged out. "Me too! Jessica Anne said she hoped we won. The way she said it, you'd think she really did want to lose."

The guards came at us with their clipboards, calling off the names signed up for the different events. 'Cia and I had to split up again. Paula made 'Cia sign up for that stupid egg and spoon race. Everybody who was running the obstacle course lined up behind the stripe of white chalk on the grass. One of the Miskatonics bumped into me.

"Don't touch the middle ring." She ran off to hide behind her teammates.

I looked out at the obstacle course. There was a set of three rings you had to swing across while you kept your feet off the ground.

"Maria Sanchez," called the guard standing at the starting line. "Take your mark."

So I got to go first. I kissed my cross and said a quick prayer to Santa Theresa so she'd know I didn't forget about her. When the guard blew her whistle, I took off running. The tires were no big deal. The mud pit hardly slowed me down at all. Climbing the net cost me some time. When I grabbed the first ring I pushed off so hard I swung all the way across and grabbed the third ring. I hit the ground going full speed and crossed the finish line. Paula waited there, holding a stopwatch.

"Way to go, Maria! They'll have to hustle to beat your time!"

While I got my breath back, I watched the other girls run the course. The third Miskatonic was good, long-legged and fast. When she grabbed the first ring, the weight of her long legs slowed her down. Her hand closed on the middle ring. A steel bolt gave and the bracket fell off. The Miskatonic girl landed on her back in the dirt. The ring thumped her right across the forehead, leaving a big red mark. Two guards had to carry her off the field. How did the Miskatonics know about that, unless they rigged it themselves?

"Tough break for them," Paula said. "She'll be out of the games completely."

I had a few minutes before the archery contest, so I grabbed a bottle of water. I found 'Cia standing in the shade by the cafeteria with some other Holy Cross girls.

"If any of the Miskatonics tell you to do something or not do it during your event," I said, "don't listen to them. I think they're setting us up."

"For what?" 'Cia asked. "Winning?"

"You got it."

"What's wrong with that?"

"I don't think we want to find out."

The rest of the afternoon passed the same way, with girls on both teams getting hurt. The Miskatonics didn't look they played sports much, but nobody could be as bad as some of them were without doing it on purpose. I didn't know what to think. A few of the Miskatonics went at it like this was the Olympics. Amanda Sue was one of them, her dreamy eyes all squinched up and her teeth clenched while she played Ping-Pong against Francine.

When the last event was over, there were twelve Miskatonics still standing and sixteen of our team in good shape. We sat at the picnic tables again, eating orange juice Popsicles while the guards added up everybody's scores. Paula and Naomi started walking toward us. Naomi looked upset.

"Come on, ladies!" Paula called. "Time for the big awards ceremony!"

"Let's get this done, girls. You're all probably tired and want to go home." Naomi glared at Paula. "I know I do."

Paula ignored her. "Camp Miskatonic has its very own lake! We'll be holding the awards ceremony down on the lakeshore. Won't that be lovely?"

So we all followed Paula. Two of the guards led us down to the shore of the lake. A boat dock stretched out into the water. Two more guards stood at our end of the dock wearing plain purple choir robes. On the far end of the dock stood two big concrete pillars. Each pillar had that squiggle painted on it in silver with a purple outline. The tops of both pillars looked like crescent moons with the points up. The sides of the pillars facing the lake curved down and out like rain gutters.

Madame du Noir made her grand entrance all dressed up in fancy purple satin robes with that silver squiggle embroidered all over them. On top of her white hair sat a tiara with the same squiggle. It must have been set with diamonds, the way it glittered and flashed in the light of the setting sun. Four more guards came with her, all of them wearing purple choir robes.

"Looks like church," Anna Chang said.

"Yeah." Even Francine looked nervous. "Hey Paula, I thought you said we didn't have to do any of this stuff."

Paula gave her a tight smile. "Don't worry about it. Just look respectful."

"About what?" I asked. "What are they going to do?"

"Just bow your heads and keep your mouths *shut*."

'Cia and I looked at each other. All of a sudden Paula didn't sound like a nice blonde church lady anymore.

Madame du Noir held up a small envelope. "These are the results of the competition. It was very, very close. Toward the end we thought we might need a tiebreaker!"

"Then we're lucky there were people left to play it." Naomi stood behind us, looking unhappy in an angry sort of way. I wondered if she knew what was really going on.

Madame du Noir tore open the envelope and pulled out the slip of paper inside. Her dried apple face split into a creepy smile. Right then I knew where Amanda Sue got all her big words. Madame du Noir had to be her grandmother.

"I am delighted to announce the winner of the First Annual Camp Miskatonic Sports Day is the challenger, Camp Holy Cross."

Our side started cheering, but the Miskatonics went wild. They screamed and hugged each other. Some of them were even crying. They were *happy* we'd kicked their asses? Of all the weird things that had happened today, that was the weirdest. Right then the wind came blowing in off the lake. It made me shiver with more than just cold. A bunch of frogs had started croaking. I hated frogs. Ugly and slimy, their necks blowing up like balloons.... The sun was going down and we were a long way from home. *Abuela* always told us to be home by sunset.

"We have some individual awards to give out." Madame du Noir raised her hand. One of the guards in a purple robe brought her a silver tray with three medals on it. "The three competitors with the highest scores overall will be awarded the title Champion. The third Champion, who came in among the top three in all of her events, is our own Amanda Sue."

Amanda Sue came drifting out of the crowd to stand in front of Madame du Noir. She bowed her head while Madame du Noir put a medal around her neck. Strung on a wide purple ribbon, the medal wasn't round like the usual kind. It was that weird squiggle.

"The Second Champion, scoring first or second place in her events, is Innocencia Martinez from Camp Holy Cross."

Even louder cheering greeted 'Cia's name. She looked across the distance between Madame du Noir and us.

"Do I have to go over there?"

Paula grabbed 'Cia by the elbow. "Get a move on, girl! We're all so proud of you!"

'Cia's medal was strung on a silver ribbon. Amanda Sue hugged her and kissed her on both cheeks. I thought 'Cia was going to punch her, but 'Cia held still and tried to smile the way Naomi said we should.

"The First Champion scored first in *all* of her events, setting a standard of excellence that will inspire us for years to come. Maria Sanchez!"

Suddenly my insides turned cold. I knew what 'Cia meant about walking all that way. I didn't want to leave Naomi, I didn't want to go near Madame du Noir, and I really didn't want that squiggle thing around my neck.

Now Paula swooped down on me. "Come on, Maria! Don't be shy! We all knew you'd take first place!"

Something about the way she said that really bothered me. Madame du Noir looked even more bizarre up close. With the silver eye shadow and purple lipstick, she made one ugly fairy godmother.

"It is my honor to present this award to you, Maria dear," she said. "These days it's rare indeed to meet a young woman of your strength, agility, and character."

Character? Me? *Abuela* loved me, but even she said I was nothing but trouble. That bad feeling I had got even worse. My medal was strung on a red ribbon. Dark red. Something told me *Abuela* wouldn't like this at all.

"No thanks."

I backed up, shaking my head, and ran into one of the guards. Madame du Noir stepped forward and hung the squiggle around my neck. It clanked against my cross. Amanda Sue reached for me. I dodged and stood on the other side of 'Cia.

"As the sun sets on this most memorable day," Madame du Noir said, "I will ask our three Champions to step to the end of the dock so we may take some photographs for our camp scrapbook."

"Naomi," Paula said. "Why don't you get the rest of the girls on the bus? This will only take a few minutes. We really should get going."

"Thank God." Naomi got pairs of our girls to help the ones who were hurt start walking back toward the bus.

I grabbed 'Cia's arm and we ran toward them. No way were we hanging around here with these psychos.

"Maria!" Paula rushed over in front of us, making me and 'Cia slam right into her. Paula pushed us both back toward the dock. "Don't be rude. Madame du Noir wants to take your picture!"

"*No lo quiero!*" I drove my shoulder into Paula, shoving her out of our way. "'*Cia! Vaminos!*"

Somebody grabbed me by the hair. 'Cia yelled. Amanda Sue stood behind us, winding her fists in our hair. She was way too strong. The fading sunlight lit up her blue eyes, turning them purple.

"Today you rise to the rank of Champion. Today I rise to the rank of Priestess. Surrender and rejoice!"

I fought Amanda Sue's grip, bending sideways so I could ram my elbow up under her chin. Her head snapped backward. She hissed words in some language I didn't understand. Pain like a thousand needles stuck me all over. 'Cia screamed. Amanda Sue dragged us all the way down to the end of the dock. The two guards in purple choir robes followed us. Amanda Sue pushed 'Cia toward one pillar and me toward the other. The two guards grabbed us by our wrists and hauled them up between our shoulder blades.

"Naomi!" I yelled as loud as I could. "*Naomi!* Help!"

Back on shore, Madame du Noir lifted her hands up and started chanting. All the guards chanted with her. Then the Miskatonics started in. They walked halfway down the dock and lined up shoulder to shoulder, packed tight as sardines. Amanda Sue turned toward the lake. Now she raised her arms too, chanting something in that ugly hissing language. Out in the middle of the lake, bubbles surfaced. Big bubbles. Something was coming up. Amanda Sue knelt down, reaching out toward the water with both hands while she kept chanting. The trail of bubbles moved toward the end of the dock and stopped about six feet away from it. Amanda Sue bent over until her forehead touched the wooden planks, then she stood up.

"And so we offer our finest, Old One. Drink of the waters of life, O Child of Dagon and Guardian of Our Home."

Amanda touched the concrete pillar in front of 'Cia. Cia's guard shoved her up against the pillar and jammed her head down into the top of it. Amanda Sue reached back under her silvery hair, inside the collar of her camp T-shirt, and pulled out a black-handled dagger with a six-inch blade. Now I knew what those pillars looked like. Not rain gutters, but gutters for blood.

"*Madre de Dios!*" I screamed. "'Cia! Look out!"

I threw my weight against the guard holding me and brought my legs up, kicking the guard holding 'Cia right in the back of the head. 'Cia jerked free and belted her guard across the mouth, knocking her flat on her back. Before the guard could get up, 'Cia rolled her off the side of the dock. I kicked down on the kneecap of my guard, then whacked her in the nose with the back of my head. 'Cia was all over her, kicking and punching until the guard let go of me. We shoved her off the dock.

The water behind Amanda Sue bubbled and churned. All the Miskatonics blocking the dock kept the other guards from getting to us. Madame du Noir shouted something in that ugly language, making stabbing motions. Amanda Sue raised the dagger.

"Submit! The blood of the victors must feed the Elder Gods!"

Maybe the girls from Santa Theresa Summer Camp didn't have much money, and maybe we didn't know much about freaky cults from horror movies, but we knew all about fighting with knives. I grabbed Amanda Sue's wrist and held the knife away from me, then turned so my back was against her chest and slammed her up against my concrete pillar. I beat her wrist against it until she dropped the dagger.

Amanda Sue sucked in a deep breath. No way was she making me hurt like that again. I jammed my elbow up under her ribs. The breath whooshed out of her. A hard right hook across that pretty face knocked her back toward the end of the dock. It was my turn to grab Amanda Sue by all that silvery hair.

"You want to feed the fish? Go for it!"

I threw her right off the end of the dock. Three bluish-purple tentacles as thick as telephone poles shot up out of the water and wrapped around Amanda Sue, dragging her under. The water churned even harder. The white bubbles on top turned red.

"My granddaughter!" Madame du Noir wailed. "My *protégé!* My successor!"

'Cia took off running straight at the mob between us and the shore. I was right behind her, using shoulder slams and elbow jabs and all those cool moves from the soccer field. We plowed through the Miskatonics like bowling balls through cheap glass. Paula stood there, arms out to stop us. 'Cia ducked under Paula's arms. I crashed into Paula and we both went down. She held on, rolling around and keeping me tangled up so I couldn't get away.

'Cia turned around. "Maria!"

"*Vete al autobus!* Hotwire it if you have to!"

"What about you?"

"Go!"

Madame du Noir pulled out another dagger just like Amanda Sue's and headed straight for Paula. "You have failed! You will pay for the loss of my beloved child!"

"No! Wait!" Paula yelled. "I've still got this one!"

"You bitch!" I called her every name I could think of in Spanish. "You sold us out!"

"That's right. For all the really good things in life. All the things you'll never have." Paula laughed. "Who'd miss two little *putas* from the housing projects? You people breed like rats."

Rats, huh? I sank my teeth into Paula's white arm, as hard and as deep as I could go. She shrieked and beat on my head with the other hand. I shoved her off me and jumped up, spitting her white blood in her face.

Madame du Noir snarled and hissed in that ugly language. The guards and the Miskatonics all started moving in on Paula. I ran for it, catching up with the bus just as it was about to hit the gates. The driver opened the door. Naomi reached out to haul me inside.

"Wait a minute," she said. "Where's Paula?"

"Paula sold us out," I said, sucking in air. "Those freaks were going to feed me and 'Cia to their pet squid!"

"It's true," 'Cia said. "Paula made some kind of deal with Madame du Noir."

"A deal?" Naomi shook her head. "I'd better go--"

"No!" I pushed Naomi down onto a seat and 'Cia sat on her.

A scream echoed over the treetops, long and horrible.

The driver floored it. As soon as we were out on the highway, Naomi got on the radio, calling for the sheriff, the highway patrol, the fire department, the forest rangers, and anybody else who'd come running. We all watched out the back windows, but none of the Miskatonics came after us. 'Cia and I both looked at the squiggle medals still hanging around our necks. We pulled them off, slid the window down, and chucked them into the ditch.

Hunger

by Alexandra Grunberg

Rolph's axe met the side of the tree trunk with a heavy thud that sent vibrations through his hands up to his shoulder. It was painful, but the good kind of pain that came with the satisfaction of performing difficult labor. He ignored his muscles' pleas for a break and dislodged the axe for another swing.

"Bad time?"

Rolph's biceps clenched as he paused mid swing, ruining his momentum. He turned to see a young man in a long black coat, shivering. Rolph dropped his axe and swept the smaller man up in a bear hug, ignoring his resistance. When the man was thoroughly embarrassed, Rolph set him back down again.

"Always a good time for you Elijah," Rolph said, sitting back on a stump. "Always nice to have a break."

It had been so long since he had seen anyone, Rolph was overjoyed to be visited by an old friend.

"It's 'Pastor' now, Rolph," Elijah corrected, readjusting his wide-brimmed hat. Rolph was pleased that it still remained slightly askew. It made Elijah look more like the boy he had grown up with, the boy who skipped classes with him to shoot at squirrels or go swimming in the river at night. Not this somber man of God, always dressed in mourning.

"You sure try to make it difficult for me to forget," said Rolph. "What brings a respectable minister like you to my humble abode?"

"Humble, indeed," said Elijah, raising an eyebrow.

"I'm not done fixing it," said Rolph.

The cabin had suffered during the recent ice storm. A tree had fallen on one of its sides, taking down part of the roof and the edge of two walls, but Rolph had thrown deerskin over the exposed corner. It would not have been livable, especially at this time of year, for most men, but Rolph was a survivor. He had lived in worse.

"I could ask some members of the congregation for help," said Elijah.

"I don't need help. And no one there would help me."

He stood up and took off his hat, placing it on the ground. Though Elijah had seen the wounds before, he still flinched. Rolph grabbed his axe and channeled his aggression into a steady swing. There was no point losing his temper with a friend.

"You're a part of my flock now," insisted Elijah. "People listen to me now. Maybe because they're afraid of me, but less than Christian means can lead to Christian ends."

"They're not afraid of you," said Rolph, as the wood splintered. "They're afraid of monsters, and demons, and Hell. Did you come here to overwhelm me with your Christian charity, or do you actually need something from me?"

"Actually, I would like to ask a favor," said Elijah. "Do you remember Paul Lawson?"

With one last strike, the tree fell with a dull thud. The snow erupted around it in a fine, lightly drifting powder, an elegant contrast to Rolph's success. But though his work was done, Rolph did not release his grip on the axe. He nodded toward Elijah. There was no sudden chill in the air, no change except for one man's name, but Rolph clenched his jaw and Elijah's cheeks flushed.

Rolph felt his grip on the axe tighten to such an extreme that the wood began to give under his hands. A pinpoint of hate stung the center of his forehead and his eyes burned and watered. He steadied his breathing, which had become a grating rasp, as he reminded himself that he did not hate Elijah, he did not want to hurt Elijah, though his pulse seemed to beat out a desire to hurt everything.

"I'm sure I've heard his name before," said Rolph, calming himself with the deep breaths as the burning sensation began to fade. "What mess has that idiot gotten himself into now?"

"Don't be cruel."

"I'm not being cruel, I'm being honest. Isn't honesty a virtue?" asked Rolph. "The man's an idiot. It's one thing for me to build my home where I can have some space and privacy. But what is the son of a judge doing, thinking he can be a trader? What's he going to trade? I saw some of his traps before. Even a beaver isn't stupid enough to fall for those. It's a wonder that his family can eat at all."

"If you don't mind," said Elijah. "I'm trying to get to the point. No one has heard from Paul in quite some time. Rolph, no one has heard from any member of the Lawson family in quite some time."

Rolph released his grip on the axe. Elijah flinched at how close to Rolph's feet the sharp blade had fallen, but Rolph did not even notice the axe leave his hand.

"For how long?"

"Three months."

"Why the hell didn't you come to me sooner? They could all be dead!"

"I wasn't sure you'd want to go," said Elijah. "You're not the first person I've asked. I wish I never had to drag you into this, or cause you any trouble or pain. But everyone I've asked so far has refused. Everyone, Rolph, and perhaps with good reason. There's something in the woods."

"Rabid?"

"Perhaps," said Elijah. "Perhaps worse. A family came into town two months ago. They had apparently lost their daughter before arriving and their son was injured. His leg was ripped apart, the remaining flesh covered in bites. The mother was hysterical, and claimed they were attacked by a monster."

"Wild dog?"

Elijah stared into the trees.

"Come on, Elijah, you're not telling me there's a rabid bear out there? I mean, I'll do what I can, I've dealt with my share of crazed animals, but that's a lot to ask of one man."

"Rolph, the bite marks looked human."

Rolph sat down on the stump and looked up at Elijah. His friend did not look at him, but continued to stare into the woods, his hands clasped together. Rolph could not tell if he was warming them or if he was praying.

"I had heard tales before," said Elijah. "A man is holed up for a long time, wintertime. He is starving, his family is starving. And he gets so hungry. He has to eat something, so he does. The flesh of his family satisfies him for a short time, but then, strangely, he is hungry again. From that point on, he is only hungry for flesh, and he will never be satisfied."

"I've heard this myth," said Rolph. "The crazy loner. It's Indian crap. They spread those lies to scare us out of their land. I know you're a superstitious man, Elijah, but you won't have me believing in monsters. However, I do believe in insanity. And right now, it sounds like the entire community, you included, abandoned Elizabeth and her daughter with a crazy man because they were afraid of a myth."

"If you don't believe it, will you go?"

"Why don't you come with me?" asked Rolph.

"The community needs me."

"That's shit, Elijah."

"Okay," said the minister, his hands clasped now in obvious prayer. "I'm afraid. I don't want to go."

"That's not my problem."

Elijah placed his hand on Rolph's shoulder. He flinched and pulled away from the touch.

"You cannot hold hate in your heart forever," said Elijah, and much more quietly, as though he was speaking to himself, added, "And you were never very good at pretending to hate her."

"You're wrong," said Rolph. "But I'll go."

For a moment he stood and looked out into the trees, into the shadows between them where he knew Elijah saw monsters. Rolph did not need myths for monsters. He did not need religious morals to do good deeds, either. To covet was a sin, but, as Elijah stated, less than Christian means could lead to Christian ends.

He grabbed his axe off the ground and picked up his hat.

Rolph walked close to his father as they were led, hands bound behind their backs, to the town square. The crowd writhed and jeered around them, spitting out hateful words and curses that fell on Rolph like hail. He worried that the crowd would start throwing actual stones soon, but they kept their distance from the two large men who had a firm grip on the prisoners' arms. Someone spat in his father's face, but he did not react. His face was calm, serene, the perfect image of peace.

They reached the town square and the men led Rolph and his father to the stocks. Judge Lawson stood by, his son, Paul, a weak little boy, standing behind him. When Judge Lawson lifted his arms to quiet the crowd, Rolph saw that he held a hammer in his hand.

A lump formed at the base of his throat, but he forced himself not to cry. He would not give the crowd the satisfaction of seeing him cry.

"My flock," said Judge Lawson as the crowd hushed to attention. "These men claim to be part of this community. They claim to be children of God. Yet they walk in darkness, masquerading as good Christians, waiting to lure the pure from the truth. These Quakers have refused conversion. They refuse to come to God. And so they must be punished."

The crowd erupted into cheers and howling.

Rough arms pushed Rolph toward the stocks, and he bit the inside of his cheek to keep from crying out. He would not scream. He would not let tears fall. He would not let them see his shame.

The stocks closed around his neck and hands. He could not turn his head to see his father, but heard the thump of shutting wood as he was identically encased. Usually this was it, a public humiliation until the judge decided the lesson was learned. But Rolph heard the sound of steady footsteps as Judge Lawson walked before his father.

There was a moment of silence, and then a loud crack, followed by steady pounding. The pattern of sound was repeated, and the crowd cheered again, though Rolph's father remained silent.

Then the judge came before Rolph.

Rolph felt his breath shorten, his heartbeat quicken. He felt the cool tip of a nail against his earlobe.

Rolph's eyes searched the crowd for some form of help, or solace, or compassion, some of the inner peace that his father found so easily but was so elusive to Rolph. He saw hate and he saw anger, shadowed faces, and open, whooping mouths.

And he saw a pair of eyes, so soft and dark, like deep black pools. Beautiful eyes that were locked on Rolph. And at the sight of those eyes, witness to his shame, Rolph could not be strong anymore, and he began to sob as the nail pierced his skin. And Rolph's heart was encased with a cold frost as the image of the jeering crowd was overwhelmed by a pair of dark eyes.

Rolph opened his eyes, and the town square faded away as he was brought back to the present, to the small cave he had dug into a snow bank to survive the night. The crowd was gone, the pain was gone, but the eyes remained, staring at him through the entrance to his shelter, staring from the darkness of the forest. Those familiar dark eyes, but the light in them had changed. There was no compassion, no hint of the love he had always hoped he had glimpsed. There was only ice. Then the eyes were gone as the creature fled, and for the first time in twenty years, Rolph cried.

Rolph reached the remains of a small cabin. The door had been ripped off its hinges, the wood around the frame bending outwards. Elizabeth had clearly broken out of the house from the inside. Or the creature that used to be Elizabeth.

Through the doorway, Rolph could only see shadows. Maybe the creature had returned to its old home. Maybe it had run back here after being startled last night. Maybe it was watching him now, waiting in the shadows for him to be a fool and step inside. Or maybe it was gone.

If it was gone, Rolph was obligated to go inside, to see if Paul and his daughter had survived. Or, if they had not survived, to gather their remains for a proper burial.

Rolph gripped his axe and walked through the gaping hole.

The room was in disarray. A table was split down the middle, the two halves fallen at jagged angles with jutting splinters. Curtains that once hung at the windows had been ripped down and torn to pieces, the blue fabric strewn across the floor and broken furniture, spotted with dark drying blood. The wind had blown snow inside and everything was powdered white. Rolph bumped against the arm of a chair and it fell to pieces, far too loudly for his liking. Rolph heard a faint thump from the next room. He lifted his axe, ready to strike, and walked toward the sound.

The room must have been the kitchen. The large open

fireplace was still mostly intact, though the logs had been scattered. The kitchen table was pushed to the far wall under a small window. It tilted in toward the room, one leg missing. Blood stained the inner edge. On the other side of the room, half-hidden in shadow, was a partially disintegrated chair covered a pile of bloody rags. Next to the rags was a cellar door.

Rolph walked over, as quiet as he could, to the cellar. He tugged lightly on the large knob, but it did not budge. He tugged harder, but stopped when it only resulted in a sharp squeak. Rolph ran his free hand over the door, searching for another way to open it, and was surprised to feel deep scratches covering the entire surface of the slippery wood. He moved back into the light and held his hand up to the window. His palm was streaked with blood.

Something tried to break into the cellar. Maybe someone was still alive down there.

He walked back to the shadows and crouched next to the cellar door, but hesitated. If he made too much noise, the creature might hear him. And did he really need to get in? It was just Paul down there.

But Elizabeth's daughter could be there, too.

Rolph had forgotten about Paul and Elizabeth's daughter, Sarah. He had not seen her since she was a little girl, but she had always reminded Rolph of Elizabeth. Now that Elizabeth was no longer Elizabeth, Sarah might be the closest thing he had left.

He banged once on the cellar door.

Twice.

Something blocked the light.

Rolph turned around and saw dark eyes at the window. He dropped his axe and skidded into the shadows, falling backwards. Rolph braced himself, but the landing was soft. The eyes at the window were gone, but Rolph was not concerned about the monster.

He had just become aware that he had fallen on a body.

He rolled over the rags that were now clearly human remains. Everything from the waist down was a ragged mess of bloody fabric and broken bones. The top of her dress was covered with blood. But her face was still completely intact.

It was Elizabeth.

Rolph gasped in the heat as the sun burned the back of his head. He and his father had been nailed into the stocks for two days, and he felt like his stomach had been replaced with an empty hole, his skin with sandpaper.

Out of the corner of his eye, he could see his father trembling, blind to the world in the throes of prayer. He wondered how his father could enter his own world like that, and wondered if right now he was immune to the heat and pain, if his religious fervor relieved the anguish. Rolph's faith had never been strong enough to bring him to the shakes that signified a deep religious experience. He wished he could find the faith to pray now, to find comfort in religion, but as the sweat burned his skin around the hot metal nail in his ear, he felt his soul sink into despair.

"Hello, Rolph."

Rolph tried to look up and winced as his ears tugged against the nails. But he did not need to see her to know who it was.

"You should leave, Elizabeth," he said. "You'll get in trouble."

"I don't care," said Elizabeth, and her voice was so warm, so calm and sure, Rolph believed her. "I brought you a gift."

Something smooth and round was pressed to Rolph's lips. He took a bite and was blessed by the tangy juice of the apple. He gnawed at it, not caring as bits of the apple flesh stuck to his chin and upper lip, while Elizabeth patiently turned it so he could get every last bite. The food did not kill his hunger completely, but Elizabeth had made his position bearable.

"Thank you," said Rolph.

"It was nothing," said Elizabeth. "But you should know, you now owe me one apple."

Elizabeth chuckled, but Rolph could not join her.

"You really should leave."

"Sending me away already?" Elizabeth teased. "I thought you'd like the company."

"I do," said Rolph. "But you know your father does not like it when you speak with me. You know that we can't be friends."

"What made you think I wanted to just be friends?"

Rolph blushed, but it was impossible to see under his

sunburned skin.

"Elizabeth, you know we will never be anything more than that. You're engaged."

"I know," she whispered.

Rolph heard the hollow sounds of footsteps on wood and his gut caved. Someone was climbing up to the stocks. He heard Elizabeth gasp and felt the rush of air from her skirts as she turned around, but instead of a murmured excuse or cry of fear, Elizabeth began to laugh.

"I'm sorry, I didn't expect anyone else to be here."

"Elijah!" said Rolph.

"I brought you something," Elijah said, unable to conceal a tremor form his voice. He was a good friend, but not fearless like Elizabeth.

"Aren't you worried about getting caught?" asked Rolph.

"Yes," said Elijah.

"You're a good boy, Elijah," said Elizabeth, and Elijah muttered excuses to the contrary.

"Are you still hungry?" he asked Rolph.

"Of course I'm still hungry," groaned Rolph, and Elijah fed him a small roll.

Rolph's friends stayed with him until the sun began to fade and the community returned from the fields to the town. At night, his father still trembled, lost in his religious fervor, but Rolph was already comforted.

Her eyes were open, those beautiful dark eyes, clouded over now with recent death. The blood was still warm on the tatters of the dress that Rolph clung to, pulling her broken corpse into a tight embrace. A shadow came across the window again, but this time the monster was inside.

Sarah had her mother's dark eyes, but they were the only thing human left about her.

Her cheeks were sunken in, the skin tight against her skull where sparse strands of hair fell to her shoulders. Her dress hung loose on her shoulders, but the fabric that once hung to her ankles barely hit the center of her thighs, where her legs seemed to sprout down like dying winter roots as her arms split out like branches that turned into yellowed, curled claws.

Rolph dropped Elizabeth's corpse and lunged for his axe. He felt sharp pain as the creatures claws raked down his back. He grabbed the axe, hacked upwards blindly, and was rewarded with a high-pitched screech. Rolph sat up as the creature stumbled back into the front room, maneuvering around broken furniture as it made its way back outside before disappearing into the forest.

He seemed to have wounded it pretty deep. Rolph was surprised that he had won that easily. It had come and left so fast. He wondered if he should run now, before it came back, or wait to finish it off.

Except he knew he could not finish it off. It would have been easy to follow it out, especially when it was wounded, and kill it. But it still had Elizabeth's eyes. Sarah had Elizabeth's eyes. And now she was gone. Now they both were gone. Little glimpses of the life he never had.

Rolph hugged his axe toward him as the snow began to fall in a sudden flurry of blinding white, a flash that burned the image of dark eyes from his mind, leaving only the hot ice of hate.

Rolph hated everyone.

But he hated one man in particular.

"Is it gone?"

Rolph turned around. The door to the cellar was open, and a small man stained with earth crawled out. As the door closed behind him, Rolph saw the deep scratches once more next to the body of Elizabeth. One arm had fallen into the light, and he could see the tips of her fingers, worn away not by the bite of a hungry daughter, but by desperate clawing at the cellar door where her husband had stowed himself safely away, leaving his wife above to die.

Rolph held his axe aloft and charged at Paul Lawson.

Rolph stared at Paul from his stooped position in the stocks as the usually shorter boy smirked down at him. His ears still throbbed and burned where the nail connected his flesh to the wood. His body ached from standing, and the back of his neck itched where the now fading sun had beaten down on him for three days. He could barely see the slumped figure of his father next to him, now eerily still. Paul, however, was right in his line of sight. The boy walked toward him and grasped his hair tightly.

"What are you doing?" gasped Rolph.

"I'm letting you go," said Paul.

"What about the nails?"

"Only good Christians get the nails removed," said Paul, and he tugged forward, tearing Rolph from the stocks.

Paul screamed and ducked as Rolph's axe sunk into the wall behind him. He pried the axe from the wood as Paul ran screaming into the front room. He should have known to be quieter. If he did not shut up, Sarah would get to him first. And Rolph really to be the one who made Paul bleed.

It was strange how good it felt, to be pursuing Paul. Rolph had been alone so long in his cabin, so isolated from the world outside. No one around to help him. Only Elijah, and Elijah was no help at all. Elijah could not feed Rolph's hate. Rolph had no desire to see Elijah's blood stain the snow. But now, Rolph could feel a frost grow from his heart and fill his body. He had been waiting for this, starving for this, and now Paul was right in front of him. This time, Rolph had the power. This time, Paul's flesh would tear and bleed.

He followed Paul into the front room, and swung with abandon. Rolph's axe left a red gash in Paul's arm, but instead of bringing him to the ground, it spurred him on into the blizzard. Rolph cursed, but his curse was unintelligible. His mouth felt odd, but he had no desire to form words beyond that incoherent gargle. He was having enough trouble focusing on his balance, as the cabin seemed to close in around him, the ceiling brushing his head as his arms reached almost as far as the door where Paul slipped into the snow.

Rolph grunted as the tree fell, the last tree he needed to complete his cabin. He had built it far enough away from the town that no one would bother him. Though Elijah had welcomed him into his flock, Rolph knew that most of the townspeople saw his father when they looked at him and avoided him. He did not miss their attention, and he told himself that he did not miss company.

He was surprised when he turned around to see a little girl standing in front of his unfinished house. For a moment he thought she was some sprite or spirit, or perhaps even a hallucination, a gift from his lonely subconscious.

But he soon recognized her from her dark eyes, though she had grown quite a bit since he had last seen her, barely more than a toddler hiding behind Elizabeth's skirt.

"What are you doing out here, Sarah?"

"Mommy wants me to tell you something."

Rolphed kneeled down to be at eye-level with the girl and smiled.

"And what's that?"

"Hi."

Rolph laughed.

"Well, you tell your mother I have a message for her too."

"What?"

"Hi."

Rolph laughed and Sarah attempted to join him, but Rolph could now see that the little girl was distracted. She chewed the end of a bright red braid and furrowed her brow. She would have looked comical, but Rolph recognized the air of desperation that had clung to him in childhood.

"What's wrong, Sarah?"

"That's not all Mommy says."

"Oh?"

The little girl shuffled her feet in the grass and picked at her skirt. Rolph noticed that her clothes were worn and thin. He knew that Paul had been spending his inheritance with abandon, and now wondered how bad it had gotten. Was the family in debt? Was Elizabeth okay?

"Mommy says you owe her an apple."

Rolph threw down his axe and disappeared into his cabin. He returned a moment later with a sack full of apples.

"You tell your mother that I'm paying her back with interest," said Rolph, as he helped Sarah get a grip on the heavy bundle.

"Thank you," said the little girl. "You're a very good

Christian."

"I'm not," said Rolph, picking up his axe. "I just don't like it when people are hungry."

Rolph searched for signs of Paul. Though the snow covered Paul's footprints, he was leaving a heavy trail of red behind him. Rolph was surprised that the sight did not help him as much as the smell of the blood, a clear beacon that led him on. Rolph staggered through the storm, following his prey into the forest.

The trees loomed above him, dark and silent, but these woods held no fear for Rolph. There was only one monster here, and Rolph was going to kill it.

He followed the trail until he saw Paul again, kneeling from fatigue in the middle of a small clearing, the snow gathering at his legs in a premature burial. He did not turn to see Rolph coming at him from the left, his axe forgotten in the woods as he reached out with claws. He did not turn to see Sarah coming at him from the right, her arms outstretched as well, mirroring Rolph and the dying trees, splintered branches that rose into the dim sky above them.

Elijah stood in front of the ruined cabin, next to the simple grave he had dug for Elizabeth. He knew that Elizabeth should have been buried in holy ground, but he had done his best to bless the land before laying her to rest. And it was easier to bury her here than to explain the state of her remains back in town.

Elijah had searched through the house, down to the cellar where he had found a well-hidden stack of preserves buried under the icy dirt, but he could not find any other bodies. Part of Elijah hoped that the others had just gotten away, travelled to a different town, but he knew better.

The snow was beginning to melt, and dripping icicles left slick puddles on the earth where Elijah could see the first blades of grass coloring the world. He looked out into the woods and was surprised to see more unnatural color in the dying winter, a pair of dark eyes and a pair of blue eyes, staring back at him from the shadows before they disappeared into the woods, into the world of myths.

Beautiful Libby and the Darkness

by Christopher Nadeau

Jody had given all that he was to the love of his life. His soul, his heart, his every *molecule* belonged to her. He'd done things for her that would have driven most men stark raving mad; people murdered with their body parts severed, entire families lit on fire, screaming and writhing. All because she'd demanded, no, *needed* it to be done.

So why, after all that, had she abandoned him? What had he failed to do for her?

Didn't she love him anymore?

Jody cried and drew his raincoat closed around his neck. He enjoyed walking in the rain. It had been their thing before she disappeared. What once had been a romantic action was now tinged with melancholy and regret. Still, a part of him held onto the hope that one day she would emerge from the storm and rejoin him.

Yet, he knew it wouldn't be so easy. He would have to find her and remind her of his usefulness.

It shouldn't be too difficult; sooner or later, she'd start decaying again and, when that happened, who else would bring her what she needed?

Jody knew what his love really was. She'd confided in him and he'd sworn to never tell. It was a miniscule price to pay for unconditional love. Jody had never experienced that until the day she found him in a most uncompromising position.

Sara Jane was a whore. A filthy, no good, lying street-walking whore. She was also his wife, which presented no small amount of problems. He'd put up with her shit for two years, but sleeping with some low-rent, truck driving asshole was the last straw.

Jody stared into his wife's hateful, dishonest face, unable to believe the words spewing forth from her mouth. How could she still deny what she'd done? She seemed hostile, hateful, even disgusted that Jody had exposed her secret. Was she insane?

Standing in the middle of their kitchen, arms held limp at his sides, Jody watched her performance until he couldn't take anymore.

"Shut up," he said. "Just stop."

She did as he said, no doubt more out of shock than any inclination towards obedience.

"What the hell is wrong with you?" He heard the desperation in his own voice and hated the sound of it. Sara Jane started laughing.

"What's wrong with me?" she said. "You think *I'm* the reason I cheated on you?"

Jody's lower lip trembled. "Then, why would—"

Sara Jane waved her hand and shook her head. "Because you're pathetic, Jody. You're short and weak and slow-witted and you never succeed at anything when you do bother to try." She cocked her head sweetly. "Does that answer your question?"

Jody didn't remember picking up the frying pan and striking his wife in the face with it. The sound of impact snapped him out of his trance-like state just in time to watch Sara Jane fall backwards into the kitchen table, most of the impact hitting the back of her head. Jody watched her roll onto the floor in a clump of unmoving flesh and only when he heard her start moaning, did he go to her. He put his ear to her mouth and chuckled at the sound of her high-pitched wheezing.

"Guess we answered each other's questions," Jody said. "Guess we got that all cleared up." He chuckled again, this time covering his mouth, lest something screechy and more hysterical come out of it.

Jody glanced down at the frying pan still in his hand and bit his lower lip. "My mom said you were a whore the day she met you. We've hardly spoken since then." He raised the frying pan above his head.

He lowered the makeshift weapon, coming within inches of dealing the killing blow, when someone yelled, "Wait!"

Jody snapped around, falling over onto his side at the sight greeting him.

She was beautiful. Dark hair, dark eyes, delicate features with full lips. She was dressed in a white gown, the kind one might have worn as a hospital patient decades ago. Jody couldn't look away from her eyes. While stunning, they also looked hollowed-out, aged before their time, as if she'd seen unimaginable horrors.

He'd never yearned for anyone more in his life.

"*Who are you how the hell'd you get in here?*" he spewed in some bizarre form of verbal vomiting.

"I was called here." Her voice was smooth, warming, sensual. "I need what she has."

Jody frowned, wondering if today would turn into a double-murder. What a shame if that turned out to be the case.

"I don't know what that means."

"She is blight and deserves the darkness."

Jody thought perhaps he did know what she meant and it sent a shiver of revulsion throughout his entire body. He looked down at his dying wife, noted her shallow breathing, and began to shake.

"Oh, God. I didn't mean to — "

"Of course, you did," the beautiful stranger responded kindly. "Otherwise, I would not have come." Her face took on a pallid, drained look. "Time is short. Will you give me what I require?"

Jody looked once more into her eyes and felt himself surrender.

"Whatever you want."

Jody swallowed bile for what must have been the hundredth time, held his breath, and went back to slowly peeling the skin from his dying wife's face. He finally succeeded in pulling the last of the upper layer off and forced himself to stand on wobbly feet. "What now?"

The stranger waved him forward. "Place it over my face."

Jody paused, realized even now he could stop this insanity, confess, turn himself in and forget all about this bizarre occurrence. Then the stranger said the one thing that helped him cross over:

"With this single act, our love will be eternal."

He lovingly applied the skin from his dead wife's face and never looked back.

On the news, they were talking about the latest serial killer on the loose. Police had no leads yet, but they had a profile. The physical description could have matched any white guy between the ages of 21-45, but his motivation, they claimed, was to make a statement in a world he found cruel and unjust. Removing skin and body parts and leaving behind the bulk of the victims was his way of saying, "See? I'm in control."

Jody was making a statement and, yes, there was an element of asserting control as well. But the idea that he was too naïve to accept an unjust world was hilarious. Jody had known this world held nothing for him for far longer than he'd been innocent. The message was for Libby. How else could he remind her of his value?

So what if he had fun doing it?

"You're beautiful," Jody said. "You're always beautiful."

Libby smiled prettily, her body shimmering momentarily, like a dying light bulb. Jody had just severed his latest victim's left hand and offered it to her. She accepted it with restrained gratitude.

"You don't like it, do you?" Jody heard his voice shake.

Libby frowned, her expression indicating reluctance and compassion. "It is appreciated, but I fear it does nothing to enhance."

Jody felt the entire planet explode beneath his feet. He'd failed her and all he ever wanted was to earn her love. He loved her and wanted her to live forever, but she also needed to be happy.

Sighing, he tossed the hand away and forced a smile. "I'll get you a better one."

He didn't notice the changed expression on her face.

The security guard screamed even with his tongue cut out. In retrospect, making him think he might actually survive unscathed was a much better idea. One look at his skin was enough to convince Jody the fat bastard had nothing to improve his beloved, let alone him. Libby had, over the years, shown Jody a few tricks to prolong his own existence.

At most, the fat security guard's splotchy, stretched flesh

might provide a Vitamin D boost.

"I have no use for your tongue," Jody says calmly. "But if you keep screaming, I'll see what use I can make of your head."

The security guard's screams died down to whimpers, his eyes wide and bloodshot. Jody gave the man his back and focused on the security camera screens, awaiting his intended victim's arrival. He'd been shadowing her for just over a week, mentally recording her patterns. He smirked, remembering his similar tactics had landed him his ex-wife. Life truly was one big circle.

Consider his victim: Her resemblance to Libby was uncanny. The thought that there could be two of them in the world…No. There was only one Libby, and she was all his and that was that.

The young woman now entering her apartment building would be Libby's wake-up call, one final sacrifice to show her who loved her.

Jody had a theory.

Libby grew used to being called sub-human. It was in much of the literature and many of the faces of the proud Aryans walking past her as if she didn't exist. Her people were not people at all, they were vermin, an infestation, and it was only a matter of time before she and her family wound up in one of the camps.

Life was no easier for Libby because she was a girl, nor did being pretty spare her the pain of camp existence. She watched and experienced levels of cruelty and brutality she'd never before imagined until the day she thought her luck had changed, inconceivably, for the worst.

She'd just finished cleaning the commandant's washroom with a toothbrush on her bruised knees when the harsh words of a Nazi guard punctuated the relative silence.

"Is this the Jewess he wants?"

"That is the one," a second voice replied. "She looks healthy."

The first chuckled in a way that made Libby's flesh crawl. "Too bad he needs her the way we found her."

Libby didn't turn around and look at the lustily chuckling man. Curiosity was one of the fastest ways to the showers with no water.

"Jew," the first one said. "The Doctor wants you."

Libby would always remember how innocuous-sounding that was, but she knew better. The doctors in the camps didn't heal the sick. Whatever plans he had for her, this doctor was going to cause pain unlike any she'd ever known.

The stupid girl kept trying to tell Jody her name. Like it mattered. Like a name would somehow dissuade him from making his offering.

"Take another look at that fat-ass security guard," Jody said.

She turned her head – difficult because of her restraints – and whimpered at the sight of the guard's still bleeding corpse.

"His name was Walter," she said.

Jody threw the metal coffee cup he'd been holding into her chest. "I don't give a shit what his name was!" He walked over to her, enjoying the way she shrank back. "Do you understand?"

"Yes!" She shrieked. "Yes, sir! I do!"

Jody smirked and cocked his head. "When she comes, you'll join something so much bigger than you ever—"

"My name is—"

"*Stop trying to relate to me!*"

The young woman sobbed and tried to look away. Jody held her face so she couldn't and shook his head. "The hell do you know about love anyway?" He laughed without humor. "Libby and me, we transcend all this shit. Morality. What's that?"

He let go of her face and turned away, thinking about how morality died on that operating table in 1943.

The doctor received Libby with all the compassion and interest of a slaughter-house worker. If her nakedness aroused him, he gave no indication, simply handing her a hospital gown and instructing her to get on the table. He was a thin, reed-like man in over-large spectacles without a hair on his head.

"You should feel honored," he said, adjusting her straps. "Today we will be trying something new and you are the first."

He walked over to a row of beakers and picked up two of them, one in each hand. "Perhaps you are incapable of appreciating this?"

Libby shuddered, her eyes coming to rest on this pompous ass.

"I thought you Jews were supposed to be smart!" he yelled, eliciting a chuckle from the guard in the corner of the laboratory.

The table was so cold and hard. She felt the world contract into a tiny point containing just her and the doctor and this goddamn table. She lay there, staring up at the ceiling, waiting, waiting.

It was as if Libby had been reborn into the world, fresh and untampered with. He could almost make himself believe this young woman was her, if not for constant whimpering. Why couldn't she just shut up and accept her fate?

"Mister, I won't say anything. Honest."

Jody blinked, an involuntary mouth twitch causing his face to momentarily contort. *She's nothing but skin and spare parts*, he thought.

"I'll tell everybody I found Walter's body when I came home and—"

Jody whirled around with such sadness and rage, it caused the young woman to freeze in mid-babble.

He lunged across the room, rewarded by the sounds of her screams and pleas for forgiveness. He grabbed her face in his hand and squeezed until she once more grew silent.

"Time's up," he said.

Libby sensed something was wrong moments after the third injection began coursing through her veins. She screamed and writhed, trying to break free of her restraints. The Doctor merely stood over here, impassive, watching. He seemed to be writing something in a notebook. Libby cursed him using ever word in her arsenal, drawing chuckles from the back of the laboratory.

For the first time in her young life, Libby felt true rage. An instant later, rage became hate.

Then everything made perfect sense.

"She is changing!" the Doctor yelled. "Look at her!"

Libby threw her head back and roared in agony.

"Her skin," the guard yelled. "Doctor, what is happening to her skin?"

"I am dying!' Libby yelled.

And she died.

And returned moments later.

The Doctor barely had enough time to scream before Libby leapt off the table, the restrains snapping as if they were made of confetti.

"Shoot her!" someone yelled.

"We'll hit the Doctor!" another replied.

Libby had the Doctor pinned against the wall, his face held firmly in her grasp. He seemed unable to move his body, eyes flitting from side to side as if seeking a sudden escape route.

"Mercy," he said.

Libby chuckled. "I though you Nazis were supposed to be smart."

His face melted like butter in a hot pan, fluids running down his chest and abdomen until all that remained was a quivering husk. Libby let the remainder slide to the floor, and turned to face two frightened guards.

"Demon!" one of them yelled.

Libby shook her head. "Your precious doctor awoke something far older than any *demon*."

The guards glanced at each other as if seeking clarification neither could provide.

Libby held up a deformed left hand. "Even now it decays. Do you know what he was trying to do?"

She told them what she'd learned about the Doctor's intentions. He'd been working on a formula he believed would create in human beings the ability to regenerate flesh and limbs. The "un-killable" soldier would fulfill all of the Aryan prophecies regarding racial superiority. And if the Jew was unable to sustain the chemical infusion, then that confirmed what they already knew as well.

"Instead he sent me into the darkness," Libby said. "And now I need what you have."

The guards tried to kill her, but their bullets might as well have been dandelion seeds for all the damage they inflicted. She took the hand from one and the skin from the other and left two decaying husks on the floor.

Libby walked out into the night, already feeling weaker. She needed someone else to do the killing for her. She headed for the building that had been her prison for the past two years and chose the one she wanted to help her.

Legends grew around the girl who killed her captors and walked out freely through the gates. As the story went, she became like a Golem, striking fear into the hearts of the Nazis and freeing those she could before moving on. But Libby was no more concerned with the plight of the Jewish people than she was with the outcome of the war. The night she walked into that building, she chose one young man named Ari who'd always smiled whenever he saw her.

Over the years, they destroyed many evil men and women, sending them into the darkness while keeping their body parts and flesh for replenishment purposes. But then Ari changed. He seemed to lose the true purpose of what they were doing. His offerings became inconsistent, displeasing.

Soon, she had no choice but to leave him.

Jody held his carving knife to the young woman's cheek and turned it so the blade was flat. He looked into her panicked eyes and smiled.

"Libby's gonna love your skin."

"I-I don't understand," she said, her lip quivering.

"I do," Jody said. "That's all that matters."

"Stop, my love."

Jody turned so abruptly, the knife's edge nicked the young woman's cheek, drawing a long, thin line of blood.

"Libby," he said. I knew you'd come. I…why are you stopping me?"

Libby's shimmering form grew darker. "I have seen this before. You've lost sight."

Jody's arms went slack and the knife fell from his hand to the floor with a loud clank he hardly noticed.

"Why are you saying this to me? I brought her for *you*. I had a theory that her resemblance might replenish you permanently."

Libby sighed. "Years ago, another man had a theory."

Jody's eyes and mouth widened simultaneously. "This is *different*! I'm not…I didn't…Why did you leave me? Don't you love me anymore?"

Libby's smile was filled with affection and sadness. "This was never about love. Love was what happened while we were killing evil."

Jody frowned, thinking back to the moment, all those years ago, when Libby appeared in his kitchen. His adulteress wife, a lying sociopath. A woman who took wedding vows and then betrayed them.

"I was called here," Libby had said.

Jody then thought of that other moment, when his offering didn't meet Libby's satisfaction. What had she said to him that time? Something about it not doing anything to enhance.

"I am so very sorry." Libby interrupted his memories. "Ari lost his way, too." Libby smiled.

Jody's eyes filled with tears. He sniffled and looked away from his beloved. He'd thought the offering of low quality, insufficient for one so wonderful and perfect, but it hadn't been that at all. It had come from an innocent.

"This child knows nothing of the darkness." Libby pointed at her look-alike. "Yet you would murder her as if she does in the name of love."

"Sorry." Jody sobbed, head lowered. "So sorry. I love—"

"And I you." Libby walked over to him. "But now you belong in the darkness with the others."

Jody looked into her beautiful eyes and wiped his own. "Will I see you again?"

Her smile widened. "When I am finished here."

Jody smiled and closed his eyes. As the flesh melted from his face, he thought of the day he would see his Libby once again. A shining light in the darkness. She would be beautiful. She would always be beautiful.

Every Act Of Creation

By Rich Larson

Waking up was like clawing out of a slippery bathtub. Elliot's head was dark and empty and aching. He tasted metal in his mouth, felt pins and needles in his hands. When he finally worked his eyes open, the canvas ceiling of the tent was splashed with wriggling projections. Vital signs. He heard the thrum of a monitor and under it the dim howl of wind outside.

"Oh. You're awake."

Elliot turned his head and something tugged deep behind his face. The doctor blurred and then sharpened. He had sallow skin and a tight-shaven red beard. Roderick, medical support.

"Can I pull this out?" Elliot croaked.

Roderick rubbed his lips and nodded assent.

While Elliot was dredging the slimed tubing out of his sinuses, he remembered the climb. They'd been on the last leg of it, nearly to the fallsite, already jawing about setting up the heaters and breaking out a blueberry vodka, when the shale started to come loose. Elliot remembered one wedge flying past his head. A warning shout. Then a blur of faces, mostly Roderick.

"You were concussed yesterday," Roderick said. "Skull fracture. Had to do a scan for brain damage." His thumb ran over his lip again and Elliot saw the skin peeling. It was cold in the mountains, except for the steaming trench the meteorite had plowed, the trail they had followed first by satellite imaging and then by helicopter and then finally by piton.

"We at the fallsite?" Elliot asked. He rolled his tongue in his mummified mouth. The tubes flicked like snakes on his chest.

145

Roderick handed him a damp sponge. His hands were raw red. "We're here," he said. "Everything is running smooth."

"Team set to go?"

"Went down this morning," Roderick said.

"Those fuckers."

Roderick looked startled. He shrugged his shoulders.

"Am I good to get out of bed?" Elliot asked.

"Physical checks out," Roderick said. "Everything's good. Running smooth." He pulled his coat tighter around himself and vanished out of the tent.

Twilight was icebox blue when Elliot stumbled outside. Dressing had taken time. His limbs were like gelatin and every part of him was sore, but now, leaned against the frame of the tent, he couldn't feel the aches. The fallsite was too beautiful.

There were no trees up here, nothing but cragged black rock and shale. Wind had worn at the mountainside, glaciers had carved it, and now the meteorite had gouged it open. Lamps and scanners were already arrayed around the jagged mouth, swatches of flickering hologram delineating the edge.

Elliot had watched the impact happen on grainy satellite imaging. He had tracked the meteor for months. He had assembled crew and followed it to the middle of nowhere.

And now they had gone in without him. Elliot walked on stiff legs to the edge of the hole. The dark was impenetrable, angled deep into the rock. His eyes roved over the scarring. There was no steam anymore. The thing had cooled quickly up here.

Elliot lit one of the cigarettes he had found in his coat pocket, then turned back to the camp. The team had set up quickly: bubblefab tents sprouted in a rough fairy circle and the comm tower swayed like a spindly insect. There was more trash scattered than Elliot would have liked to see. He supposed the blueberry vodka had been cracked without him.

Roderick was feeding scraps into a brazier. His face looked hollowed out by the flickering shadows.

"Guess you weren't expecting to treat a head injury on day

one," Elliot said. "Glad we had you along."

Roderick rubbed this thumb along his bottom lip. He blinked.

"Raise them on the radios yet?" Elliot asked. "Where's your kit?"

"There's a vein of something in that big old space rock," Roderick said, handing it over. "Messing with the transmissions. They've been cutting in and out. Jackson said he'll rig something up tomorrow."

Elliot wiped the screen with his glove. Nothing showed from the head cameras. No noise but static. He wouldn't even get to watch footage from the tent.

"Last check-in?" he asked.

"Two hours ago," Roderick said blankly. "They're on their way up."

"They better have samples," Elliot said. Roderick nodded and Elliot tried to remember his psych profile. He hadn't been so nervous on the way up, but maybe it was the fallsite. It was cold and empty up here and the hole was like a monster's mouth.

Elliot wandered back towards it. There were caverns under the mountain and the meteorite had plunged deep and maybe fragmented. It would have been slow going under there, shoring up the walls and testing stability all the way. But seeing the meteorite would have made it all worth it.

Elliot took a last drag from the cigarette and flicked the butt over the edge. It fluttered out of sight like a dying firefly.

Roderick went back to the hospital tent to clean things up and Elliot took a survey of the camp. Things were not right. Tent struts had been bent and repaired. Small tears had been taped over. Too many discarded food cartons. Something was swelling inside Elliot's skull, a disjointed feeling, but maybe it was the concussion. Maybe it was the painkiller.

The weather had changed too much from yesterday. Elliot looked at the hospital tent, the yellow glow. Roderick's silhouette moved like a shadow puppet inside. With the sky darkening over his head and the radio kit still dead in his hand, Elliot went to the supply tent. He unzipped the door, and thoughts began to collide as he found it was all but empty. The food, the water, the liquor, and medstores.

Elliot stared over his shoulder and saw Roderick still moving around the hospital tent, now lifting something up to the light like a supplication. He looked back into the supply tent. It was dark and he didn't want to strike the glowstrips. Elliot ran his hands along the stripped shelves. His fingers found a plastic bag. He unsealed it and rubbed coarse hair between his fingers. Small sharp crescents fell out with the strands, fingernail clippings.

Elliot's head twinged in the bandages. He made a line for hospital tent, eyes blurred by the wind. Roderick's elongated fingers were holding up a pointed shadow and tapping it gently. Elliot broke into a shambling run. The syringe's silhouette descended. Elliot tore down the door and found Roderick with the needle plunged deep in his wrist, eyes wide and shot with pink.

Elliot tore the syringe away and bowled him to the floor. A flying arm knocked his teeth together, sending another tremor through his skull, but after they landed Roderick did not fight. His skin was waxy pale and tears were leaking down his nose, into his beard.

"You cut my hair before I woke up," Elliot panted. "You cut my fucking hair. Why would you do that? Why would you have to do that?"

Roderick shook his head mutely.

"And this?" Elliot held up the syringe. "You're doping off our supplies? Where's the food?"

"There's still some food," Roderick said faintly.

"How long have I been on that fucking cot?" Elliot demanded.

Roderick's chest heaved under him like a bellows. He was crying.

"Roderick, what's the date?" Elliot saw, again, the cigarette butt tumbling down into the dark. "Roderick. How long have they been down there?"

"They never came back," Roderick sobbed. "A month. They never came back."

Elliot knotted the sheet from the cot and used it to truss the doctor's hands and feet. He left him in the hospital tent and went back to the supplies. Two of the probes were gone, but a third was still nestled in plastic. He ran the start-up and it flashed red laser light across the tent's ceiling. Cradling the metal sphere in both hands, Elliot stalked back towards the hole.

"Won't work." Roderick had wriggled to the door of the hospital tent. A slice of his ruddy face showed through the gap. The saline had frozen around his eyes. "It never works."

Elliot shoved the doctor's head back inside and zipped the door. He went to the hole, the dark mouth, and dropped the probe. Its rotors hummed to life on the way down. Elliot sat cross-legged on the edge with the kit in his lap, willing the feed to appear. The sound of the probe faded. The screen stayed blank. Elliot cursed.

The doctor was lying on his back in the middle of the tent, watching the ceiling. Elliot sat down across from him. He turned the dead radio kit over in his hands.

"How long since you had contact?" he asked. The knots around Roderick's ankles had come undone.

"They went down on the third day. When you didn't wake up."

"And the radios didn't work."

"I waited and waited and waited." Roderick gave a wooden laugh. "I wanted to go down after them. I really did. But I couldn't. You were my patient." His glassy eyes were pleading. "I couldn't just leave you, could I?"

Elliot remembered the empty medstores in the supply tent. Roderick was doped to the eyes, maybe had been for weeks. He looked over at the fallen syringe.

"The comm tower?"

"No." Roderick's head flopped back down. "I tried. I don't know. Maybe I broke it. Maybe it's the, uh, the radiation. Whatever's coming off that rock. I don't know."

"Didn't even fucking look."

"What?"

"You didn't even fucking look for them," Elliot snapped. "You fucking coward. What if there was a slide? Did the seismic scanners go off?"

"Nothing's working," Roderick said. "Nothing close to the pit."

"We're going down there in the morning. For now I'm going to the comm tower." Elliot stood up. He looked at the syringe again and felt sick. "You've probably let three people die, you know. To watch me nap. Three people."

"They aren't dead," Roderick said, with a delirium grin. "I hear them sometimes."

He started to sob again as Elliot left the tent.

Disassembling the comm components took longer than Elliot anticipated. He brought them in from the cold and worked in the hospital tent. Roderick had fallen asleep with saliva trickling down his scabbed lips. Wind was picking up outside, shrieking through the metal struts of the tent. Elliot cranked the light as bright as possible. There was nothing wrong with the hardware.

A few tins of coffee were left. Elliot filled a thermos and drank it black as he sifted through the logs. They had followed the protocols. They had staked out the pit and dropped probes. He listened to small bundles of audio and picked out the voices: Jackson, Somberg, Ranna. When they couldn't wait any longer, they had descended.

He bundled a thermal under his coat before he went back out. Night had fallen fast, and the perimeter lights were a sickly low-power green. Elliot trudged to the comm tower and rigged it back up with frostbitten fingers. No signal came in. No signal went out. The structure bent and creaked in the wind like an old man's spine.

Elliot went to the pit. He squatted at the edge and peered down, one ear cupped with his hand. If there were voices carrying up into the wind, they were only screaming.

In the morning Roderick geared up like a condemned man. He wasn't babbling or crying anymore; his eyes were flat and empty. He was chewing his lips.

"Ready?" Elliot asked, tightening the straps of his pack.

Roderick shook his head and Elliot opened the tent. The light outside was watery pale. Elliot led the way through the barren camp to the pit. The dead scanners arrayed it like broken teeth. He unspooled a line from his pack.

"In case things are shifting," Elliot said, driving the piton. He looped the line through his harness. Roderick slowly did the same. Moist air was coming in plumes from the entrance, a faint organic smell. Elliot swallowed bile. He'd never dug bodies from a rockslide, but in the military he'd seen bomb wreckage. Blots of gore in shattered concrete.

"Like the labyrinth," Roderick said dully, tugging the line.

"Be ready with the medkit," Elliot said. He flicked the torch wrapped around his helmet and they started to descend.

Darkness. The pale rake of the torch only blackened the shadows more completely. They crouch-walked down the incline, sediment sliding with each footfall. Light from the entrance dwindled fast and then was swallowed completely as the meteorite's jagged path deepened. The rock was preternaturally smooth under Elliot's hands, fused and then cooled like a vein of obsidian. A few minutes in and Roderick started muttering.

"Quiet," Elliot said.

The voice kept on in the dark, a muffled one-way conversation. Elliot turned and caught Roderick in the beam. His pink eyes were wide. His mouth was shut. Elliot felt ice in his gut.

Must be getting close, wish the probe was working. Must be getting close. The voice came faint, impossible to pinpoint.

"Jackson?" Elliot called. "Hey! Jackson?"

Must be getting close, wish the probe was working.

"We have to leave," Roderick said. He squinted into the torchlight. "We have to leave, we have to leave. Please."

Rich Larson

"Playback," Elliot said. "His helmet's down here. Close."

Jackson's voice faded. Elliot faced forward again and started shuffling downward. Sweat was slicking his palms and the air felt strangely damp. After a moment, he heard Roderick follow. Line rasped against harness in the dark. The rocks were jagged and progress was slow. Every part of Elliot's bedridden body was aching when his torch found the meteorite.

It hulked like an ancient idol, gloss black and unscarred. In the light of Elliot's torch it gleamed with an oily sheen. He saw a scattering of bent picks and sampling tools at the base. He didn't see Jackson's helmet.

"What the fuck?" Roderick asked the question in a sob. "What the fuck sort of rock is that? We shouldn't be here. None of us should have been here."

The line jerked and Elliot stumbled, light slashing across the wall. It lit up a jumble of pink-tinged bones, a disconnected jawbone, a hollow socket, and then the line jerked again and Elliot fell. The helmet clattered, spilling wild shadows. Something rushed in the dark. Elliot's heart thumped into his throat as he scrabbled for the helmet, the torch. He swung it up and around and Roderick's panicked face was an inch from his.

"How can he talk without a jaw?" Roderick whispered. His forehead glimmered with sweat and he made to scramble away but Elliot grabbed at his leg. They struggled on the sloped floor, grinding against the rock. Roderick was wheezing and kicking like an animal. When Elliot finally pinned him, the torch revealed his pupils were impossibly wide.

"How can he talk without a jaw?" Roderick repeated. He gave a pained laugh. Elliot looked at the fallen medkit, thought of the scalpels, the drills.

"Did you do this?" Elliot demanded. His head turned to the bones again, the crumbled lattice of ribs and limbs. Nothing decomposed that quickly. "Where's his gear?"

He turned the torch back to Roderick. The doctor's lips were hanging in shreds now, picked apart by frantic nails. He was shaking his head.

"I don't know," he pleaded. "I don't know. Maybe. Yes. I did it. Take me to prison. I did it. Yes."

Never seen space rock like this. Fucking odd.

Something moved behind the meteorite. Elliot snapped his head up and the torch illuminated reflective strips, a shoulder disappearing into the gloom. He knew that gear.

"Somberg? Andrea, is that you?" His voice came out wavery. He looked down at the doctor muttering prayers. Elliot dug a piton out of his pack. The point was blunt.

"I told you they're alive," Roderick said. "I told you I hear them."

"Stay. Don't fucking move." Elliot gripped the piton in his sweaty fingers and edged his way around the smooth rock. "Andrea? We're down here. The doctor's here. What's happened?" He heard a footfall. Another. Elliot wormed his way around and saw Andrea's empty gear, collapsed like she'd vanished from it. He stared at the caved fabric, the empty sleeves. Wet air licked his face and he looked up.

Behind the curve of the meteorite, the cavern went on. His torch might as well have been a lit match. They'd known the mountain had hollows, but this was truly massive. Elliot looked down at the gear again. He felt his head twinge and wondered about the concussion. The drugs. What had Roderick been putting in his drip?

Never seen space rock like this.

When he rounded the corner, the doctor was sitting upright. The medkit was strapped to his back.

"You kept me under for a month," Elliot said. "There was no coma."

Roderick stared. His eyes were blank now, like an animal's.

"You drugged me," Elliot said. "You killed them and you drugged me. Woke me up so I could back your fucked up story about the pit." He had a sudden sharp image: Roderick crouched down here, flensing flesh off a corpse, biting his lips raw.

"I don't know," Roderick said. His voice was a void. "I don't know. I've been using. More than I usually do. It's fogged, all of it."

"That's one body," Elliot said. "Take me to the others."

Looks like the impact cracked it open.

The voice spun him back to the crashed meteorite. He looked at the glossy black surface. Ran his hand over it. There were no cracks, and he was hearing things.

"You walk in front," Elliot said. He gripped the piton in his hand and tried to dredge up facts on manic strength, painkiller addictions. Roderick unclipped from the line. Elliot traded places with him.

"I want the light," Roderick said.

"I'm right behind you. Just go."

The air was turning damp when they found the second body. Ranna was naked and bloated, stretched out on the rock like Prometheus for the vulture. There were tight surgical holes in her belly. Elliot had his hands around Roderick's throat in an instant. The doctor was boneless, limp and Elliot thought he knew how much more pressure would fold the windpipe. He let go.

Roderick wheezed and sobbed. "I couldn't have. I don't have a laser. I couldn't have."

Elliot unrolled a blanket and threw it over Ranna's corpse. Nerves jangled in his hands. Her scalp was bare, glistening. Elliot thought of his ziplocked hair in the supply tent. He made himself look under the blanket a second time. Her fingernails were missing. Other things. Gas and bacteria had swollen her stomach, but her skin was coated in something gleaming.

What the fuck is that?

Elliot's head snapped up. "Hear that?"

Roderick gave a low moan. His fingers were digging at his cheeks, pulling at his beard. His lips were bloody.

Shine the light. Over here. Shine the light.

Elliot prodded Roderick to his feet. He clutched his head with one hand and shoved with the other. The harness caught and Roderick pulled it away from his thigh, stumbled. They managed a few more paces before the line ran out and the screams began.

Roderick started screaming, too, howling back at the dark, and Elliot knew he wasn't hearing it in his head. He clapped his hand over the doctor's mouth.

"Don't," he hissed. Roderick kicked once, then ragdolled. Elliot pulled his hand back and found it stained red. He tore the torch off his helmet and swiveled it through the dark, bouncing off wet rock and nothing else. The screams came fainter, then louder. They shrieked through the cavern like angry ghosts. Elliot was frozen to the floor.

Even when the sounds subsided, Elliot heard them echoing in his ears. His heart thrummed furiously . The torchlight had caught something further on, something wriggling like a fish. Elliot began to crawl, hand over hand, and he heard Roderick follow.

Red and gray bundles of sinew, packets of putty-colored fat, all glistening under some neoprene coating. Jackson wriggled again, and Elliot vomited. His head spun. He made himself crawl forward, through his own sick, and he saw that Jackson's tongue and eyes were gone.

"Get something," Elliot gasped. His nose burned with the vomit. "Fucking get him something. Roderick." He looked over his shoulder and Roderick was hunched over the medkit, unzipping with shaking hands. He looked like an animal in the harsh light, beard clotted, eyes wide. The syringe came out and Elliot reached out his hand for it, no longer able to look at the skinned thing on the floor.

Roderick's breath came in gasps. He looked at Elliot and shook his head, then plunged the needle so deep the metal whispered. The vein of his wrist bulged. He toppled backward.

Elliot stared until the doctor stopped breathing. He heard the rasp of limbs sliding on the floor. He reached numbly for the medkit and groped inside for something, for anything. His fingers found the cold edge of a scalpel and he closed his eyes.

The medkit duffel covered Jackson's head. Elliot's pack sat on his chest, where Elliot put his knee. The exposed neck bobbed, and Elliot saw for the first time the intricacy of all the small tendons, all the parts moving in concert. He held the scalpel tightly but his hands were shaking and it would not be quick.

The blade of the scalpel touched the glossy coating, the membrane that was preserving the thing, this thing that had been Jackson, and it rippled. Another banshee scream. The body bucked and squirmed. Elliot jabbed with the scalpel, twisting it back and forth, carving through the membrane.

Jackson's head jerked and Elliot realized, bile burning his throat, that he would have to pin it down. He spread his hand and clamped it over Jackson's ruined face, feeling contours under the duffel bag. He worked the scalpel until blood gouted up onto his fingers, dark and slick and copper-smelling. Not enough, not nearly enough.

Elliot went deeper and dragged it from side to side, eliciting a new sound, a wet drowning howl. Elliot's jaw clenched so tight he felt it in his forehead. Jackson's head thrashed again and Elliot felt his fingers slip into the caverns where his eyeballs had been. The howl came again, choked and burbling. Elliot dug deeper. The thrashing came slower and then not at all.

When it was done, Elliot crawled back the way he'd come, slicking the stone with his passage. The torch was slippery in his hands. It jittered with his trembling, he couldn't hold it steady now.

Jackson? Hey! Jackson?

The curve of the meteorite loomed, jet black. As Elliot stumbled to his feet, there was a porous hiss and the surface began to slide apart. Something gushed out onto the floor of the cavern, silvery and thick. It danced under the torchlight, writhing and weaving together, and Elliot realized it was knitting bones. More of the quicksilver slid upward on the skeleton, hanging organs, cording muscles. Elliot's face began to build itself in front of him.

"Playback." The voice was coming from behind incomplete lips. "His helmet's down here. Close."

A final layer slid up onto the Elliot-thing, a coating of skin, and then flowed into empty sockets to form gunmetal eyes. The anatomy wobbled, solidified. It took a heavy step forward, holding together for a moment longer, and then burst into a cascade of scuttling motes, all slipping and sliding over each other, up Elliot's nostrils and down his throat, snaking through his body like thread through a labyrinth.

Silence

By Dawn Napier

The silence wasn't deafening. That phrase never made sense to me anyway. How can silence make you deaf? And if you did go deaf from all the silence, how would you know? After all, it was already silent.

The silence wasn't deafening. It was just—silent. Not a single person spoke; not a single page rustled. That was odd. Libraries are quiet places, but they are far from silent. Someone is always moving books around, turning pages, or reading out loud under his breath. very so often there's a burst of real noise, like a child throwing a tantrum or some rocket scientist surfing the Internet without head phones.

I shifted around in the huge, comfortable easy chair that was my favorite hangout. I loved coming to the library, and I especially loved these chairs. There were only three on the entire floor, and it was a rare treat to get to snag one. But nobody was nearby, watching and waiting for me to get up for a drink or a pee break so they could snake my spot. Tonight there was nobody around at all.

I put my book down and looked around. The lights were still on. The clock on the nearest wall said 7:26. The library wasn't due to close for another half hour, and there were always three or four warnings on the intercom when the library was about to close. I hadn't heard the first one yet. So why was it so quiet?

I shrugged and went back to my book. Maybe everyone had cleared out early. That would make it easier on the closing librarians. I felt sorry for them when ten or fifteen people all decided to wait until seven-fifty-five to check out and leave. They always wore pleasant smiles, but you could see the irritation in their eyes.

I lost myself in the fantasy novel, savoring the quiet like a rare steak. After a crazy-long day of carrying pizzas and grinning like an idiot, it was a beautiful thing to be able to relax and veg out. Soon the library would close, and I would have to go home to my crappy little apartment with its bad heater and strange smell I hadn't identified yet. It was quiet there, since I had no kids and no husband yet, but it wasn't like the library. The quiet in my apartment was the quiet of Nobody Cares. The quiet here was the quiet of We'll Just Leave You Alone. It was warmer here, and kinder. I loved the library. I felt like I could live here.

The main character in my novel vanquished the evil queen, freed his trusty pet dragon, and set off to reunite with the Girl He'd Left Behind. I skipped ahead a few pages. Most of the action was over, and I just wanted to find out if the girl would take him back. It seemed likely, but this author had surprised me before.

Yep, she took him back, but not before making him cry like a girl. Good for her. He might be a hero, but he'd still ditched her during the peak of harvesting season, leaving her a hand and a horse short. And he never did return the horse; his trusty dragon had eaten it. Although as it turned out, a dragon made a pretty good farm hand.

And they all lived happily ever after, I finished silently, closing the book. Stories didn't end with those words anymore, but they should. I looked up at the clock. It still said 7:26. It must have stopped.

My neck ached and my back popped as I slowly stood up. It had to be closing time by now. I wasn't that fast of a reader. But I still hadn't heard the usual warning: "The library will be closing in fifteen minutes. Please bring all check-out materials to the circulation desk." And then again in Spanish.

I put the book back on the Leave It Here cart. I felt weird doing that, since the librarians would have to put it away after I left, and I knew right where the book went. But those people meant business; they didn't want anyone but themselves putting the books away. I understood. It was easier to put a book away from the cart than to sift through stacks and stacks of books, rearranging those put back incorrectly.

There was nobody at the circulation desk. There was nobody in the check-out area at all. That was weird. Usually there were two or three of them, standing around and shooting the bull. Even if they weren't immediately visible, there was an office with a huge windowed office behind the circulation desk, and there should be someone back there. I didn't need to check anything out, so it was no big deal, but it was still weird. The lights were all still on, and the steel security gate was still locked into the wall where it belonged. I hadn't fallen asleep and somehow missed closing time. I'd bet my life on it.

Ah, well. Time to go either way. Morning came early, and I still wanted to update my profile on three or four job-hunting websites. The library had Internet, but the library wasn't for work. I came here to relax and enjoy the silence, and I couldn't do that plugged in.

The sliding door didn't work. I almost walked right into it. I put up both hands and managed to stop myself before I bonked my nose on the glass. I stopped short and looked around for witnesses to my embarrassment. There were none.

I stepped back and tapped on the sensor mat with my foot. Nothing. I stomped on it. Nothing. I did the Macarena; at this point I was still treating it as a joke. My mad dancing skills were for naught. The door didn't budge.

There was a huge red sticker that read, "In case of emergency, push on right side of door." This didn't feel like an emergency yet—I wasn't scared, and who ever heard of getting trapped in a library?—but I was uneasy. Broken clock, no librarian watching the front, and now the door didn't work. The weirdness was adding up. I shoved on the right side of the door as hard as I could.

It still didn't budge, and now I was getting a little scared. I banged on the door with my fist. It rattled like a landslide in the smooth silence.

"Hey!" I shouted, knowing as I did so that it was useless. What I could see of the parking lot was dead empty. "Hey!"

Nothing happened, and nobody came running to see what the racket was about. There was no doubt now that I was alone in here. My heart started to pick up a little.

Closing time had come and gone, and somehow I'd missed it. Maybe I'd fallen asleep, and they didn't see me there in the chair. The closing librarians were mostly younger, careless kids in their early twenties. I was barely thirty myself, but somehow that three and zero conferred a magical sense of maturity and superiority. Those kids were in too much of a hurry to get out and start their evening. Nobody had seen me or thought to wake me up. My fear backed off a little in respect for my growing irritation.

They hadn't shut off the lights nor closed the gate. Whoever was in charge of closing properly was going to get their ass reamed come morning. If I was still here, I was going to be the one to do it.

I walked back to the circulation desk and looked around. Everything looked so normal. Both of the computers were still on; I could see the little flying bats and dancing bubbles that indicated a screen saver in operation. I leaned over the desk and moved the mouse. The bats and bubbles vanished, and a password prompt appeared. I considered typing in something witty like FUCKSTICK69, but instead I walked away. I needed to find a phone.

I found one at the reference desk—the computer had the same dancing-bats screensaver, it must be standard issue—but when I hit the Talk button, there was no dial tone. I looked behind the computer and under the table; everything was plugged in. The power button was lit. The phone just wasn't working.

Fear took note and shoved irritation into the back seat. This was creepy.

I went back to the circulation desk and past it to the office behind. The light was on in the office. I already knew that I wasn't going to find anyone and I was right. I opened the door, which was thankfully unlocked, and went looking for a working phone.

There was another cordless on the desk next to the computer, identical to the one at the reference desk. It, too, was dead. I supposed that a rain storm or an accident could have knocked out the phone line and killed the power. That might even explain all the stopped clocks. But the lights were still on. None of this made sense.

My heart was cooking along at a healthy gallop, and my mouth felt dry. There was a reasonable explanation for this; I knew there was. I'd feel like a damn fool once everything was clear. I was looking forward to feeling like a damn fool.

I looked at the clock on the office wall. Seven twenty-six. But it was much later than that. My gut was telling me so.

Maybe I should just settle down and camp out for the night. The library would re-open at eight am, and then I could go home and embrace my ugly little apartment that I hated so much and badly wanted to see again. I'd be late for work, and there was no way around it. But I hadn't missed a day in six years, so they could just deal with it. This definitely qualified as an extenuating circumstance.

There was a miniature snack bar here in the office, and I feasted on chocolate bars, baked potato chips, and fruit snacks. I wasn't hungry, and it was hard to swallow past the lump of fear in my throat, but I forced the food in. I needed to feel as normal as possible. I needed to pretend that there wasn't something deeply, desperately wrong here.

I went back into the stacks and browsed for something to fall asleep to. Everything was neat as a pin; for a bunch of slackers who couldn't be bothered to pull a gate closed, they'd done an awesome job of cleaning up the books. I found a book of dirty knock-knock jokes; that looked suitably mindless. Give me something to read that I don't have to think about and I can get comfortable anywhere.

I settled back down into the big, soft chair and kicked off my shoes. I opened up a bag of chips that I'd snagged from the snack bar and opened the book. If the librarians gave me any shit about eating in here, after what they'd put me through, I was going to dish it out.

"Mommy, there's a dead lady in that chair," Haylee told her mother.

Shannon looked up from her perusal of the young adult shelf. She had to work fast, because if her older daughter caught her picking out a teenybopper romance, she'd give Shannon hell for weeks. McKayla was sixteen and considered herself too mature for teen fiction. Shannon was thirty-eight, and she'd never live it down.

"What dead lady?" Shannon barely noticed what Haylee was saying. Which mind-candy would taste better, a sexy vampire or a sexy werewolf?

"Dead lady in that chair." Haylee pointed to the large recliner

that looked to be made out of down pillows. Shannon thought that she wouldn't mind napping in that thing. It looked damn comfortable.

"There's nobody in that chair, honey." Werewolf, definitely. Vampires were overrated.

"She's asleep. But she's not breathing. And there's blood on her face."

Now it was sinking in. Damn it, McKayla must have told Haylee about that woman who'd died here two years ago. A patron had fallen asleep reading one night and never woke up. Shannon thought she'd heard it was a brain embolism that did it. Quick and painless. Not the worst way to die. She probably never knew what hit her.

McKayla was a great girl, but sometimes she forgot that her half-sister was only six. Maybe they'd made a game of telling scary stories and it had gotten out of hand.

"The dead lady went away to heaven, sweetheart," Shannon said. She believed in heaven about as much as she believed in magic beans, but it was all she could think of to say.

"She's right there, sleeping," Haylee insisted.

Well, whatever. At least Haylee didn't seem afraid. Shannon would grab one more book and then they'd find McKayla and head out. And hopefully Haylee wouldn't remember next time they came to the library. The last thing she needed was Haylee's father giving her shit for "filling my daughter's head with nightmares."

Haylee kept looking over her shoulder as Shannon hustled her away. The little girl's face was calm and curious, but just a little troubled.

I woke up with a snort and a jerk. The joke book was lying open across my chest, and a small drizzle of drool had narrowly missed its pages.

I yawned and looked around, confident that I would find a scared librarian tapping anxiously on my shoulder. They'd probably forgive my library fines for the rest of my life as an apology.

There was nobody there. I stretched my back and stood up. I'd been sleeping for a long time; my joints were telling me so. But the place still looked empty and silent.

All the clocks still read 7:26. It was very frustrating, not knowing what time it was. I went over to the nearest window and looked out into the night. Not a single car drove by. It was as though I were the only person left in the world.

The silence was deafening.

I have no idea how long I stood there, watching and waiting for I knew not what. The darkness and silence were hypnotizing. My mind seemed to zone out, aware of its surroundings but uncaring and free. I was floating.

Finally I shook myself loose. It must be very early morning, since there was no traffic. I thought that I ought to be hungry, so I went back to the office behind the circulation desk.

It was fully stocked again. I stood very still. I'd ransacked those snacks, eaten at least two chocolate bars and three bags of chips. I ran back to my chair. The book was still there, but the bag of chips I'd fallen asleep with was gone. This made no fucking sense. Back to the office. The garbage can under the computer desk was clean and empty of wrappers.

Had I slept the whole clock around? Had an entire day passed, and I just slept through it all?

But the place was still lit, and from here I could see that the gate still wasn't pulled. I could see the library being improperly closed one night, but two?

I ate some more snacks, since I didn't know what to do. My heart was racing, fueled by sugar and fear, and I decided that it was time to do something drastic.

I found a metal folding chair in a corner behind the circulation desk. I unfolded the chair and carried it like a lion tamer to the glass sliding door. With a deep, nerve-gathering breath, I raised the chair and swung it at the glass door as hard as I could.

Bong! The chair bounced out of my hands and clattered across the floor. The door was untouched. It didn't even ripple under the force of my blow.

Now I was angry. The library was a special place to me, this atheist's version of church. I'd broken a personal commandment by attempting to do damage here. And nothing even happened. No lightning, no fire and brimstone, and no shattered glass. I was scared and angry and seriously pissed off.

I picked up the chair and swung it again. And again. I beat

that metal chair against that smug sheet of glass that refused to even acknowledge my efforts. It didn't even fucking crack.

I ran to a window in the corner of the back office and threw the chair against it. It bounced off the window with a clang and hit the computer monitor, knocking it to the floor.

That wasn't enough. I was still angry and scared. I ran through the library with both arms out, sweeping books, CDs, and boxes of magazines onto the floor. I picked up a computer monitor and dashed it to the floor. Then I threw another. This wouldn't be possible, had the library not recently received a grant that enabled them to replace their ancient monitors with fancy new flatscreens. They flew like china dishes.

Panting and exhausted, at last I stopped. When the librarians came back, they would see this mess and raise the roof. I might go to jail, but at least I would be out of here. After that, I could go home.

I went back to my favorite comfy chair for a rest. The book of dirty knock-knock jokes was still there, and I read a few pages before falling asleep.

"The dead lady's mad," Haylee announced.

Shannon shook her head. McKayla had sworn that she hadn't told Haylee anything about the woman who'd died here. Shannon believed her. McKayla was an upfront kid when it came to screwing up. Haylee must have picked it up at preschool, or maybe from her father's girlfriend. Shannon didn't really care. All that mattered were that Haylee wasn't afraid to come to the library, and that Chris had no ammunition with which to attack Shannon or her older daughter.

"Why is she mad, honey?" Shannon asked.

"Don't know. I think she needs coffee."

Shannon laughed. Haylee had watched The Wizard of Oz at age four, and she'd commented, "That green lady needs her coffee." It had been a running joke ever since.

"Dead people don't drink coffee, sweetie." She selected the sexy-vampire novel she'd passed up last week. The werewolf had been a disappointment.

"Is that why she's mad?"

"Maybe."

"I wanna say something to her."
"Okay, but stay where I can see you."

When I awoke, it was still dark outside, and the nearest clock still read 7:26. There was a kid looking at me.

"Hi," she said.

I sat up and blinked. My head felt muzzy and confused, but nothing hurt this time. I must be getting used to sleeping in this damn chair.

"Hi," I said. The kid was cute, brown-haired and brown-eyed. She looked at me with a very intense expression, like she was a scientist studying a weird bug and thinking about dissecting it.

"Why are you mad?" she asked.

I looked around. There was no evidence of my destructive rampage. The computers were back in place, the books neatly lined up. I wanted to cry. God I was so tired.

But hold on. There was no mess, but the kid knew I was angry. Interesting. Also weird and creepy.

"Because I'm stuck here, and I want to go home," I said. "Where's your mom?" Maybe there was a way out after all, if this little girl had found a way in.

"She's over there." The little girl pointed, but I saw nobody. "Why aren't you in heaven?"

I jerked back, and then I shook my head. "It's not time for me to go to heaven," I said. "People go to heaven when they get really old and sick. I need to get out of here and go home."

"Rusty go'ed to heaven, and he was just four. Doggie doctor said he had carsey-noma."

"Well I don't have carcinoma. Can you show me how to get out of here?"

"That way." The girl pointed toward the main entrance.

I sighed.

"I can't get out that way. I've already tried. How did you get in?"

"That way," the child insisted, still pointing.

I stood up and walked away from her. I had to; the frustration was building again, and I didn't want to take it out on an innocent kid.

"Where's your mom?" I asked again. "How did you get in here by yourself?"

"I already showed you that." The child looked as annoyed as I felt. "She's over there. And we comed in through the door."

I looked around carefully, scanning everything in sight. There was nobody else in the library. It was still dark outside and dead inside.

"You should be in heaven," the girl said. "In heaven, nobody's mad. In heaven, Rusty chases all the squirrels, and the squirrels like it because they're so happy. Everyone is happy in heaven. Even the squirrels."

Good God, what if the kid was right? I felt cold inside, and I shuddered. What if I really was dead? And the library was empty and haunted—by me.

I just wanted to go home. The apartment was a shithole, but it was mine. My computer was there, and all the photos I'd taken for Photography class. I'd hated everything about college except that class. I still had every picture I'd taken on a CD slideshow. I wanted to watch it one more time.

I began to cry. "I want to go home!"

The little girl patted my knee. "Maybe heaven looks like home."

"I don't know how to get to heaven," I said. The cold fear was getting bigger and harder in my chest. Maybe I was stuck here because I hadn't earned my way into heaven. Maybe this was purgatory. Or hell.

"Heaven is up," the child said. "You should take the evelator."

"We're already on the top floor," I said, but I followed her anyway. And a little child shall lead them, I thought crazily. None of this was real. None of this was happening. This new weirdness was the final proof.

The kid took me to the elevator in the main lobby. The door opened as we approached, but there was nobody inside. "Push UP," she said.

"But this evelator—elevator—only goes down," I said, peeking inside. It looked like any other elevator. Small and square and just a little bit scary. "It goes to the lower level of the library."

But I was mistaken. There were two buttons side by side; one said DOWN in red, and the other said UP in green. I stepped inside, and before I could lose my nerve, I pushed UP.

The fear tightened in my chest until I could barely breathe. The doors were closing, and the little girl was waving.

"Wait!" I shouted. I put my hands out and shoved the closing doors, and they re-opened easily. Then I got off the elevator.

"You don't wanna go to heaven?" the girl asked.

I looked around the lobby. It was still empty, but there were traces of color in the air, as though I was seeing shapes through a filter. Faintly, I heard voices.

"I don't want to go," I said.

I walked back into the stacks, and the little girl followed. The voices were a little louder here, and out of the corner of my eye I saw a woman walking with an armload of books.

"I like it here," I said finally. "I don't think I'm ready to leave here."

"I like it too." The little girl smiled up at me.

"Haylee!" A low hiss from nearby. The girl's smile faded.

"Gotta go," she said, and just like that my savior took off. I was alone again.

But I didn't feel alone. I took a deep breath, inhaling that lovely old-book scent. I was in no hurry to leave.

Then I started looking for something to read.

To Rest

by Melissa Mead

Ava stared into her teacup. She hadn't meant to break her lunch date with Lisa. She just couldn't bear any more talk about baby names, the perfect shade to paint the nursery, and what a wonderful godmother Ava would be. So she passed Lisa's house and kept on driving.

Leaving town hadn't helped. All around her, other people sat at the café's tiny sidewalk tables, enjoying the sun. People with babies and toddlers, children and teens. Across the street a crumbling brick building, a school or something, with an adjoining cemetery, filled her vision, confronting her with far too many tiny headstones behind its iron gate. Turning away only meant facing the same view, reflected in the café's window. The tea reflected clouds and bright sky, a wavering glimpse of Heaven.

The sunlight made her eyes water. It had been a sunny day like this ten years ago when she'd stopped on some urgent errand that she couldn't even remember now, leaving three-month-old Abby strapped safely into her car seat. In the 15-minute parking, with the car window opened what she thought was the perfect amount. Too small to let a kidnapper's hand in.

Too small to let baking-hot air out.

Her neck was getting stiff. She raised her head to see a boy wandering along the sidewalk. No one spoke to him, or even reacted when he leaned over diners' shoulders to examine their newspapers or their lunches. His ramblings brought him steadily toward Ava, the way cats seem to gravitate toward the one person in the room who's allergic to them.

He looked maybe eight years old. Or ten. His expression looked older, though. A skinny kid, and was that a nightgown he was wearing? He was barefoot, sickly-pale, and as far as Ava could see, utterly alone.

Ava slipped out her cell phone and opened it. If she could get a picture she could run a match to see if anyone was looking for the boy. Easy enough to upload a picture to some official alert site. No fuss, no questions from the police. Just a quick call, before the kid got hurt, or worse.

The boy froze as though she'd pulled a gun on him. He sidestepped out of the picture. She refocused.

He turned and bolted into the street.

"No!" Ava screamed. She cringed, expecting to hear the thud of flesh against fender. Traffic screeched to a stop. But when Ava looked up, shaking, no body lay in the road. The boy was gone. Not so much as a fender-bender, although one driver made a pointed gesture at her and drove off, leaving behind a taint of burnt rubber and profanity. The other diners stared at her.

Blushing and apologizing, Ava paid her bill, left double her usual tip, and hurried back to her hotel room to spend the rest of the afternoon and night hearing the echo of shrieking brakes in her mind. When she closed her eyes, she saw that pale face.

Ghost-pale.

Nonsense.

Bedsides, she already had her own ghost, tiny, yet filling her whole heart. She had no room for any more lost souls.

Ava swore she'd never go near that cafe again.

She came back before breakfast. The shop was closed, but the boy was there, standing by the table she'd abandoned the day before.

"You saw me, yesterday," he said.

He looked unhurt, and less shaken than Ava, who felt ready to explode from sleepless anxiety.

"I thought I saw you get killed! What were you doing? Didn't your mother ever tell you not to run out into traffic?"

Her outburst didn't frighten him. In fact, he nearly smiled. "No, ma'am."

"Well, she ought to…" Ava clamped her mouth shut. As though she had any right to judge what this boy's mother ought to do. "Is that a nightgown you're wearing?"

He drew himself up indignantly. "It's a nightSHIRT. I'm twelve, not a baby."

Twelve? A pretty scrawny twelve. Poor kid. Probably hadn't had a decent meal in ages. Amazing what some people got away with where kids were concerned.

"Where are your mom and dad? Do they know you're running around town barefoot in a nightgo… nightshirt?"

"They're dead." He locked eyes with her, daring her to say something. Before she could open her mouth, her cellphone rang. Lisa.

Ava expected the boy to run away while she apologized for not showing up and assured Lisa that really, she was fine. He didn't. He stood watching her, his expression rapt.

"It's like magic," he said when she signed off. "How far away were they- the person you were talking to?"

"Ten miles, maybe twenty. You haven't got a cellphone?"

He shook his head.

"Well, you're twelve. I might not've let Abby have one either, if… when she got to be twelve." She choked on her daughter's name, and glared at the boy as though he'd tricked her into saying it aloud. "What's your name?"

"Caleb." He was giving her that look again, sizing her up. Looking for something, but she couldn't tell what. Ava suppressed an urge to squirm.

"How far away can you talk to people?" he said.

"Depends on the reception. What's your last name?"

He looked down, suddenly enthralled by a crack on the sidewalk. "Don't have one."

"Come on; everyone has a last name. What's yours?"

"Ward," he said after a moment. "Who's Abby?"

Was he paying her back for insisting on knowing his last name? "My daughter," she said, typing "Caleb Ward" into her Search function. "My baby girl."

No alerts. No record of anyone like him at all. Of course, he'd probably lied.

"Where is she?"

Sadistic little urchin. "She died."

"Oh." After a long, thoughtful pause he said "I'm sorry."

"Me too."

"Do you love her anyway?"

Ava flinched as though he'd punched her. "Of course I do! Did. What kind of question is that? Just leave me alone!" He did. No screeching brakes this time. She turned away to dry her eyes, and when she turned back, he was simply gone.

Part of her hoped the boy wouldn't be there the next morning, but he was. Waiting for her. Ava sat down at the little metal table.

"I know what you are."

He looked startled. "You do?"

"Yep. You're a projection. I read up on it. I'm only seeing you because I'm missing Abby. That explains it."

Although it didn't explain why her subconscious had conjured up a male street urchin who looked like Wee Willie Winkie. Even if ghosts aged, Abby wouldn't be twelve now, only ten. Ten and three months.

"I suppose that could be why. Nobody else sees me." Caleb looked thoughtful. "Is a projection the same thing as a ghost?"

"There's no such thing as ghosts," said Ava, more harshly than she'd intended. She scooted her chair away from him. "Besides, it's broad daylight."

Caleb didn't blush, but he ducked his head, obviously mortified. "I'm scared of the dark. I always made Nurse Summers leave a lamp burning. The other boys hated it."

Ava choked on a laugh. "Kid, you're priceless."

He edged closer, reached out a hand.

"Don't touch me!"

"Why not? I won't hurt you. I promise."

"Because... Just don't."

His hand fell to his side.

"You're the only person who's seen me, and you don't even like me."

"Look, it's nothing personal. I'm just not good with kids. Really. I mean it. Go away."

174

"I'll have to come back. I'm sorry. I can't help it."

"Why won't you leave me alone? If I have to be haunted, why not by my own little girl? I'm sorry. I said I was sorry. Over and over again, I said it. I'm sorry, Abby, sweetheart…"

The boy touched her. Just a quick, cool, light touch, like a barely-felt breeze. Just enough to make her look up, notice a few early customers eying her uneasily, and follow the strange boy. She staggered across the street and clung to the cemetery gate. The onlookers, satisfied that she was a harmless, grieving mourner, went back to their business.

"I didn't mean to make you cry," said Caleb. "You could see me, that's all. Everyone else is gone. I'm the only one left, and you're the only person who's seen me."

"What do you mean, 'The only one left'?"

He pointed at the brick building. "Come inside. Please. Maybe you can find out what happened."

"That's trespassing! I haven't gotten so much as a traffic ticket in a decade, and now I'm supposed to start breaking and entering?"

"You won't break anything."

"I won't enter anything, either."

"I'll have to come back. Every day. Everywhere you go. I didn't even know you'd be here today, but I had to come. Even when I tried walking the other way, I still ended up by your table."

"Her" table. So had she, even though she never wanted to see the place again. Ava shuddered. If she drove back home, would something drag her back here tomorrow? Back to the tiny headstones, over and over, for the rest of her life?

"Let's get it over with, then." She trudged down the sidewalk to the gate. A blue historical marker declared the building to be the Woodside Children's Home.

"Abandoned following the influenza epidemic of 1899," Ava read aloud.

"You won't get sick now," Caleb assured her from the other side of the gate. "There's nobody else left."

Ava had a harder time getting across. Caleb showed her a secluded corner with a gap in the fence, and she emerged muddied and scraped, with a tear in her blouse.

Melissa Mead

The back door, boarded over but half crumbled from dry rot, was easier to get through. Ava stepped carefully over the dusty floor, expecting her foot to plunge through the decayed boards at any moment. Caleb led her to a room lined with iron bedsteads and crumbling mattresses.

"This is the dormitory." His voice trembled. "Can you see anybody? Henry or Clyde or Nurse Summers? Even Nurse Groth?"

Ava looked around the empty room. Cobwebs, peeling paint, but no other pale, nightshirted figures.

"There's no one here, Caleb."

He urged her through the parlor, kitchen, dining hall. Last of all, he came to a smaller room with a washstand and a single bed in it. "That's the infirmary. You won't find anybody else there."

A scrap of white cloth, like Caleb's nightshirt, caught her eye.

"Wait; I think there's something in the b… Oh God."

Ava turned and fled with her hand to her mouth.

"I told you I wouldn't hurt you!" Caleb called. "I promised!"

Ava didn't listen. She didn't stop running until she was out of that building and heaving lungfuls of clean air. When she looked up, Caleb was standing in front of her.

"I told you there was nobody else there. Just me."

Ava forced herself to look at his pale, hurt face without seeing the desiccated thing on the bed.

"There was no one else left, was there? They fled and left you alone."

"But they should be here now! We should all be… all be the same by now. Where is everyone?"

Ava swallowed. "I think somebody needs to… to lay you to rest. I'll find someone." She laughed a shaky laugh. "Maybe you can even help pick out your own spot. How many people get to do that?"

"No! Please don't go. It'll be dark. If it doesn't work, I'll be alone in the dark forever."

He was crying. Which was nonsense, Ava reminded herself. That… that thing she'd seen hadn't cried for over a century. She was trespassing. The last thing she needed was a visit from the police. All she had to do was turn and walk away.

Like she'd done on a bright summer day ten years ago.

176

"I'll stay. But I can't do this alone," she said, and dialed Lisa's number with shaking hands.

Lisa came. She brought a shovel as well as gloves and a clean sheet, which Ava hadn't thought to ask for. She got through the fence and out of sight from the road before demanding to know what was going on.

"Good thing I'm not showing yet," she laughed. "Ava, what on Earth are you up to?"

Ava had meant to tell her a few bare facts, maybe even some lie about a vow to a distant relative. But with Caleb's eyes on her it all poured out. About Caleb. About Abby. The jail time, the therapy, the nightmares, the guilt. When it was done she just stood there, waiting for her friend to turn and walk away.

"So that's why you didn't show up," said Lisa after a moment.

"Yes. I understand if you think I'm nuts, if you don't want to talk to me after this, if you won't want me around the baby, but I swear I didn't mean to."

Lisa held out her arms, and Ava sobbed on her friend's shoulder.

"This explains so much," said Lisa. "No wonder you're seeing little kid ghosts. Let's get you home."

"No!" said Ava and Caleb at the same time.

"I can't abandon Caleb," said Ava. Lisa's brow furrowed, but she followed Ava to the infirmary.

"Oh, the poor thing," she said.

"I'm not a poor thing," Caleb muttered. "I'm just dead."

Ava kept her eye on him while Lisa, matter-of-fact as always, made a bundle with the sheet.

"Do you have a favorite spot, Caleb?" said Ava when they were outside again.

Caleb stared at the grass and refused to answer.

"What did he say?" To Ava's gratitude, Lisa sounded perfectly serious.

"He won't talk to me. C'mon, Caleb. Please?"

"Great. A ghost with the sulks." Lisa sat down on a nearby bench, the shrouded bundle at her feet.

"I'm not sulking! I'm scared."

Ava took a deep breath. "Caleb, you heard what I said to Lisa? About Abby?"

He nodded.

"I understand if you can't trust me."

"You didn't mean it. I just don't want to be alone. I want to stay with you."

Ava choked.

Ava?" said Lisa. "Are you okay?"

Ava nodded fiercely. "Caleb, it means so much that you trust me, that you'd want to stay with me, but..." Her voice cracked.

Lisa stood up. "Listen, kiddo, I can't see you. I can't hear you. But if you can hear me, and if you care so much about Ava, you could do her a mighty big favor by bringing Abby a message from her mom."

Caleb wouldn't look at Lisa, or the shovel she carried, but he edged closer to Ava.

"Will you stay until we're sure it worked?"

Ava nodded.

"I won't leave until I know you're not alone."

Lisa raised an eyebrow and mouthed "How would we know?" but Ava gestured for her to hush.

With a resigned look on his face, Caleb led them to an apple tree in the back corner of the yard. "Here. Nurse Summers used to say I ate so many apples I'd turn into an apple tree."

Ava dug until her palms stung and she couldn't tell if the wetness on her face was tears or sweat. Lisa laid the sheet-wrapped bundle in the hole and hefted a spadeful of dirt.

"I'll do this part, Ava. You say goodbye to the kiddo."

"Should you be doing that? In your condition?"

"Ava," said Lisa with a smile, "you worry about your little fellow, and I'll worry about mine."

"He's not mine," said Ava, but she glanced at Caleb and said "If you're sure, I'll sit with him while you finish."

"Wait!" said Caleb. "Not yet. It's going to get dark. Maybe we should do it tomorrow."

Ava sat down, took out her cell phone, and flipped it open.

"See? Lighted display." She held it out. Lisa, put this in, would you? With the light on."

"You aren't seriously going to bury a perfectly good phone, are you?"

"Please. For Abby."

Lisa sighed, but settled the lighted phone gently atop the sheet. Ava motioned for Caleb to sit next to her, and after a moment's hesitation, put her arm around him. He laid his head in her shoulder. It felt as though she leaned against a cool feather pillow.

"Is it all right if I don't watch?"

"Of course, Caleb."

The dirt parted with a gritty rasp, fell with a muffled thud. Ava felt Caleb shiver. Lullabies she thought she'd forgotten came from her throat, lessening the relentless dull thumps.

"I'll tell Abby you're a good mom," said Caleb. His eyes closed. Ava finished the verse and looked up to see Lisa leaning on the shovel.

Ava looked from her to the sleeping boy on her lap. "But… It should have…"

"Ava? We should get out of here."

Ava's eyes stung. She kissed the pale forehead. "I'm sorry, sweetheart."

The boy in her arms smiled and murmured something. She prayed that it really was "Hi, Abby." He vanished. Ava scrambled to her feet and picked up the shovel. The way her knees were wobbling, she needed something to lean on.

"You OK, Ava?"

"I will be. And so will Caleb."

"Where is he?"

"Gone. But at least he's got a light. And a new friend. I'm sure of it." Ava started walking. "Lisa? Let me tell you about my daughter."

Ghosts in the Gaslight

By Andrew Knighton

Perched on the end of her badly sprung bed, Josephine lit the lamp and waited for Conrad to appear. Every night after work she went through this ritual – the hiss of the gas, the flicker of the flame, the excitement at waiting to see him and the anxiety that he might not come.

He always did.

The flame shifted in the breeze blowing through a chink in the window. Conrad's smile appeared, and then his eyes, glittering like rubies, making her heart flutter. Teaching filled her with joy, with pride at a job well done, with love for the children in her care. But none of it moved her like Conrad's smile.

"'You lit the flame for me, my sweet," he murmured.

"Of course." Josephine reached out so that her hand almost cupped his face. The heat made her fingers throb, but she could bear it to be this close to him.

"I brought you something."

She reached round on the bed, layered skirts rustling as she turned, and picked up the brightly colored scrap of paper. Careful not to smudge the chalk, she held it up so that he could see.

"Mr Timpson gave the school colored chalks from his works," she said. "This afternoon, instead of handwriting I had the whole class draw pictures of flowers. This was Mathew's."

"It's wonderful to see such colors." Conrad gave the sad half smile that she was so familiar with, the one that made her heart ache. "I just wish I could be free of here, could see all the colors of the world with you, touch you, feel you against me."

Josephine blushed at such talk, but made no attempt to stop him. These were her thoughts too, had been since she first met him. What was the point in modesty? Had he not seen her in her under-dress that first time, before she turned round and found him in the flame, wide-eyed with amazement that she could even see him.

Every night Josephine dreamt of her wedding, of a perfect day with her friends and her perfect love. She dreamt of being for a moment as beautiful as her mother, of leaving this house and her bitter old father behind. For years the groom in those dreams had been faceless, but not any more.

"Have you found my mother among the other spirits?" she asked, prizing open her silver locket and peering sadly at the picture inside. "I would love to see her. It might even help calm father's temper."

"No, I'm sorry." Conrad's face swayed from side to side. "But I'm sure she moved on to heaven years ago."

"Poor you, trapped between this world and the next." Was it just the tears welling in her eyes, or was he growing harder to see? "Is something happening to you?"

"I'm fading away, my love." For a moment, he became all but invisible. "My spirit is being consumed by the fire."

"Oh no!"

Horror filled her at the thought of losing him, of being left alone with only father's fists.

"I think I have found a way you can save me." There was a glint in his eye which she could only take as hope.

"Tell me!" If he could be saved then Josephine would do it. She could face any hazard for love.

"I think that the trapped spirits go into the gas at the Albert Street gasworks. If you can stop it, I might be free."

"We could be together?"

"Of course, my sweet."

"I'll go at once."

All excitement, she grabbed her coat from back of a rickety chair and pocketed her house key.

"Wait!" Conrad said. "Don't just leave me."

She looked at him in bemusement. She loved him, but what else could she do?

"You'll need me at the gasworks," he continued, "to show you what to do."

"But how can I take you?"

Conrad's face creased up in frustration.

"Fine," he snapped. "I'll follow you through the street lamps. Look out for me, and listen to what I say."

"No need for that tone." She tried not to smile. He might lose his temper from time to time, but he always came back from it sweeter than ever.

"I'm sorry, my love." He shook off his frown. "I'm just anxious. For us."

She rushed down the creaking stairs and into the cramped parlor. Father sat by the hearth, one hand held out to the flames, the other around a cup of gin. His face glowed like the devil in the ill-lit room.

"Where are you going?" he growled, struggling to shove himself upright.

"I am going for a walk," she said.

"Are you indeed?" Father lurched to his feet, his saggy face wobbling. He stank of sweat and his angry little eyes were bloodshot. "What about my dinner, eh? What about the cleaning and the bedsheets? You've duties here girl."

"Dinner is in the pot." She glared at him. "I will sweep tomorrow. And you can change your own bedsheets."

"What would your mother say to this, gallivanting off into the night?"

A ball of fury welled up within Josephine.

"How dare you use mother against me!"

"Don't you take that tone. Get to the sweeping or I'll take my belt to you."

He raised a gnarly fist.

"Please don't." Her heart was hammering. How could this skinny wretch still fill her with fear? "I pay the bills, remember?"

He sniggered and slumped back into his chair.

"That what you're going out for?" he asked. "To pay the bills?"

Josephine stifled her tears as she ran out the door.

At first she assumed that the man at the gasworks gate must be a night watchman. He was dressed in a long black coat and letting himself in with a heavy set of keys. But as she approached down the empty street he turned, revealing the white of a dog collar at his throat.

Josephine sighed with relief. Surely a vicar would help her.

As she strode towards the gates, Conrad's face appeared in the flames of a nearby street lamp. She couldn't hear his soft greeting over the scraping of the gates, but she smiled back. Soon they would be together.

"Excuse me," she called out.

The vicar was halfway through pulling the heavy iron gate shut behind him. He peered at her through the bars.

"Yes, my child?" He pushed a pair of wire-rimmed spectacles up his narrow nose.

Could you let me in please?" Needing an excuse, she thought of the children she taught, of the kinds of things they might come up with. "I left something inside."

The vicar shook his head.

"I'm sorry, you'll have to come back tomorrow."

"But it's important, Reverend..."

"Russell. Reverend Russell. And keeping the sacred trust that has been invested in me is also important."

It seemed a funny thing to say, but Josephine was busy grappling with another thought. This was a man of the cloth. He believed in the mysteries of faith, in the power of love. Of all the people she might meet, surely he would take her story seriously? Surely she could trust a priest?

But what if he didn't believe her? What if he called her mad?

She thought of Conrad and pushed down her doubts. She needed to get in.

"Something terrible is happening in there," she said. "You may find this hard to believe, but souls are being trapped in the gas, burning in the flames."

"Oh, that isn't so hard to believe," Reverend Russell said.

"Thank you." She was so relieved she might have hugged him, if it weren't for the iron bars between them.

"You see, they deserve to burn." Russell pulled the gate to with a clang, turned the key in the lock. "They are the unworthy, the sinners, and they shall burn in earthly fire. Why else do we have all this industry, if not to fulfill God's will on Earth?"

"But you've trapped an innocent!" Desperation replaced her broken hope.

"That rabble-rouser and fornicator in the street-lamp?" He pointed a bony finger at the flames where Conrad flickered. "He got everything he deserved. Leave him, child. He's not worth it."

"But I love him."

"More fool you. Now be gone, or I'll call the police on you for trying to trespass."

He stalked away between the brick buildings and brass pipes of the gasworks.

She turned to Conrad.

"What did he mean when he talked about you?" she asked.

"I was a union man." Conrad looked thoughtful. "The likes of Reverend Russell defend the establishment, not the people."

"And the other part?"

"I'm sorry, I didn't know how to tell you." Conrad lowered his gaze. "I have been in love before. But our parish priest would not bless the union of his daughter and a radical."

"That's awful!" Josephine's anger rose at the injustice of it all. "And for this he's trapped you here, letting your soul be eaten by flames?"

"Yes, my sweet." Conrad looked up at her. "So it seems."

"Well, I won't stand for it." She strode along the fence, looking for a weak point or an opening, Conrad's face appearing in one street-lamp after another beside her.

"You'll still set me free?" he asked, all eagerness.

"Of course. Then we can be together."

"Yes," he said. "Together."

A thought crossed her mind. If Conrad had died, and this was Russell punishing his soul, then surely Conrad had no body.

"How will we be together?" she asked. "Once you're free, I mean. If your body is gone..."

"I've seen it in others, my sweet," he replied, gaze darting back and forth along the fence. "When a soul is let into the world, a body forms around it. A little like when a child is born, but not a child's body. The soul made manifest."

She paused, trying to think this through, to picture it at work. But her thoughts were interrupted by an excited cry from Conrad.

"Look!" His flame swayed towards a dark corner of the fence, a place where a rusty bar had been broken loose by some previous trespasser. It left a narrow gap, but after a moment's hesitation Josephine squeezed through, suffering nothing worse than crumpled, dirty skirts.

Ahead of her a small gas lamp flickered on the corner of a building, presumably lit by Russell or a night watchman. Conrad appeared in the flame.

"This way," he hissed.

She scurried from shadow to shadow trying not to be seen. She could hear voices howling in the pipes, other spirits just like Conrad, trapped here by this awful man.

"Does it hurt?" she whispered, looking at Conrad.

"Of course," he said. "Every minute of every day I burn."

"Why didn't you tell me?"

"You couldn't work it out?" he snapped, then immediately seemed to regret it. "I'm sorry, love. I just..."

"I understand."

Living with her father, living with the loss of her mother, those things hurt Josephine every day, but she spoke of them to no one. She stayed strong. Like Conrad. Like her mother.

She laid her fingers on the locket, let her love pour over her mother's memory.

Then she rose and strode confidently forwards, not worrying about the shadows. With her mother's memory to strengthen her, she could face her fears.

"Come on," she said.

Conrad's face didn't appear in the next lamp. She turned to see him back behind her, flickering nervously in the flames.

"The fires are hotter further in," he said. "What if I burn up?"

"Just think of your freedom," she said. "Think of us together."

"Freedom." A look of resolve filled his face. "Lets keep going then."

They circled round a towering gas tank. Ahead, the windows of the Retort House glowed orange. Peering round the open doorway, Josephine saw a series of large brick chambers like baker's ovens, a fire raging in one. Reverend Russell stood silhouetted against it, Bible open in one hand, chanting prayers into the fire.

She crept towards him, and to her left a gas lamp sputtered into life, Conrad appearing in the small, weak flame.

Russell seemed preoccupied with his work. He reached into his pocket and pulled out a lock of hair.

"Esther Brighouse," he intoned, "I condemn ye to the fires you deserve. Con-woman, thief, harlot. May you burn in His holy wrath."

He cast the hair into the flames and a shriek filled the room, making Josephine jump.

"I know you're there." Russell turned to face her. "I expect you'll join them too, when your time comes."

With the option of subterfuge gone, Josephine reverted to more comfortable tactics – a direct challenge and the certainty that she was right. She placed her hands on her hips and glared at the priest.

"You let Conrad go," she demanded. "He doesn't deserve this."

"Oh doesn't he?" Russell said.

"Just because they wouldn't let him marry-"

"Wouldn't let him?" Russell's laughter was like nails across a chalkboard. "Conrad Marple never showed any interest in marriage. Just ask any of the girls he led astray. Just ask my Bess. He had his way with her, took her from the bosom of her family, then left her for some common slut. He took my daughter's innocence, ruined her reputation, just for his base needs."

Josephine turned, shocked, towards Conrad.

"I'm sorry, my love," he said. "I couldn't bear to tell you the truth. I was a terrible person before I met you, lustful and selfish. I deserved what I got here. That's why I never mentioned the pain."

Tears ran down Josephine's cheeks, whether at his anguish or her own heartbreak she wasn't sure.

"You changed me," Conrad said, his voice rising to a high plea. "Made me hope I could be someone better. That I could come back."

Josephine looked at him. He had lied to her once, was he lying again? She didn't know if she could trust him, but she knew that she loved him. Was that reason enough?

"Do you really think this is God's will?" Conrad asked. "Souls burning to nothing on one man's whim? There are men trapped here for protesting their wages, women condemned for how they fed their families, children who just stole to stay alive. Can this be right?"

Josephine's heart was torn over Conrad. But she knew how she felt about such injustice, about children punished for being born poor.

"I'll do it," she said. "Whatever needs doing. For them, and maybe for you."

"Josephine, I—" Conrad's eyes went wide with alarm. "Behind you!"

She turned and raised her hand just as Russell swung a shovel at her. It smacked her across the arm and face with a terrible crack, sent her sprawling on the ground. Her arm felt numb from the elbow down, and blood poured from her nose down her throbbing face.

"No one's letting that sinner out!" Russell towered over her, shovel raised. "No one!"

Fire flashed from the lamp and Russell staggered back across the room, frantically beating at his flaming hair.

Josephine rose, her arm dangling useless by her side.

The flame in the lamp was even weaker than before, Conrad's

face fading almost to nothing. She could see him trying to shout to her, but all she heard was a distant hiss. He must have thrown so much of himself into attacking Russell, into protecting her from that brute, that there was barely anything left.

"How do I save you?" she pleaded. "I don't know how!"

Footsteps scuffed the floor behind her and she turned to see Russell approaching once more.

"Getting weak is he?" Russell said. "Fading away? Good. Maybe there's not enough love left to hold him any more. Not from you, not even from how much he loves himself."

"Love?" With her good hand Josephine wiped a smear of blood from her locket. "What do you know about love, you spiteful old brute?"

Russell laughed again, a wretched, hollow noise that rasped in his chest.

"All of this is built on love," he said. "Love for God. Love for my poor, lost Bess who this wretch took from me. Love for my fellow man. My love powers this work, holds it all together. It traps the undeserving, that they may be punished for the good of the rest, that mankind may be redeemed. For my love may be great, but His is greater, and He put us here to carry it through."

"That's not love," she said. "Love is kind. Love is patient. Love is friends and family, not strangers seeking to teach you your place. Love endures."

"Oh, you must know something about love, if you can see them trapped in the flames." Russell had to raise his voice to be heard. The ghosts were all around them, howling through the pipes. "You must have some powerful love in you. But don't preach to me about how I feel. Don't tell me what's right and wrong."

"Why not? That's what you're doing."

The locket was hot in Josephine's hand. That one piece of metal held more love than all his angry rants. All the love she felt for her mother, poured out in the years since she had died.

But was that really what love was for? To freeze some fragment of the world, to cling on to what should pass? She thought of Conrad and Gladys, of people still in the world who needed her more.

"You say love built this," she said, pulling back her good arm. "Maybe love can unmake it too."

She flung the locket with all her strength. It hurtled through the air, a gleaming point of light against the darkness of the room, and landed in the fiery retort. It trembled in the flames, seemed for a moment to swell, then collapsed, unleashing a blinding white flash.

Russell screamed and clutched at the crumbling remnants of his hair. Josephine barged past him and out into the night. She couldn't bear to be in that place, to see what she had done to her mother's memory.

But as she stepped outside she knew that she had done right. She watched in elation as flames burst from the mouth of every pipe in the gasworks, faces soaring up through the smoke, vanishing into the night in laughter and song.

Conrad hovered in the nearest flame, grinning so wide his head seemed about to split in half.

"Free!" he said. "You set me free!"

"We can be together," she said, her tears now those of joy.

"I'm sorry," he said, and for the briefest moment she thought he meant it. "I needed someone to get me out. You were just easy."

He rose from the flame up into the air, a fading afterimage against the darkness, his voice vanishing into the night.

"If it wasn't you it would have been someone else. But thank you."

Josephine sank to her knees in the dirt, sobbing so hard that her whole body shook. She had thrown away her mother's locket, betrayed her memory, and all for this? For a man who didn't want her? For some terrible womanizer to whom she was just nothing?

"You ruined everything." Russell stood over her. "But God sent me to punish the wicked, and I shall not stray from His path." He raised the shovel once more. "Make your peace with him, for whatever it's worth."

Josephine hadn't the strength even to pray. She just looked up and waited for it to end.

There was a hiss like leaking gas. Fire flashed up Russell, igniting his clothes, charring his skin, sending him reeling away from her with a hideous scream.

A remnant of flame danced across the ground in front of Josephine. Conrad's eyes glittered like rubies against amber skin.

"I'm sorry, my sweet," he said. "You deserve better than me."

And he was gone.

Josephine pushed the door open, stepped into the parlor. Father sat by the fire, an empty bottle at his feet, snoring like a horse.

Josephine lifted the poker with her good hand and prodded him awake. He blinked up at her in the dawn seeping through the doorway. She realized she must strike a disturbing image, with her battered face, her singed hair, her own blood spattering her dress.

"Go now," she whispered, so cold and hard that she surprised herself. "And never come back."

He rose and staggered, bleary-eyed and terrified, out into the street.

Josephine put the poker down, turned to stare at herself in the grubby mirror.

"You deserve better," she said.

The Murder in the Steel Skeletons

by Gerri Leen

The towers reach for the sky, most are nothing more than shells of the buildings they once were. The sides and windows fell off long ago. Cement crumbled but steel remains—for now.

The city is normally quiet, except for when a building lets go, or that's how Aaron likes to think of it. He's watched several buildings die. Going from one state to another with little fanfare, just a creak here and there before louder squeals sound as metal and glass rub other materials.

Then the first piece falls. Sometimes it is a cluster of pieces. He has to be sure to be far enough away to avoid the spraying glass. The larger sheets could cut him in half if they fell just right.

He knows how to be safe, though. He knows which buildings are solid—or at least reasonably so—and which are not. He only has to follow the crows.

Flocks and flocks of them. "Murders" he remembers his mother called the groups of crows, though he has no idea why. He doesn't call them that; they've saved his life more times than he can remember with their caustic cries alerting all around to danger.

If you know how to listen, the empty city is full of sound.

If you don't, you'll find out how quickly the other survivors can find you. Not all of them are nice. In fact, most of them aren't.

Aaron's lumped them into categories. The solitaries are people like him. They live alone, make their way as best they can, and don't bother anyone. He knows four of them, but not well. Enough to nod if they happen to pass each other in this huge city that once housed so many people it was impossible to walk down the street and not pass someone.

Then there are the mentals. They were on the street to begin

191

with and that hasn't changed. They should be easy prey for the predators, but they've survived so long alone and unwanted that they were best suited for getting by when the chemical bombs went off.

When everyone but a handful died.

When the city started to crumble.

Aaron wasn't there, of course. No one alive remembers the cities full and vital. But his grandparents did, and they passed the knowledge on to his parents, who told it to him. Along with their particular words of wisdom.

"Never turn your back on a stranger."

"Always know where water is."

"Groups bring trouble."

He wonders if that last one is true. He watches the crows, after all, and they have huge flocks. They appear to be fine together. Safer together. They appear to have fondness for each other.

Mates and plenty of food and an early warning system.

What does Aaron have? A backpack full of food he has scavenged, a knife, and his firesticks. Little to tempt the predators, the groups of people who roam the city and to whom he owes the long scar on his face.

He got away from them. That's all that matters. His face is ugly now, but he's alive.

He hears the squeal-scratch from the building above him, so he crosses the street to get clear of falling glass and metal. He keeps walking, hears a strange sound that he realizes is singing.

Up ahead, a figure crouches against the wall of a doorway, holding a smaller bundle, singing a soft, sad song. The figure looks up: a woman. It has been some time since he's seen one. He realizes the bundle is a child.

"Don't hurt me." She doesn't move, doesn't run, doesn't pull out a makeshift weapon that she must have hidden somewhere on her body—no one survives in this place without at least one weapon.

She goes back to the baby, and he sees that the child is not crying, not moving, eyes staring sightlessly.

It is dead. Yet she sings to it. Is she a mental?

"What happened?" he asks.

She keeps on singing.

He should walk on. Keep going and be safe, be strong—alone, the way his parents taught him.

He stays where he is. "What happened to your child?"

"He's not mine."

Did she pick him up when he was dead? Carry him around like a doll? A mental for sure.

"He's my brother's."

Oh. That sounds better. Saner. "He's dead."

"I promised I'd keep him safe." She tucks the ragged blanket around the baby. "I told my sister-in-law I wouldn't let anything hurt him."

"Hard promise to keep in this city." He decides to sit a little while, eases down on the sidewalk next to her—but not too close. She's still a stranger, sad story or no. "Where are your brother and sister-in-law?"

"Dead." She looks down at the baby, and her eyes change, as if she's really seeing him for the first time. "Just like him."

"Sorry." He isn't sure what else to say. Kids are fragile. They get sick and they die. They go hungry if they're too little to eat scavenged food, and this baby looks very young, even to his untrained eyes.

A hoarse caw sounds over them. Then another. Two crows are sitting on twin columns of twisted steel. The sun finds a space through the bones of the city, lights up their feathers like black opals.

"They mourn their dead, crows do. Did you know that?" She struggles to her feet. "I always liked them. Hated that so many didn't."

"The crows got the last laugh. They're all over the place here."

She nods. Then she takes the blanket and covers the baby's face.

"His name was Johnny."

"Do you want to bury him? The easiest way is a stone mound. Use the pieces of shattered concrete to pile over the body, so animals can't get to it."

"Real dirt. Not just a pile of rubble. With a marker."

Markers are easy. Markers are fast and then he could be on his way again. It's what his parents would tell him to do if they were here.

But he doesn't say it. He says, "There's a garden not far from here. The plants are bursting out all over, but there's dirt there. And they probably have a shovel. Maybe something to make a marker from."

She nods. "Show me where it is. Thanks."

He knows he could just tell her. It's a couple of blocks down, two more over. He should let her go.

But predators might get her.

Or she might not be a good digger.

And she's so pretty.

He holds his hand out. "I'm Aaron. I'll take you there. I'll help you."

"I'm not stupid." Instead of her hand, a knife is pointing at him. "Just tell me where it is."

"I don't think you're stupid. I can be headed that way as well as any other. There's a whole bunch of crows there, so I like the place. One of my bolt holes is in the building." He meets her eyes, sees only fear.

He wonders what her parents told her.

He's not sure their parents were right, not sure that's how you make a future, all alone for the rest of your life.

"Let me help?"

He hasn't helped anyone since his mother died. He has no idea why he's helping now. He only knows he wants to.

The two crows are sitting on a girder now. His father used to know things about buildings, like how they were made and what the different materials were. The two crows put their heads together, like they're having a conversation, like his mother and father used to do.

He's spent a lot of days thinking about how they had each other so being alone really wasn't that at all, was it?

"Crows mate for life," she says, and he realizes she's figured out what he's watching. "The crows have kept me alive."

"Me, too. Sometimes I wish I were a crow. That I had a place to go, with that many other souls to belong to." It is an odd thing to tell her—it's true, but why is he sharing it?

"Yeah. Flying would be nice, too, most days."

194

He nods. "Okay, well, if you don't need my help, I'll be moving on. The building is two blocks down, two over. The signs have all fallen down, but the building is an older one—old style, I mean. Big white place. The garden is in the back."

She puts the baby to her shoulder. "Lot of big white places there, I bet?"

"I guess so."

"Hard to find it, maybe? Better with someone who knows where it is?" She almost smiles.

"Groups bring trouble. That's what my mother told me."

She nods. "Groups do—my parents told me that, too. But maybe we're not a group. Maybe we could be a...pair." She holds out her hand.

He decides to take it, to squeeze her hand, to feel the skin against his.

How long has it been since anyone touched him?

Suddenly the two crows fly up in a great flapping of wings. The sound of feet comes toward them.

"Predators," he says, and pushes her into the building they stand in front of. "Don't make a sound."

She doesn't, just stands by him, and he can hear her shallow breathing as they sit and wait.

"The crows hate them," he whispers. "They know the predators hunt them. They never forget."

"I know. I count on that. I thought the crows would keep me safe." She looks down at the bundle in her arms. "Keep him safe, I mean. Me—I go on whether I want to or not."

He reaches into his pack, pulls out some berries he found and holds them out to her. "Hungry?"

By the way she snatches and gobbles them down, he can tell she is starved.

"We might want to stay here, wait until the predators are good and gone. It'll be dark soon. We can bury him in the morning." He pulls out some more berries. "I have food."

"I'm not going to pay you for it." She is looking at him in a way he doesn't understand.

"Not a lot to pay with."

"My body. That's the payment the mentals want."

"I'm not a mental." Although he thinks her body is a nice one—not that he's had a lot of experience. One time, hiding out in a building like this from predators—before he had his scar—he and a young woman who never told him her name found some solace. She left him before he woke; he's never seen her since.

"Here."

He dumps the rest of the berries in her cupped hands and settles down on the ground. "I'm going to sleep, so you can stop being afraid. Don't murder me in my sleep, okay?"

He hears her laugh, and it's an unexpected sound—maybe as surprising to her as it is to him. "I won't."

He hears her sitting down. Not too close, but not very far away either.

As he drifts off, he hears her say, "My name is Jennifer."

Busting Faces

By Charles Payseur

Ban woke in the early morning to bust faces, grabbing the hammer from the work table where he had left it the previous night. No voice rose from the house to call him back to bed, no soft hand to draw him back inside after he had burst through the front door and toward the main square. Erik was gone three years now, ever since the Sickness had swept through the capitol and taken so many of them. Ban was one of the few, the survivors, the Remnants or whatever the others were calling themselves, the ones that had moved east and into the future.

Ban remained in the past and busted faces. The trip to the main square wasn't far, just a twenty minute walk, one of the reasons he had moved in with Erik in the first place, aside from the man's easy smile and rising fame. Ban remembered those early days, his constant surprise how the hands that shaped marble and stone could be so soft and gentle, and he had gone with Erik to every unveiling, to the great artistic revival that was sweeping through the city, trying to bring back the glories of a past age.

"We have to remember where we come from," Erik would say, echoing the popular thoughts of the time, the same thoughts that kept him in business, kept him sculpting. "We have to remember the past or we're destined to repeat it."

And then a smile would inch across his face and they would laugh. Erik wouldn't have cared if he was sculpting for a museum or a whore house as long as he got to do it, as long as he could tease the faces out of the stone and clay. Ban would watch him as he worked in the basement of their home, drawing up the ghosts of people who had lived hundreds of years ago, pulling at the past like it was his mother's dress.

"As if they really knew what these people looked like," Erik would say, voice hotter now, hands at work on the stone. "They just like the past because it's passive, the way I like a mound of clay or block of marble. They see what they want in it and draw it out, and as much as I am the one to shape these things, it's them that give them life, like raising the dead to dance."

So Ban walked in to the main square of the capitol, aware that he was the only one alive for miles and miles. The fighting had been fierce here, in the streets, as the old men on their balconies had watched the dying march on them. Ban had been home, doors barred, locked in the basement with Erik, who was clinging to life, still working. Ban reached the site of the Founding, an enormous work with sixty-five individual statues that Erik had overseen for the bicentennial. The Founders, the heroes of the nation, or what had been the nation before it all collapsed and the fight had moved into the east.

Walking past the first row, which he had already seen to earlier in the week, Ban came to a face, one that he didn't recognize. He imagined that it was like the old men on their balconies, the panic in their eyes. In the last days of the Sickness there had been a cure, a solution, but only for a few, only those that could pay. And Erik had refused, had demanded the cure for everyone, for the young and the bright. He had spoken before the Sickness drove him into the basement with Ban, urged the people to act.

"I could give myself a stronger jaw," Erik had said, working on that last sculpture, a bust of himself. "Or I could make my lips fuller. You always complain that they're no fun to kiss. I don't want people thinking that of me."

It was a lie, a joke, but Ban couldn't find it funny. He just watched as the face took shape, strikingly accurate, each detail correct. And when Erik fell into his final sleep Ban had looked at it. He could see the smile in the lips though they were still and even, could hear the laugh and the wit though there was no voice. There was a hammer on the work table that he had taken, that he had risen above his head.

His arm shivered at the impact as he brought the hammer into the face of the statue in the square, the Founder whose name

Ban did not remember. Again and again he hit the stone surface, cracking the nose, ruining the brow, the ears. Again and again, erasing the face from the statue, letting the ghost of the past rise like vapor into a breeze and lose itself. There would be no past to reclaim when the people returned from the east, when nostalgia tugged at them to revive the dead to dance.

"We have to remember the past," Erik had said, "or we're destined to repeat it."

It was lie. Learning from the past was like a prison, a closed circle that never went anywhere, that only brought them back to where they'd already been, to something old. Better they have to make it up from scratch, all new. The past spoke only in echoes of the present, reaching back towards something familiar, flawed. Ban had heard it, holding Erik's bust.

"I love you," the stone had whispered to him, and Ban had swung the hammer and busted the face until it couldn't speak.

Government Waste

By J. S. Bell

The dog appeared from the empty desert, the heat shimmer giving way to light and shadow taking form.

Before his eyes focused on the apparition, in that split second between first sight and recognition, Tom Bugh thought: *They found me.*

The arid breeze ruffled the dog's fur and raised an exhausted whirlpool of dust. It lifted the edges of the paper – the last of his meager hoard – spread on the card table in front of his trailer. The guts of a Holly four-barrel carburetor leaked solvent in bloody patches onto the paper, ruining it for anything but fire starter. *Couldn't let it get on the table, of course.* The nagging voice of Shyla Bugh, twelve years dead, cursed him from the grave, "Don't get that shit on my table!"

Tom said to the dog, "Haven't seen you in a while. Are they coming again?" The sound of his voice spooked him a little. It came out raspy and dry and mean, like a crotchety old man's.

Surprise, surprise.

The mutt sat on its haunches, tongue flopped to the side, panting. More hound dog than anything else, with maybe a little dobie in him. Tom snorted. The sum total of his knowledge of dogs: Four legs and drool. The critter could be a South American ring-tailed mastodon, for all he knew.

"Water?" Tom challenged the mutt with a lifted chin. The Doberman-hound dog-mastodon cocked an eyebrow at him, in an almost human gesture of curiosity. He stayed planted, though, about ten yards away, as close as he ever got.

"Food? You're outta luck there, my friend. I ain't got no food."

"Don't have any," he corrected. Shyla in his head, always after him to speak properly. "I'll get you some water, though. Least I can do for a desert traveler such as yourself."

Tom scooted back from the table, working at not collapsing his rickety metal lawn chair. Body parts creaked and popped, but he made it to the trailer, climbed inside and retrieved a gallon jug of water from the fridge. Sediment from the well settled at the bottom of the jug; he took care not to shake it up. He rummaged under the sink for the beat up pan he used to catch the roof leak when it rained.

When he came back through the door, the dog was gone. Tom blinked and focused on where he last saw the mutt.

Nope. Nothing but sand and scorpion shit.

Behind the spot where the critter came from – to the west – a distant, jagged streak of purple marked the beginning of the mountains separating Old Texas from Old Mexico, a territory now called Nuevo Sonora. For a bazillion miles in any other direction, there was nothing but flat ground covered in scrappy little trees that were good for nothing but snagging your clothes and lighting fires.

Tom put the pan down next to the trailer and filled it with water, in case the dog returned, then went back to his carburetor rebuild.

In front of Tom's makeshift campground of twelve years, a two-lane road, covered in powdery dust and dried armadillo shells, slowly crumbled into asphalt ruts. A 1971 Chevrolet Camaro with a jacked up back end, Cragar mags, and racing slicks crouched with its hood up, going nowhere with a bad-ass attitude.

He checked the desert again, but the dog failed to reappear. Nothing stirred beyond the humming of a thumb-sized fly, cruising between the mesquite branches on fly business.

Tom cocked his head, tuning it like an old-fashioned antenna. A sound, light as a feather's shadow, whispered closer. Drifting from the east, as if heat waves had a voice, a low whine tickled the edges of his hearing. It faded, then grew, Doppler-shifted away and broadened.

He frowned.

"Well, Hell's bells. I guess they're coming after all."

The whine amped up to the irritating hum of an electric

vehicle, unmistakable and unavoidable. There was only one road across these plains, and though an anti-grav car could skim over the surface, drivers rarely cut across country. The chances of a battery dying in the middle of a helluva lot of nothing was too great for most people to want to risk it.

"There's always hoping they won't stop," Tom grumped. Just in case, he climbed back inside the trailer and fetched his short gun, which he tucked down the back of his pants. Six bullets left to his name, and those almost as old as he was. Getting ammunition proved harder than finding usable gasoline, and more dangerous. The Feds caught a man buying ammo on the black market, they'd lock him in Camp Brady until he turned to worm dirt.

"And speaking of Feds . . ."

Standing in the door of his trailer, Tom experienced a flush of cold sloshing over him from head to toe. The solid drab blue of a government-owned Ford Gravitas skimmed through the brush and slowed to a stop in front of his camp. It sighed to the ground; the whine terminated with a click.

At least the dog has sense enough to hide.

The hatch cracked open, levered up like a bird with one wing. A woman emerged, wearing a one-piece business suit and a frown. Head shaved except for a brunette scalp lock, like an old-fashioned ponytail, her brown eyes pinned Tom from thirty feet away. The woman touched the air in front of her with the index finger of each hand.

At first, Tom thought she was pointing at him, or trying to communicate in sign language, but realization dawned when he remembered the newest version of the iBrain had a holographic interface. The woman entered or retrieved data from her implant and manipulated a keyboard only she could see.

The woman's frown cut deeper into her face, and her gestures grew more emphatic.

"No signal," Tom called.

"What?"

"No signal out here. Your iBrain won't connect." The gun in his waistband had magically swollen in mass. It felt like a rocket launcher hiding in the back of his pants. Any second, it would fall out, and this government minion would see it. She'd jump back in her car and head for reinforcements, either from Juarez or Nuevo Tucson. Feds would fill the air, armed to their shiny eyeballs, all geared up to capture one old man with a six-shooter.

"My database says Bugh, Thomas J," the woman said. She had a clear voice, high and prim. It was the kind Tom associated with school principals and lawyers. "That is your correct name?"

"It is." Desert air dried his throat. He coughed and said it again, louder and with air behind it this time. "It is."

"I am Mechelle Saint-James and I am with the Bureau of the Census. I need to ask you a few questions."

"You're from the government, and you're here to help."

"What was that?"

"Nothing, ma'am—"

"Please don't call me ma'am," Saint-James snapped. "You may call me Sah Saint-James, or just Sah."

"Sah?"

"Short for the gender-neutral term Sapient."

"Yes, ma—sah." Tom coughed again. "Why don't you sit in the shade? What shade there is, I mean. You want some water? Tea?"

Her eyes narrowed, but Saint-James left the side of her vehicle and came closer.

"Nothing, thank you."

Tom gestured for Saint-James to take his metal folding chair, which she eyed with the same enthusiasm as she would a hot, smoking cow patty. The alternative was a five-gallon bucket, up-ended, which Tom appropriated.

Saint-James scuffed and shuffled the chair around under the one decent tree in the yard until she found the position she wanted, wrinkled her nose at the collection of parts on the table and poised her fingers in the air in front of her. Without looking at him, she said,

"It is time for the annual census, Sah Bugh. The census is an important tool in your government's on-going efforts to . . . ."

Tom tuned out her canned spiel and studied the woman from the Census Bureau. Thirty, maybe thirty-five years old – it was hard to tell these days with the DNA labs pumping out new anti-aging regimes every day – Latino complexion and no trace of makeup anywhere.

". . . so I just need to ask you a few questions," Saint-James concluded.

"Fire away."

"For confirmation, you are Bugh, Thomas Jefferson?"

"Correct."

"DOB 30 June, 1998?"

"Yep."

"Race?"

"Redneck."

The woman rolled her eyes. "Please Sah Bugh, the census must be taken seriously. How should you be racially identified? Latino, of Mexican/South American descent? Latino, of other descent? Native Amer—"

"Caucasian."

Saint-James raised one eyebrow a micro-millimeter, moved her fingers to enter the data. She said, "Sex—"

"Not anymore, but thanks for the offer."

She froze him with a look. "If I might continue, sah. Sexual identification? Mono-sexual, bi-sexual, asexual, or other?"

"There's something other? Wait, never mind. Forget I asked. The first one there. Mono-whatever."

A new bead of cold sweat trickled down Tom's ribcage and found every shiver-nerve on that side of his body. He clenched his teeth and held still. An axiom from his childhood: Never let 'em see you sweat.

Saint-James paused with her hands poised in the air. Tom followed where she looked and saw the bowl of water by the trailer. "You have a pet, Sah Bugh? That's not in the database."

"No, no pet. I put that out for wee ones. Y'know. Fairy people."

He had to give the woman credit. She barely flinched. Her eyes widened a little, that was about all. "You're clowning around, aren't you Sah Bugh? Don't you know how important it is for the government to maintain accurate data on its citizens? Allocation of federal funds—why, everything from roads to healthcare—is determined by the census. We can only serve our population if the data is up-to-date."

"But what if I don't use those services?"

Double-blink.

"What?"

"Look around you, Miss—Sah Saint-James. Do you see any hospitals? Roads, to speak of?" He jerked a thumb over his shoulder. "That one don't count. I don't need police protection, education, energy, or damn near anything else the government provides. So why should I take the census seriously?"

Saint-James gaped at him. "But, Sah Bugh, that's craz—not right. I mean, think of the anarchy. Without the military police keeping order, citizens might riot, there would be, ah, no control. Without federal adjudication and firefighters and, and, you know, proper licensing of vehicles . . . things would fall apart."

"Woman, I'm ninety-six years old." His voice had taken on an edge. He hated trying to argue with these people. It was so . . . pointless. "For the past twelve of those years, I've lived out here"—he waved a hand again—"on my own. Working for what I need to buy, and bartering when I could. In all that time, I've availed myself of no government service. So why don't you take me out of your database and leave me be."

Saint-James mouth grew rigid as her spine. Her eyes narrowed to slits and she worked her fingers through the air like casting a complex spell.

"Do you mean to say," she hissed, "that you've paid no taxes in twelve years?"

Tom sat back and slapped his thighs. "Now you're getting it."

The young woman's fingers paused in mid-air, then she pointed an index finger and stabbed repeatedly at an unseen button. Frustration became evident by the flush building up from her neck. "What the hell . . .?"

"You keep forgetting," Tom said. "No signal."

"What?"

"You're trying to call the IRS Quick Response Team, right?" That was when she saw the gun he'd drawn from his waistband. Saint-James yelped and scraped back, pushing up so fast, her chair fell over with a clatter.

"No! Why would you think that?"

Tom sighed.

"It's what they all do."

"Ah—All?"

"All you government types." Tom pointed to a row of markers near the brush where the dog came from. Coffee can lids, nailed to wooden posts, knee-high to a short child. "They come out here, bothering me, babbling their government this and government that. I've had the EPA, Social Entitlement Administration, the Lifetime Medical Care Agency, FDA, Health and Human Services, DHS, even a goddamn skinny fellow from the Farm Bureau." Tom sighed. "Parasites, every one."

Horror blanched the tan woman's face, as if somebody added a lot more *au lait* to her *café*. "You k-k-killed them?"

"Yep. Afraid so."

"And b-buried them? There?"

"Buried them? No, those are just markers. Can't waste taxpayer money and just throw out government assets. I mean, why let 'em go to waste, right? Plus, there's a dog lives back off there somewhere"—Tom gestured to the desert—"takes care of the leftovers."

In the end, Tom saved himself the cost of a bullet. When Mechelle Saint-James tried to run, he brained her with the base of the Holly carburetor. Which meant more cleaning, but hell, it wasn't like he'd ever get the thing to run again anyway.

He tinkered with Saint-James' GPS, set the auto-pilot and sent the vehicle on down the road. The car would travel another two hundred miles before the battery ran out—longer if the solar panel array stayed in the sun. Like all the others, Saint-James would disappear somewhere in the desert, another mystery of the plains.

Long after purple twilight faded to twinkling blackness, the dog returned. Tom's fire had died to coals, but fat dripped from skewers and sent tendrils of smoke into the air, which were snagged by the breeze and scattered into the desert. The Camaro was back together, hood down, and Tom had even gotten her to fire up and run for a few minutes.

All in all, a pretty successful day.

"Take this, you mangy mutt," Tom said.

He tossed an ulna to the dog, who snatched it out of the air and trotted away from the firelight.

"I hate to see government waste."

From the darkness, crunching.

Acknowledgements

Acknowledgements

Dragon's Roost Press would like to extend our sincerest gratitude to a number of people.

First, a hearty thank you to the 21 authors featured in this, our first anthology. We appreciate your willingness to share your literary babies with us. All of the material in between these covers is absolutely magnificent. You have captured, each in your own unique way, the themes of isolation, abandonment, and loneliness which we hoped to convey.

We would also like to thank the numerous authors who submitted, but whose stories were not selected. We were overwhelmed by the number of submissions we received. No one expected the response to have an international element. There was a lot of amazing fiction that, for one reason or another, we were not able to include. We wish the best to all of the authors who submitted to our anthology.

A big thank you goes out to all of the people who contributed to our crowdsourcing campaign on Indigogo. Peter Barber, Bert Cieslak, Laura Cieslak, Marie Cieslak, Michelle Dixon, Sara Gale, David Hayes, Chris Pullen, Melanie Talbot, Annette Vida, Ariel Vida, hmar**@********, patuk**@******, and those who chose to remain anonymous. Without you we would not have been able to provide payment for our authors, the art design, or the publishing fees. We appreciate all that you have done for us. Your perks are on the way!

Thank you to everyone who supported the project throughout its various stages. Your smiles, social media likes, and words of encouragement are truly appreciated.

A special nod goes out to the members of the Great Lakes Association of Horror Writers. A writer could not hope to find a better group of fellow authors, artists, film makers, and horror enthusiasts. You are all magnificent.

A raised glass to Sara Gale of Exit 57 Graphics, without whom this book would have a blank cover. You managed to turn the vaguest description ever into something outstanding. The artwork you provided is amazing.

Belly rubs and bacon to the best assistant editors anyone could hope for, Tesla and Titus. Thank you for being so patient while your Papa spent hours at the computer.

Finally, thanks and love to Ruth Pinto-Cieslak who supported yet another of her husband's crazy ideas. With you beside me I know I can accomplish anything.

About the Contributors

J. S. Bell ("Government Waste") is a part-time writer with publication credits for fiction at *The Western Online* and *Cast of Wonders*.

Gustavo Bondoni ("Lords of Dust") is an Argentine writer with over a hundred stories published in ten countries and four languages, and winner of the National Space Society's "Return to Luna" contest and the Marooned Award for Flash Fiction in 2008. His fiction has appeared in a Pearson High School Test Cycle in the US, three Hadley Rille Books Anthologies, *The Rose & Thorn, Albedo One, The Best of Every Day Fiction,* and others. He is the author of two short story collections *Tenth Orbit and Other Faraway Places* and *Virtuoso and Other Stories* and the short novel *The Curse of El Bastardo.* His website is at www.gustavobondoni.com.ar, and his blog is located at http://bondo-ba.livejournal.com/.

Michael Cieslak (Editor) is a lifetime reader and writer of horror, mystery, and speculative fiction. A native of Detroit, he still lives within 500 yards of the city with his wife and their two dogs Tesla and Titus. The house is covered in Halloween decorations in October and dragons the rest of the year. He is an officer in the Great Lakes Association of Horror Writers. His works have appeared in a number of collections including *DOA: Extreme Horror, Dead Science, Vicious Verses and Reanimated Rhymes*, the GLAHW's *Erie Tales* anthologies, and *Alter Egos Vol 1*. He is the current Literature Track Head for Penguicon. Michael's most recent endeavor is the Dragon's Roost Press imprint. Michael's mental excreta (including his personal blog They Napalmed My Shrubbery This Morning) can be found on-line at thedragonsroost.net.

At age 5, Lillian Csernica ("Camp Miskatonic") discovered the Little Golden Books fairy tales. Her very first short story sale, "Fallen Idol," appeared in *After Hours* and was later reprinted in DAW'S *The Year's Best Horror Stories XX.* Ms. Csernica has published stories in DAW'S *Year's Best Horror Stories XXI, 100 Wicked Little Witch Stories, Insatiable, Sorcerous Signals,* and *Midnight Movie Creature Feature 2.* Her Christmas ghost story "The Family Spirit" appeared in *Weird Tales* #322 and "Maeve" appeared in #333. Ms. Csernica has also published an historical romance novel, *Ship of Dreams.* Ms. Csernica has also written nonfiction in the field of science fiction, fantasy, and horror. She has been a columnist for *Speculations,* writing "The Fright Factory" and "The Writer's Spellbook." Her controversial column of literary criticism and short fiction reviews, "The Penny Dreadful Reader," ran in the print edition of *Tangent,* earning praise from such leading lights of the field as editor Ellen Datlow. Now Ms. Csernica reviews short horror fiction for Tangent Online. Born in San Diego, Ms. Csernica is a genuine California native. She currently resides in the Santa Cruz mountains with her husband, two sons, and three cats.

Kurt Fawver ("Every Weeknight at Seven and Seven-Thirty") is a writer of dark fantasy, quiet horror, and the generally weird. He has been published in a number of anthologies (from publishers such as Necro Publications, Omnium Gatherum, Blood Bound Books, etc.) and spec fic magazines. He also has a collection of short fiction available from Villipede Press. He is a member of the Horror Writer's Association. He also holds a Ph.D. in literature and writes scholarly articles on the subject of horror and dark fantasy as well as teaching composition and literature at the collegiate level.

Sara Gale (Cover Art and Exterior Design) lives in South-East Michigan with husband Jeff and her shadows: her dog Misty and Hook, a Blue and Gold Macaw. They share the house with a number of full sized horror characters including Michael Myers, Jason Voorhees, Freddy Krueger, Chucky and his bride Tiffany, and her collection of 23 pairs of Converse Chuck Taylors. She is a huge fan of horror and rates Stephen King just below "The Man With The

Chin," actor Bruce Campbell. Sara has over 17 years as a graphic designer and is the owner of Exit 57 Graphics. For more information or to to contact her for a graphic design project, please visit: http://www.exit57.com.

Ken Goldman ("Deleted") is a former high school English and Film Studies teacher (Horror and Science Fiction in Film and Literature) at George Washington High School in Philadelphia, Pennsylvania. Since 1993 he has published over 700 stories. He is an affiliate member of the Horror Writers Association. His recent novel, *Of A Feather*, was published in January 2014 by Horrific Tales Publications.

Camille Griep ("Robodog") lives and writes near Seattle, Washington. In addition to magazines such as *The First Line, Bound Off,* and *Every Day Fiction*, her work has been anthologized in *Blaze of Glory* (Song Story Press) and *Witches, Stitches, & Bitches* (Evil Girlfriend Media). Find her at www.camillegriep.com.

Alexandra Grunberg ("Hunger") is a New York City based author and actress. Her work has appeared in *Daily Science Fiction, Fiction Vortex, Plasma Frequency Magazine*, and more. You can find links to her stories at her blog, alexandragrunberg.wordpress.com.

David C. Hayes ("Misty Hills of Dreamer Sheep") is an award-winning author, editor, and filmmaker. Most recently, he has written stories for Dark Moon Books, Strangehouse Books, Evil Jester Press, Blood Bound Books, and many more. His first collection, *American Guignol*, was released in 2013 and he is a multiple genre anthology editor. He is the author of *Cannibal Fat Camp, Muddled Mind: The Complete Works of Ed Wood Jr.* and the *Rottentail* graphic novel as well as many screenplays, stage plays (his *Dial P for Peanuts* won an Ethingtony in 2011), articles and more. His films, like *The Frankenstein Syndrome, Bloody Bloody Bible Camp, A Man Called Nereus, Dark Places*, and *Back Woods*, are available worldwide. He is the co-owner of Cinema Head Cheese (www.cinemaheadcheese.com), a geek culture website, and you can visit him online at www.davidchayes.com. David is a voting member of the Horror Writers

Association and the Dramatists Guild. He likes creepy hugs and all kinds of cheese.

Tory Hoke ("Alpha") writes, cartoons, and eats too much sugar-free candy in Los Angeles. Her short fiction has appeared in *Crowded Magazine* and is forthcoming in *Strange Horizons* and *LORE*. More of her work, including a word-a-day vocabulary comic, can be found at www.thetoryparty.com.

Sierra July ("Affection, Inconceivable") is a University of Florida graduate. She holds a bachelor's degree in animal sciences. She strives to honor and support animals of all shapes and sizes, whether through veterinary medicine or through her writing. Her fiction has appeared in *Every Day Fiction*, the Fast-Forward Festival, and *365tomorrows*. Her poetry has appeared in *Star*Line* and *Songs of Eretz*. This story was inspired by her shelter dog Wesley, the original honey dog.

Sharon D. King ("Follow the Music") holds a Ph.D. in Comparative Literature (UCLA) and (as Sharon Diane King) is a character actor in film and TV. Past publications include an essay in the critical anthology *Of Bread, Blood and The Hunger Games* (McFarland, 2012) and a satirical novella, *The Younger Games* (WitsEnd Publications, 2011); forthcoming works include an essay for a critical anthology on the TV series *Supernatural* (*Supernatural, Humanity, and the Soul*, Palgrave, 2014) and a fantasy story ("Read Shift") in *Kaleidotrope* (2014). King's humor-filled presentations for the ICFA and WorldCon include "I'm Not Really Dead, I'm Just Drawn That Way: Victims and Their Vernissage in Art-Horror Film" and "The Boundary Beneath: A Glimpse at Underwear in Speculative Literature and Film." She has twice staged theatre of the Grand Guignol (horror plays and sex farces) at WorldCon. Since 1989, her theatrical troupe Les Enfans Sans Abri has performed short 15th-17th -century French and Spanish comedies in translation in the US and Europe. She and her husband volunteer for the nonprofit organization Reptile and Amphibian Rescue Network (www.rarn. org). They are ministered to by five terrestrial dragons of varying shapes, sizes, and appetites...but all to scale....

Andrew Knighton ("Ghosts in the Gaslight") lives and occasionally writes in Stockport, England, where the grey skies provide a good motive to stay inside at the word processor. When not writing he battles the slugs threatening to overrun his garden and the monsters lurking in the woods. He's had over forty stories published in places such as *Wily Writers, Redstone SF,* and the *Steampunk Reloaded* and *Steamunk Revolution* anthologies. You can find out more about his writing at andrewknighton.wordpress.com.

Rich Larson ("Every Act of Creation") was born in West Africa, has studied in Rhode Island, and at 21 now lives in Edmonton, Alberta. He won the 2014 Dell Award and received the 2012 Rannu Prize for Writers of Speculative Fiction. In 2011, his cyberpunk novel *Devolution* was a finalist for the Amazon Breakthrough Novel Award. His short work has since received honorable mention from Writers of the Future and appears or is forthcoming in *Asimov's, Lightspeed, DSF, Strange Horizons, Apex Magazine, Beneath Ceaseless Skies, AE* and many others, including the anthologies *Futuredaze* and *War Stories.* More about Mr. Larson can be found at Amazon.com/author/richlarson.

Gerri Leen ("The Murder in the Steel Skeletons") lives in Northern Virginia and originally hails from Seattle. She has a collection of short stories, *Life Without Crows*, from Hadley Rille Books, and has had stories and poems published in such places as: *The GlassFire Anthology, Entrances and Exits, She Nailed a Stake Through His Head, Sword and Sorceress XXIII, Dia de los Muertos, Return to Luna, Triangulation: Dark Glass, Sails & Sorcery*, and *Paper Crow*. She also is editing an anthology of speculative fiction and poetry from Hadley Rille Books that will benefit homeless animals. Visit http://www.gerrileen.com to see what else she's been up to.

Raymond Little ("Plastic Lazarus") was born in London, and has had short stories for teens and adults published in both the UK and the USA. He is currently working on his first adult horror novel, *Doom*, which he expects to finish this summer.

Melissa Mead ("To Read") lives in Upstate NY. She currently has no pets, but hopes to have some again someday. Her Web page can be found at http://carpelibris.wordpress.com/.

Christopher Nadeau ("Beautiful Libby and the Darkness") is the author of *Dreamers at Infinity's Core* through COM Publishing as well as over two dozen published short stories in such august publications as *The Horror Zine, Sci-Fi Short Story Magazine, Ghostlight Magazine* and more anthologies than one could take out with the toss of a single hand grenade. He was interviewed as part of Suspense Radio's up and coming authors program and collaborated on two "machinima" films with UK animator Celestial Elf called *The Gift* and *The Deerhunter's Tale*, both of which can be viewed on YouTube. He received positive mention from Ramsey Campbell for his short story "Always Say Treat," which was compared to the work of Ray Bradbury and has received positive reviews from SFRevue and zombiecoffeepress. Chris has also served as special editor for *Voluted Magazine's* "The Darkness Internal" which he created.
His novel *Kaiju* was recently released through Source Point Press and *Echoes of Infinity's Core* is slated for 2014 release. An active member of the Great Lakes Association of Horror Writers, Chris resides in Southeastern Michigan with his wife Lorie and two petulant long-hair Chihuahuas

Dawn Napier ("Silence") grew up in Waukegan, Illinois and upstate New York. Her earliest memories are of re-imagining favorite cartoons on paper and inventing her own. She has a husband, three kids, and a ridiculous number of pets. She reads adventure fantasy, horror, science-fiction, or anything else that takes her away from it all. She hopes that her stories can do for others what they have done for her. She is the author of the fantasy novels *Nameless* and *Storyland* as well as the *Many Kingdoms* trilogy. Her fiction blog entitled Mom's Secret Horrors can be found at http://www.http://convozine.com/moms_secret_horrors.

Charles Payseur's ("Busting Faces") work has appeared in *Mustang's Monster Corral, Perihelion Science Fiction,* and is forthcoming at *Wily*

Writers. He grew up in the suburbs of Chicago, but has since moved to the frozen north, and currently lives with his partner and their cat in Eau Claire, Wisconsin.

Abra Staffin-Wiebe ("Belongings") has sold stories to publications including *Jim Baen's Universe* and Tor.com. She specializes in optimistic dystopian SF, modern fairy tales, cheerful horror, liquid state steampunk, dark humor, and heartwarming grotesqueries. She spent several years living abroad in India and Africa before marrying a mad scientist and settling down to live and write in Minneapolis, where she is currently a fiction writer, freelance photographer, part-time work-from-home employee, and full-time mother. Her next project is learning to fold time and space to make this all physically possible. Discover more of her fiction at her website, http://www. aswiebe.com, or find her on the social media site of your choice.

Calie Voorhis ("Aphrastos") is an internationally published fantasy, science fiction, and horror short story writer and poet. An alumnus of the Odyssey Fantasy Writing Workshop, she holds an MFA in Writing Popular Fiction from Seton Hill University. She has a BS in Biology from the University of North Carolina at Chapel Hill. Residing in coastal North Carolina, she is the Assistant Technical Director of Thalian Hall Center for the Performing Arts.

About Last Day Dog Rescue

Last Day is more than just a name, it's the situation all the dogs were faced with. Because of LDDR these wonderful dogs get another chance at life. All dogs coming into their rescue were saved from high-kill animal shelters or being sold for research.

A Little About LDDR:

Last Day Dog Rescue is an ALL volunteer based organization. They do not have a physical location; all of their dogs are placed in the care of foster homes until they are adopted.

The group focuses on rescuing dogs from the "Urgent" list in shelters and pounds across lower Michigan and parts of Ohio with an emphasis on those shelters who euthanize by gas or those shelters who sell the dogs in their care to research labs where they are used for barbaric and most times painful testing and experiments. They hold a special place in their hearts for the big and black dogs, even 'ugly' dogs (whom they don't find ugly at all!) and the special senior dogs. These dogs most often get overlooked and passed up in shelters and pounds everywhere for puppies, small breeds, and the "prettier," lighter colored dogs.

Dogs found in shelters are there for many reasons; some are owner surrenders, strays, cruelty or abuse cases, and some dogs are found abandoned, left to fend for themselves in vacant homes, fields, ditches, and some have even been tied out in the woods and left to starve. Last Day Dog Rescue does not discriminate and feels that each of these dogs, no matter their size, age, color, or the reason they are there, deserve a second chance at life...they help all those they can.

Donations via check and money orders:
Last Day Dog Rescue
P.O. Box 51935
Livonia, MI 48151-5935

Donations also accepted via PayPal:
http://www.lastdaydogrescue.org/info/display?PageID=14086

About Dragon's Roost Press

Dragon's Roost Press is the brainchild of author Michael Cieslak who wanted to do something to honor all of the dogs he has been fortunate enough to share his life with. At the same time he wanted to give something back to the Last Day Dog Rescue Organization from which he and his wife adopted their current furry companions Tesla and Titus. Plus he wanted to see what it was like to put together an anthology.

A portion of the proceeds of all sales of <u>Desolation: 21 Tales for Tails</u> will be donated to the Last Day Dog Rescue Organization.

This is the first book published by Dragon's Roost Press. Look for future titles soon. For more information, please visit: http://thedragonsroost.net/styled-3/index.html.